NOW OR NEVER

This chamber was definitely, unequivocally, artificial. Dierdre Jamail had discovered genuine alien artifacts. In fact, the whole *cave* she was in was an alien artifact. And then there were the discs.

There were two of them, on the opposite wall, about shoulder height and a meter apart. In a half-daze, she walked across the small room for a closer look. The discs were set in holes in the stone wall, about ten centimeters in depth. They were, she estimated, about twenty centimeters in diameter, and they looked metallic. Each had a vertical ridge across its diameter.

She reached out and touched the right hand disc. With her left hand she touched the other disc.

She heard a voice in the distance, someone calling her name. Okamura. If she was going to do something to make her name immortal, even if it killed her, she had to do it fast. She forced he s she turned bo

And the wo

Eric Kotani &
John Maddox Roberts

DELTA PAVONIS

This is a work of fiction. All the characters and events portrayed in this book are fictional, and any resemblance to real people or incidents is purely coincidental.

A Baen Books Original

Baen Publishing Enterprises
260 Fifth Avenue
New York, N.Y. 10001

ISBN: 0-671-72020-1

Cover art by Peter Scanlon

First printing, October 1990

Distributed by
SIMON & SCHUSTER
1230 Avenue of the Americas
New York, N.Y. 10020

Printed in the United States of America

For Eleanor Wood,
Stephanie Hall, Maritha Pottenger, Lee Anne Willson,
Blake Powers, and Doranna and Jim Shiner.

ONE

The planetside base was an untidy sprawl of ugly, functional buildings made of extruded foam. Out of respect for the local environment they had been tinted in mottled patterns of gray and green, but it didn't help much. At the southern edge of the base, a score of scoutcraft idled their engines noisily. On a mountain plateau half a kilometer north of the base, ships from the orbiting republics landed, discharged their personnel and supplies, and took off, loaded with specimens and material, with returning scientists, explorers and students.

In a quiet corridor of the administration building, Dierdre waited nervously. The gravity didn't help. No matter how many thousands of hours of "weight" a spacer experienced during acceleration and deceleration, or during training in centrifuge chambers, the real thing felt different. Somehow, the body knew.

It was late afternoon by local time. She had arrived early that morning, the first time she had set foot on any planet. Even the best of holographic training hadn't prepared her for the new sensations: the far horizons, the vast volumes of space at hand, the incredible variety of smells, most of them organic, that changed from one moment to the next as the wind shifted. The wind itself was a new experience. She would have been enthralled by it all, had it not been for the anticipation of this interview. One slipup and she could be on the next ship back to orbit, and all the years she had spent learning her skills would be wasted.

"Dierdre Jamail?" She looked up and saw a young man, perhaps two or three years older than herself. He wore a Survey uniform and had that ineradicable grad student look about him.

"That's me."

"Personnel Director Merchant will see you now."

That sounded bad. She had always been taught that when people went by titles terminal decadence was setting in. She followed the man to an office that was little more than an air bubble in the foam. The sign on the door said, "Personnel Director Esmerelda da S. Merchant". Dierdre filed it away for future use. The director wanted people to know that she had been born a da Sousa, a member of one of the founding families. That kind of vanity could always provide a useful handle.

The woman who looked up as she entered had features as sharp as a machete. She smiled, but it looked as if she had found it an unfamiliar expression. She wore the olive-drab Survey coverall, with the addition of several pieces of antique jewelry.

"Dierdre Jamail?" the woman queried.

Who else would it be? Dierdre thought, since the director had sent her flunky specifically for Dierdre. Somehow, she knew that this was not the time for a sarcastic answer.

"Reporting as ordered, Director." She put on her best superior-pleasing look: respectful, attentive and eager.

The woman wasn't buying it. "Your resume is about as marginal as they get without being an outright condemnation. Let's see," she took on the abstracted look of someone scanning an eye-implant readout, "frequent absences from class, even more frequent disciplinary problems. You once broke your biology professor's jaw."

"That was Schlucter. He wouldn't keep his hands off me. I had a perfect right to deck him."

"It doesn't seem to have taught him anything," the director said. "An aggrieved husband killed him in a duel last year."

"Good riddance."

"Nonetheless, assault on a professor is a black mark. So is larceny. It seems you and some sorority friends stole a ship and took it to Avalon."

"But we'd have missed the party if we'd waited for a regular transport!"

"Oddly enough, the laws don't specify that impatience to attend a party constitutes justification for theft. Especially when the vehicle in question is a heavily-armed military craft. You're lucky Avalon's autosecurity systems didn't cut you to scrap."

Dierdre snorted. "Anyone who can't outsmart an outdated system like that deserves to get killed. Anyway, they got the ship back."

"A good thing they did. It only cost you ten days in the Avalon lockup, which in turn meant you had to repeat a planetary navigation class."

Dierdre was becoming very uncomfortable. "Look, it's my grades that should count. Aren't they good enough?" She desperately wanted a planetside assignment. She was certain that another year of schooling on probation would drive her insane.

"They're not bad, considering your record of absenteeism. Still, the work we do down here requires tight discipline and close cooperation. Teamwork doesn't seem to be your forte."

"I'm sure I could fit in if there was a *reason* for it. It's just that all the drills and regulations seemed so senseless in the classroom!"

The director looked at her coldly. "You'd be surprised. Most often, if you can't cut it in training, you can't cut it in the field, either." She was silent for a few minutes, pondering something while Dierdre struggled not to do anything foolish, like scream or go into attack mode.

"All right," the director said at last, "I'm going to give you a chance. Just one. Screw up and you'll probably be in orbit for another five years."

Dierdre felt relief pouring over her like a zero-g shower. This called for some false humility. "Thank you, Director. I promise not to disappoint you. I truly appreciate this chance."

"Tell me that when you come back alive. I'm cutting your orders for the Suleiman Archipelago."

Dierdre tried to picture it from what she remembered of her planetary geography. She didn't want to reach for her handset and she had never been able to afford one of the eye-implants that could project directly into the optic nerve. She could remember the continents and major islands, of course, and the largest rivers, but so many other features were being discovered, named, and mapped every year that she couldn't keep up with them all.

"Don't be embarrassed if you've never heard of it. It's our most remote exploration so far. The first-in teams got all the cushy, temperate-zone assignments. You latecomers are stuck with the arctic and tropical jobs. It's a string of islands off the southeast coast of Atropos. Between the archipelago and the mainland is the Iliad Sea. Got it located now?"

She nodded as the picture formed in her mind. Atropos was one of the larger islands, not quite impressive enough for continental status. It was well within the tropical belt, where the average daily temperatures at sea level ran almost forty degrees Centigrade, ninety-something in the old Fahrenheit system, with humidity to match. Flora and fauna could be anything, but always abundant.

"The Survey Chief for that area," Merchant went

on, "is Derek Kuroda. His base is at Cape Troy, on the mainland. Do you accept the assignment?"

"Yes!" Dierdre said, desperately. If she'd turned it down, there would be no other chance. The tropics were said to be rough, but she feared the arctic more. She hated cold.

"Good. Did you bring your gear down?" Dierdre nodded. "No need to delay, then. Get your stuff and report to Mission HQ. It's down by the scoutcraft base. Take this." She tore a flimsy readout sheet from her desk and handed it to the younger woman. "This has your orders and specs. You'll get a uniform issue and a briefing and you'll be assigned transportation. Eat while you have the chance. It's a long flight."

"Thank you, Director. I don't know. . . ."

"Good luck," Merchant said, abruptly.

Dierdre took that for dismissal and left. Jubilantly, she ran from the building and picked up her gear where she had left it on the stabilized dirt walkway in front. She squatted, slipped her arms through the straps of her backpack, stood, hoisted her duffel bag to one shoulder, and set off for the sounds of the scoutcraft. The muscles in her thighs protested, but she knew she would have to get used to it. She had trained most of her life for work in a planetary environment.

Besides the noise, the scoutcraft base was distinguished by a sharp chemical reek. Having been raised in the artificial environment of the spacegoing republics, the smell was homey to Dierdre. It was the complex of organic smells from the nearby forest that seemed alien.

All around her, people bustled importantly. Most of them wore the olive Survey uniform, making her self-conscious of her red and yellow clothes. Most of the uniforms bore the patches and insignia of various expeditions.

Before she had walked for five minutes, sweat

began streaming down her scalp. She checked her wrist set. It read twenty-three degrees Centigrade, with low humidity. These, she knew, were virtually idyllic conditions in the high latitudes of a temperate zone. What would the tropics be like?

Flatbed cargo shuttles purred along between the buildings. Some of them were, absurdly, still labelled "Sigma Pavonis Expedition." When the expedition had left the Sol system, nobody in the Island World administration had noticed that the star had been mislabelled back in the twentieth century in the popularly used table of the nearest stars, with a typesetter mistaking the lower-case Greek letter sigma for delta. The mistake had been perpetuated in the catalogues for all the ensuing decades. After the expedition had been well under way, an astronomer had pointed out to the Avalonian chief administrator that they were headed for what was actually Delta Pavonis. Only the name of the star in the catalogue was in error and the coordiates, spectral type, parallax, and identification number listed therein were for Delta Pavonis. Also, since more up-to-date references had been used in astrogation, there had actually been little risk of the expedition's mistakenly heading for the *real* Sigma Pavonis. Still, there once was a fellow named Columbus who thought he had reached India. . . .

The thought amused Dierdre while she looked over the scenery, but nobody stopped to offer her a ride. Maybe, she thought, it was their way of displaying disdain for a newcomer. The veterans had, or at least affected, a swagger that said they were used to gravity and wind. There was no way she could even attempt a swagger carrying her load, but she made a note to practice it when she could be sure nobody was looking.

Mission HQ was another ugly building of extruded foam, but weather shelters of any sort were still a novelty to Dierdre, so she found them fascinating.

They had a quality of *insideness* that was indescribable. It was almost as strange as being outside. All her life, she had been in enclosed spaces, although she was rarely aware of it. Even when working on the surface of an asteroid or outside a ship, a spacer was still enclosed inside a spacesuit. At least she seemed to be adjusting well. Some first-time arrivals came down with severe agoraphobia.

The building had a number of entrances, but she found one labelled New Arrivals and went in. A man sitting behind a desk, feet propped up and watching something on a small holoset, looked at her and smiled.

"Just off the shuttle, eh?" He seemed friendly, even in stating the obvious.

"Yes. I was told to report here. Something about uniform issue and briefing."

"If you'll let me see your orders, I'll try to help." He scanned the sheet, then frowned slightly. "All the way over on Atropos? How'd you draw an assignment like that?" He looked slightly embarrassed. "Not meaning to pry, of course."

This wasn't looking good. "I think it had something to do with all the demerits, back at the Academy."

"I guess that could do it. Derek Kuroda's expedition, huh? He's a good explorer, even if . . . well, never mind. You see this yellow line on the floor?" He pointed at one of a dozen lines of varying color. "Just follow the line. It loops around an area of hangars and maintenance facilities—those look sort of like ship bays back home—and you'll come to a wing full of classrooms and supply rooms. It's confusing, but you'll find a lot of that around here. Apparently, we've been living in space for so long that we sort of lost the knack for laying out flat-ground facilities. Uniform issue is the next door on the right after the dispensary. They'll direct you to your next station from there."

She retrieved her orders. "Thank you." After a few more pleasantries, she began to follow the line. The building was huge and, as the man had suggested, badly planned, with wings and facilities added on as necessity dictated. She tried to remember what she knew of Derek Kuroda. What everybody knew, of course, was that he had made the original discovery of the Rhea Objects, the alien power packs that had made the Great Leap Outward possible. After that stupendous event, he had faded from public view. She vaguely remembered him addressing a few classes back at the Academy. So he was in exploration these days? And he had been sent to the most remote and undesirable part of the planet? That sounded ominous, especially since she was bound there herself.

Uniform issue turned out to be a long, low-ceilinged room manned by a single technician, a fit-looking young man who appeared to be out of place in such a job. When he came from behind his counter, he was limping heavily. His left leg was in an inflatable cast from ankle to hip.

"Let's see," he said, scanning her orders, "you need some tropical-weight clothes. Do you have boots?"

"I was told it was a good idea to get them on Avalon, so I did." She displayed her feet, well-shod in boots guaranteed by the salesman to be ideal for all weathers and terrains. They had been ungodly expensive, but explorers she had spoken with at the Academy had been unanimous in advising that durable footwear was an absolute necessity when working planetside.

"Good move. This thing here," he slapped the big machine that took up much of the room, "does fine with clothes, but it can't make boots worth a damn. They fall apart after about ten days. Maintenance is always going to send somebody over to fix this thing, but I'll believe it when I see it. Step on inside and let it get your measurements."

She stepped into a boothlike niche lined with low-intensity lasers. The invisible beams of the instruments took a set of remorselessly accurate measurements. "Did you get that injury on an expedition?" The machine told her to hold her arms out and she complied.

"Yeah, like a damn fool. We were checking out some cliffs in that big southeastern bay in Takachiho. Believe me, no matter how much training you've had up there, it takes a lot of experience to judge when you're too high to jump. Misjudge and you end up in a job like this for a few months."

"Were you rappeling?"

"Right. We got almost to the bottom, just a few meters. That's when I found out that two meters is an easy jump, but three is too much, if you land wrong. That's another thing. Natural surfaces are always uneven, and sand can be a real killer. Soft, and there's always rocks and things buried in it, so you stumble easy. That's what happened to me: I came down on a patch of sand with a rock under one foot. Ended up with a fractured femur and torn ligaments in my ankle and knee."

She left the niche. "Does that sort of thing happen often?"

"All the time. Just check in at the hospital. Leg, foot and knee injuries are the most common type. It seems that in spending several generations in space, we lost our fear of heights. People are always overestimating how long a fall they can take."

"I'll remember that. Thanks." The machine coughed a bundle of cloth into a bin.

"There're your uniforms. Four sets, coveralls, underwear and socks, all in tropical weight. Your expedition colors are embroidered on the shoulders."

She pulled the bundle apart and began folding all but one set. The underwear looked incredibly archaic; a short-sleeved singlet and voluminous shorts in some white, nubby fabric. "Do they really expect us to wear these?" She held up a pair of the shorts. The thought of wearing them was vaguely embarrassing.

"They're not designed for fashion. They're to soak up sweat and keep your coveralls from rubbing you raw."

She made a face. "Sounds primitive."

"It is. Could be worse, though. Back on Earth, the tropics meant all that sweat drew bugs and caused fungus infections. Nothing here like that. What's here is plenty strange enough, though."

"So I understand. What else do I need to pick up?"

"Nothing here. Your first uniform issue is free from Survey. When you replace them, you buy them. Gear's something else. Do you have a tent and sleeping bag?"

"Uh-huh. One-piece unit, cost like hell."

"Let me see it." She pulled the unit from her duffel bag and he looked it over. "This is a good one, but it'll cook you in the tropics. This bag is made for temps down to minus fifty. Even if you left it wide open at night, you'd burn up. When you get to Supply, tell Leva, the supply man, that you want to swap it for a tropical model. Don't let him snooker you. The tropic model costs about half what this one does. Get him to give you the difference in credit or in lagniappe from the supply room. You have good knives, tools? Rope?"

She dumped her pack and duffel bag and he went through the contents. When he was satisfied, he helped her repack them. "You're pretty well set except for the sleeping bag and tent. Have you had antisolar treatment?"

"Sure." It was a variation of the antiradiation treatment that most spacers had anyway. The skin cells were encouraged to manufacture a natural block against several forms of hard radiation.

"Good. You have brown eyes, so that's a help. Here, one last thing." He punched something into the console of the fabricator and it kicked out one more piece of cloth. The man picked it up and handed it to her. "Wear it in good health."

She turned the thing over in her hands. It was of olive cloth, like her new uniforms, with a central part that was shapelessly cylindrical and an outer part that was stiffer, discoid in shape. "It's a hat!"

"That's right. Everybody wears them in the bush. Your antisolar treatment won't cut the glare, but this will. It gives you portable shade. Both sides pin up if you want them out of the way. You can fan yourself with it and when you get mad you can throw it down and stomp on it. You'll get mad a lot, out there."

"Thanks." She tried it on, feeling ridiculous. She had never worn a hat. Spacers never wore such things. "How do I look?"

"Great. Except you've got it on backwards." He made the proper adjustments. "There. Now, there's dressing rooms down at that end. Go change into one of your new uniforms and nobody'll be able to tell you from an old-timer."

She went in and made the switch. When she stepped out, she found that clothes didn't make the explorer. She felt exactly as she had when she left the shuttle: like an awkward, stumbling beginner. It didn't help that the underwear felt so strange. She had the absurd feeling that people could see them beneath her coverall.

"Perfect," the uniform issue man said. "Now go to Supply, and don't forget what I told you about getting your credit back."

She thanked him and went to Supply, thence to Medical. Eventually she found herself in a large auditorium with about twenty other newcomers, awaiting a final briefing before taking shuttles to their duty assignments. They fidgeted in their seats for a few minutes, then fell silent as a woman came in and mounted the podium. She was dark-haired and wore a white lab coat over her Survey uniform.

"Welcome to Delta Pav Four," she began. "I'm Antigone Ciano, director of environmental engineering." Dierdre sat up and took closer notice. This was interesting. The Cianos had been a crucial family in space pioneering. This woman had the intense, slightly mad look common to that family.

"In the next few hours," Ciano went on, "you will all be winging to your various assignments. If you've paid attention in your classes, you know that we've discovered a planet that's better than we had any right to hope, and stranger than anything we could have imagined." She clasped her hands behind her back and swayed like a reed in a gentle breeze.

"The whole planet teems with life, but it seems to have evolved here in a fashion completely different from the same process on Earth. The flora and fauna of the different continents and islands differ as radically as if they had evolved on different planets. The same seems to be true in the oceans, although we've barely begun to look at those. Various theories are being tested to account for the differences, mostly concerning extreme isolation during the very beginnings of life on this planet. It's a moot point, because the geology here is just as strange as the biology . . . mountain ranges where they have no business being, things like that. Well, you'll see for yourselves. The thing to remember is that whatever you learn in one place may do you no good in another."

The newcomers looked dismayed, but she brightened. "There's a good side to all this. Nothing here has evolved to bite you, for instance. There are no equivalents for mosquitoes, ticks, fleas, and that sort of thing, no bloodsuckers or parasites. I was on Earth many years ago and believe me, that improves things a lot. We can't eat anything that lives here, but that means nothing can eat us, either." She smiled at them. "Of course, you still have to be careful. Some predators attack motion or heat. It's no comfort to watch them gag after spitting out a big bloody hunk of your anatomy. They may not *know* you're inedible, so be careful.

"Conditions here are rather Earthlike, in that they run the gamut from paradisical to hellish. Most of you will be going to fairly pleasant areas, but a few will draw the hardship posts. Whichever you get, try to maintain the proper spirit of scientific discovery; it makes up for a lot of pain. Remember that your worst enemy is your own inexperience. Be very, *very* careful and watch closely what your more experienced colleagues do. Planetary conditions are new to almost all of us, and those few of us who were on Earth or Mars before the Jump were mostly in civilized and controlled areas. This is entirely different. We've had some deaths already, and many injuries."

She looked at a list in her hand. "I'll now give you your flight numbers and times. Answer when I call your name." She proceeded through the list, adding bits of information and advice along with the destinations. Dierdre waited tensely as, by ones and twos, the others got up to go meet their flights. At last, she was the only one left in the seats, wondering if she had somehow been missed.

Antigone Ciano stared at her list for several moments. "Miss Jamail? I see you're headed for those islands in the Iliad Sea."

"That's what I'm told." She wondered why she had been singled out.

"It's two hours before your flight leaves. Would you care to join me in the cafeteria? You'd better eat in any case. Your flight will take more than sixteen hours."

"Certainly," Deirdre said. She felt flattered. An invitation from one of the legendary Cianos on her first day on-planet. "I'd love to." Here was a chance to get some inside information.

"Just come along with me." The walk to the dining facility was a long one, especially lugging all her gear. Ciano kept up a running patter, making acerbic comments about nearly everything they passed. Most of her ire seemed to be aimed at Survey administration, which she considered to be inefficient and overrun with bureaucrats. Dierdre wasn't sure how much to take seriously, since scientists and engineers always talked that way.

The cafeteria had tables and chairs made of the all-purpose extruded foam, ugly but functional. The food was little better: bland-tasting synthetics, mostly with the character of tofu.

"Until we get valid agriculture going," Ciano said by way of explanation, "this is what we'll have to put up with. Shuttle cargo space is too costly to bring down much in the way of luxury foods. You'll find that rationing is pretty strict here."

"Can't they set up a big hydroponics operation?"

"Sooner or later. Don't hold your breath. We really couldn't start work until we knew what local conditions we'd be facing. At least the atmosphere is Earthlike and the gravity's not too far off. Soil nutrients are the big problem and even for hydro-p we can't just manufacture them out of nothing. It's going to take some time. Fortunately, we have plenty of that."

"From what little I've heard," Dierdre said tentatively, "I'm headed for one of those hardship posts you mentioned."

"I'm afraid so. That's why I wanted to give you, in particular, a little advice. The others were all going to relatively easy assignments where they'll have some leisure and fairly good companionship to learn the ropes. It's going to be much rougher on you. Not meaning to pry, but I take it you had some difficulties back home?"

"I guess you could say that. I seem to have a facility for making people mad. My parents got me into the Academy mainly to keep me out of trouble at home. At the Academy I set some sort of record for demerits. I almost wasn't given a planetside assignment at all."

"That's about what I expected. Well, you're going to meet some kindred spirits where you're going, but that's not going to make them easy to get along with." She ran her fingers through her tangled hair. "I know what they taught you in school: how we're all a happy band of siblings cooperating in the great adventure of spreading human life and culture through the galaxy. To be honest, it's not as simple as that. We brought a lot of our old problems with us. One of them is politics. Back on Earth, then in the old Island Worlds, later in the asteroid colonies that made the Jump, and now down here on Delta Pav Four, it's all riddled with politics from top to bottom. Power groups, interest groups, administrative bureaus, they're all fighting and clawing for limited resources. Each wants to expand its own operations at the expense of the others. We thought we were escaping that sort of thing first by leaving Earth, then by leaving the Sol system. But we couldn't outrun human nature, it's as old as tribal societies. All we did was separate ourselves from certain outdated politico-economic systems."

"What's this got to do with my assignment?" This was beginning to sound brutal.

"There's an ancient practice that runs through all sorts of organizations from nations to military systems to corporations: there's always a place to send the screwups. Some outfit acquires a reputation for inefficiency or uncooperativeness or maybe just bad luck. Pretty soon, anybody with a bad record gets sent there. It stays a legitimate part of the organization, because you need a human dumping-ground. It's in the nature of bureaucracy that it's much easier to arrange a transfer than to hold a court-martial or a firing or whatever. The source of trouble is put out of sight, out of mind." She picked up her synthetic tea and sipped with an expression of distaste.

"And that's where I'm headed?" Dierdre asked in a dead voice. "But the district chief is Derek Kuroda. I thought he was . . ."

"Derek Kuroda has been, for his entire adult life, one of the biggest screwups and trouble makers in the whole Diaspora. He does fine work but he makes enemies at an appalling rate. He tells his superiors what he thinks with reckless disregard for their feelings. He's worse in that respect than I am, and I've never been noted for forbearance. All of which is why he's stuck in South Atropos, with that ghastly-looking string of islands as his next assignment." She leaned forward and spoke earnestly. "It's great work and it'll be good experience for you, but it's a dead-end for your career if you stay too long. Take my advice and transfer out once you have a chance. If you compile a good record, you'll have your pick of assignments."

"I'll keep it in mind. Tell me, how does Dr. Kuroda feel about all this?"

She sat back with an abstracted look. "He thrives on it, the idiot. I've harangued him for years, but he never listens. He has a romantic image of himself as a rebel, a maverick. He just never grew up. Did I mention that he's my husband? I guess I didn't." She made an airy gesture with a beringed hand. "We love one another dearly, but we prefer to keep a certain distance most of the time. Half a planet is about right. With luck, you won't be seeing much of him. He'll be at his headquarters on the mainland, mostly." Abruptly, the older woman stood and held out her hand. "Good luck out there. Be careful and you'll make out all right. Send me word of how you're doing from time to time." She sounded as if she had meant it.

"I will," Dierdre said, deciding that she meant it, too.

An hour later, she stood on the airfield, her gear piled next to her as she shuffled forward in line to board her scoutcraft. It was a racy name for a clumsy-looking cargo vehicle. Its body was a barely-streamlined rectangle twenty meters in length and five meters high. At each corner was a rotating rotor pad, held clear of the ground by landing struts. A man wearing flyer's wings checked off the passengers as they boarded.

"Dierdre Jamail?" She nodded. "Southeast peninsula, Atropos?" She nodded again. "That's the last stop. If I was you, I'd stay aboard and ride back."

She was getting tired of this. "I asked for the assignment. I'm looking forward to it."

He looked as if he doubted her sanity. "You're sure welcome to it. Hop aboard, you'll be there in a little under seventeen hours."

She hoisted her duffel bag and climbed the steps into the scoutcraft.

TWO

She was sure she would go insane long before she reached her destination. She had pictured an aircraft ride as being not greatly different from a voyage in a small spacecraft. She was wrong. First of all, the noise was unbelievable. The interior was designed for cargo, with the only concession to passenger comfort being fold-down seats along the sides of the hold. There was no insulation to dim the noise from the engines, and the fumes from fuel and lubrication were almost as bad. She had wanted to talk with her fellow passengers, but the noise precluded even that small pleasure.

The motion of the craft was violent, jerking up, down, or to any side with every atmospheric disturbance. The thing had been designed for efficient cargo hauling, not for smooth flight. She was glad that the pilot had passed out anti-nausea pills before takeoff. Even the view from the tiny ports was disappointing, being mostly the tops of fluffy white clouds or monotonous seascape.

Every couple of hours they landed and discharged cargo or passengers. These brief respites allowed her to get out of the craft and stretch, breathe clean air and talk a little, but there wasn't much to learn.

Most of the other passengers were newcomers like herself and had little to tell her.

The terrain changed from one stop to the next, but it was dark after the third one. The last stop before the fall of night had been at the base of an immense mountain range, and she was deeply impressed. Holos could be incredibly realistic, but they were no substitute for knowing the mountains were actually *there*. They made her feel dwarfed in a way that a big chunk of rock floating in space never could.

Somehow, toward the early morning hours, she managed to sleep a little. All too soon, something shook her shoulder.

"Wake up, Sleeping Beauty, we're here. Come on out and see your new abode."

She snarled something sleepily and rubbed her eyes. A brief struggle freed her from her straps, and she collected her belongings and made her way to the hatch. The sky was growing dimly blue, so there was little to see, but there was plenty to feel and smell.

The heat struck her like a rubber hammer as soon as she left her transportation. The humidity matched the temperature. It was like breathing under water. If this was early morning, what would it be like at midday?

Even without a trace of breeze, the air bore distilled essence of organic decay. The air at the base had been rich with it. Here it was concentrated a hundredfold. She was sure that daylight would reveal a devastated landscape in the wake of some unthinkable catastrophe, because it smelled as if everything for a hundred kilometers around had been dead and rotting.

"Where is everybody?" she asked the pilot. "Who do I report to?" He was controlling a robot stevedore that methodically unloaded and stacked plastic crates from the hold.

"Somebody'll be along when it gets light. They

know about this delivery, they're just too lazy to come out this early. That looks like all of it. Make sure to stand clear of our takeoff. See you."

She saw no particular reason to say goodby, so she walked away from the scoutcraft as its engines began to whine in an ascending pitch, kicking dust and debris all over her, blowing off her new hat. She turned to chase it, but it was lost in the dark. When she turned back, the scoutcraft was climbing, its lurid running lights blinking in varicolored patterns. For five minutes it dwindled into the northwest, then was gone.

Dierdre walked back to the crates and sat on one. Between the fatigue of the trip and this virtual abandonment, she felt infinitely depressed. In her whole life, she had seldom been alone, rarely more than a few meters from others. Even in solo jaunts on small ships, there had always been remote communication. This was different. Now, there was no way she could summon another human being.

A loud squall from somewhere near set her nerves jangling and reminded her that she wasn't quite alone. She decided that the arrival of the scoutcraft had silenced the local fauna, but now that it was gone they were resuming their chorus. She tried to remember if she had ever read or heard any report on the animal life of southern Atropos, but she could recall nothing. All around, things were croaking, chittering, whirring.

She leapt to her feet and spun when something roared behind her. Suddenly, she was terrified. There was something out there that wanted to eat her. She had no way of telling it that she wasn't edible. With trembling fingers, she fumbled the torch off her belt and switched it on. The beam illuminated several meters of ground but washed all color from it. Then she saw movement. Something leapt into the light. It was about the size of her palm, wedge-shaped, with no visible eyes. It had six legs, the four at the broad end of the wedge long and muscular, the front ones small and terminating in tiny pincers. It swelled until it looked like a pear, its small, toothless mouth opened and it emitted the ear-splitting roar that had so shocked her. It paused as if waiting for applause; then, disappointed, hopped out of the light in a single bound.

Dierdre let out her breath and sat back down, trembling this time with relief. Not just because there was no danger, but because nobody had seen her panic. She was beginning to doubt that she would live through this.

Fifteen minutes later, she realized that she could see for at least a hundred meters. Soon colors began to emerge, and the nocturnal noises abated. Things didn't look promising, but it was a welcome change. She was in a clearing, and all around her was dense jungle. The profusion of flora fascinated her, but she wasn't about to go in there alone. To the east was what appeared to be a path. She wasn't sure whether they were called roads when there was no hardened surface. This one looked like plain dirt.

When it got bright enough, she found her hat and put it on. She needed it, because sweat was already running down her face. At least the scare had taken her mind off the heat. She waited some more, and was about to try out some of her emergency signalling equipment when she heard something mechanical. The noise was from the direction of the path and she watched to see what might be coming.

A minute later a quaint-looking vehicle trundled into view. It rolled on six fat tires, its jointed body and the rough surface making for what struck her as comical progress. It bounced its way over to her stack of crates and stopped. The driver dismounted, and he was only slightly less picturesque than his vehicle.

"Who arre ye, lass? We were no tol' tae expect a new replacement." She knew that accent. He was from Iona, a tiny asteroid that had made the Delta Pav Jump. Everyone else considered the Ionan brogue to be hilarious and many fights resulted. His bushy beard and hair were red, and framed his face like an archaic baby bonnet. His clothing consisted of boots and a ragged pair of shorts. There was nothing comical about his belt, though. It sported a large pistol and a larger machete.

"From what I hear," she said, her temper already frayed, "nobody tells your outfit much of anything."

"Och, and is that no the truth! I hope this load has yerr rations, for we've little to spare ye."

She sighed. "Well, I guess it's not your fault I was sentenced to Devil's Island. I'm Dierdre Jamail, from Deryabar, by way of Avalon and the Academy."

He accepted her hand. "I'm from Iona, as you'll no doubt have discerned. Ma name's Bela Szini."

"Really? I was expecting something more . . . well, more Celtic."

He grinned, revealing a gap between his front teeth. "Yerr own accent's no terribly Lebanese."

She laughed for the first time since touching down on planet. "I'm told my ancestors came from darkest San Antonio before they got sense and left Earth."

"Let's throw yerr things onta the donkey, then ye can help me wi' these crates."

Five minutes of relatively mild labor had her gasping. "Is it always like this?"

"It gets much worse. Ye'll acclimatize, though. You never get really used to it, but in a few days it'll no' bother ye so much. Climb on in and we'll be awa'."

With some trepidation, she climbed into the rider's seat. Bela stepped on a pedal and the donkey whirled in a circle and headed back toward the path. She had to grab the seat to keep from being thrown out and made a note to watch out for these centrifugal effects. Once they were going, she found that the ride wasn't as upsetting as that in the scoutcraft. In fact, it was rather exhilarating, and the artificial wind it created was refreshing. She also discovered that the cord dangling from her hat was to be tied beneath the chin, and that it was necessary. After it blew off and they had to stop to retrieve it, Bela showed her how the cord worked.

A few minutes' drive brought them to the seashore, a spectacle that took her breath away. So much water was simply unbelievable, even though it smelled as bad as the jungle. That was followed within minutes by another unprecedented sight: her first sunrise. Once again, a lifetime of holos had not prepared her for the splendor of the scene.

"It's fabulous!" she yelled. "Does it happen like this every day?"

"Aye. And almost as pretty when it sets. By then ye'll be happy to see it go."

She sat back down from her half-standing position. "Have I really been condemned to the lowest circle?"

He held out a hand, palm downward. It was a spacer equivalent of a shrug. "Ye're lucky to be awa' from they Survey loons. Here we've the best folk on this benighted planet. O' course," he amended, "ye'll find they're not all as easy to get along with as meself." He thought for a moment. "We run, you may say, to strong personalities."

Another ten minutes brought them to a huddle of flimsy-looking structures built on the shore. They were partly of the ubiquitous foam, partly of what looked like local materials. There were a few people walking about dozily, blinking and rubbing their eyes. Most were as casually dressed as Bela, except for those who had not bothered to dress at all. It was obvious that uniform standards were a bit slack at this outpost.

They wheeled to a stop in front of a shack built mainly from what appeared to be the bones of an enormous animal. It was roofed with vegetable matter, probably gigantic leaves, she thought. A sign by the door said: GO AWAY.

"Here we are," Bela said. "Let's see if the boss is up." He hopped out and Dierdre followed. The interior was dim after the glaring sunlight outside. It was quiet and relatively cool and she flinched when Bela howled at the top of his lungs.

"Chief Kurz! Rouse yersel' from yer drunken stupor, mon!"

A blocky, purposeful man came from a back room, buckling a kilt around his waist. "I'm awake, you idiot. Did you get the cargo?" His eyes narrowed when he saw Dierdre. "Who's this?"

"Dierdre Jamail, yer excellency."

"Dierdre? I didn't order any dierdres. What did you do, kid, kill somebody?"

She glared at him, hand on her belt knife, picking a spot to start carving. "No, but the idea has its attractions."

Kurz rubbed a hand down his face. "Sorry. It's too early for civilities. Fact is, we have a full complement and we've suffered no fatalities, a record I intend to maintain. Were you given a reason for being . . . oh, hell, I guess you screwed up like the rest of us. We'll find a slot for you. Have a seat, Dierdre, and I'll get the bureaucratic formalities out of the way." He turned slightly. "Barbara!"

A woman came from the back room. Her hair was short and wavy, and she wore a tiny loincloth and a string of big, wooden beads. She looked like something from an ancient jungle film. "What do you need, hon?" She caught sight of Dierdre and smiled. "Oh, someone new! God, it'll be good to have someone else to talk to. Do you play bridge?"

"I'm afraid not."

"Try not to be too appalled," Kurz said. "When we're out exploring, we're all business. Not too much spit and polish around camp, though. Barbara, this is Dierdre Jamail." He squinted at her orders. "Just out of the Academy, with a degree that's of no particular use. Don't feel bad, Dierdre. Down here hardly any academic specialty is much use. What you need is a sound body and an open mind. Says here you specialized in topographical analysis. I guess you know that it doesn't work very well here."

"Until a couple of years ago, we had only Earth to go by. I think maybe we just need to find the key, and everything down here will fall into place."

Kurz nodded. "I hope you're the one who finds out what it is. Barbara, put Dierdre down for rations and housing, and enter her on the payroll. Might as well list her as apprentice explorer. That suit you, Dierdre?"

"I have to start somewhere." Actually, she thought it sounded exciting. "Explorer" sounded much more adventurous than her former designation, "student."

"I'll put you in Ray Forrest's team. That's Team Red. Our exploration teams have color designations. Since we're going into the Iliad Sea my command is designated Task Force Iliad. So, when you report over the comm, you'll start off with, 'This is Iliad Team Red, Jamail reporting' or something like that."

She liked the sound of that. It sounded professional. "Where will my team be working?"

""We're just finishing up our exploration of the peninsula. The day after tomorrow, we cross the strait to the islands. The first one is Priam and Forrest's team will be the first to land."

"You can bunk in your team's barracks," Barbara said. "Or if that's too crowded for you, you can build your own shelter. I wouldn't recommend that since you'll be leaving so soon."

"There's a lot to learn in a short time," Kurz went on. "But a few basic rules you have to know right away. First, never go anywhere alone. Second, when you do go somewhere with somebody, make sure your team leader knows where you're going. Keep your comm unit and your medkit with you at all times. Everybody hates rescue parties. If you get in a fight with any of the other personnel, don't let it come to my attention. I'll send you both back with a bad report." He turned to look at Barbara. "I guess that's about it. Can you think of anything else?"

She smiled. "That's enough for one day. I'll take her down to Team Red barracks. C'mon, hon." From a peg by the door the woman took a belt that bore, among other items, a medkit and comm unit, settling it about her hips.

Dierdre followed, back out into the light and heat. She admired Barbara's easy, long-legged gait and glossy, golden skin. She wondered whether the skin was a derm treatment or the natural effect of sunlight. She had always felt her own body to be, at best, sturdily functional. Her height of 1.6 meters made her feel small in a gravity environment. It occurred to her that her stature, an irrelevancy in space, might be a handicap in exploring a planet.

The buildings were situated on a shelf of harder ground above the shifting sand that felt, to Dierdre, dangerously unstable. Barbara stopped before a long, low-roofed structure that was little more than a ragged half-cylinder of extruded foam. Its dingy brown color blended well enough with the nearby dirt, but that was its only saving grace. There was no sign or marking of any kind, so Dierdre figured that everyone just had to memorize where everybody else was. They ducked through the low doorway.

The interior was dim and relatively cool. The translucent foam and the small windows permitted enough light to make artificial illumination unnecessary. The building was lined with a double row of bunks, some of them occupied. Faces blinked toward the bright light of the doorway. On the first right-hand bunk, a man sat doing something with a pair of boots.

He set the boots on the floor. "Morning, Barb." One eyebrow went up at the sight of a second entrant.

"Ray, this is Dierdre. She'll be joining your team."

"I have a full team now. We jump off for unknown territory the day after tomorrow and we don't have time to break in a replacement just off the shuttle." He picked up his boots and with a look of profound disgust went back to whatever he was doing. "Find something for her to do at HQ where she can keep out of the way until she knows which way the gravity pulls."

"Kurz assigned her to you," Barbara said. "You want to give someone a hard time, go give it to Kurz." She turned to Dierdre. "I'll see you later. You'll do all right here."

When she was gone, Forrest glared at Dierdre. "What do you do?"

"Topographical analysis, and don't bother telling me it's no use down here; I already know. What was your specialty when you arrived?"

He hesitated a moment before answering. "Biology."

"And that's done you a hell of a lot of good, hasn't it?"

"Look, the rest of us were sent down to one of the big bases and we worked on safe operations until we knew the ropes. The dangerous operations are supposed to be handled only by experienced people."

She looked around at the ramshackle interior of the barracks. "That's not how I heard it. I've been told that people ended up here by screwing up."

He said, grudgingly, "Usually, it's just a personality clash."

"I'll believe that if you'll believe I won't be a drag on your team."

He sighed. "Hell, it's too early to argue. You're on. That last bunk on the end is unoccupied. Go on down and set up housekeeping." He returned his attention to his boots. To her admittedly inexperienced eye, they looked good for about another half-kilometer before utter disintegration.

Dierdre dragged her gear the length of the barracks, deciding that she had handled the interview rather well. She had always been good at projecting a confidence she didn't feel. There seemed to be twelve people in the team, which meant that she made it thirteen. She remembered that there was supposed to be something unlucky about that, but she didn't know why.

The bunk was a tubular metal frame with plastic webbing slung between the upper rods. She untied her sleeping bag from her pack and tossed it onto the bunk, where it unrolled and inflated. Her tent unit she left in its undeployed state, where it made a passable pillow. With unutterable relief, she sat on the bag and leaned back.

"New team member?" The speaker sat on the next bunk. "I'm Colin. Glad to have you here. Now somebody else gets to be the new member." Colin was even smaller than Dierdre, fair and apparently, although not necessarily, male.

She took his hand. "Dierdre Jamail. Does everybody get the leper treatment when they first arrive?"

"It depends on how badly they need manpower. Also whether they come from another expedition or right off the shuttle like you. That shiny new gear gives you away." Colin wore a tight-fitting blue coverall complete with a hood that covered everything but his round face. He looked about fourteen years old, but she knew he had to be older. The outfit looked stifling.

"Where are you from?" It was a standard conversation opener, but she was trying, obliquely, to discover the reason for his odd appearance.

"I was born on Malta, before the beginning of the Jump. I was born with some defective genes; that's why I wear this suit. It regulates my body temperature. I know, there aren't supposed to be birth defects anymore, but they figure it was caused by some sort of solar radiation prior to the Jump phase. There were some others, but no one like me."

"It looks hot." She wasn't sure how sensitive he

might be. She had never met a defective and wasn't certain how to talk to one without being offensive.

He smiled at her. "I'll bet I'm a lot more comfortable than you. I don't feel the heat here like everyone else."

"What's the routine here? Things look pretty relaxed, not quite what I'd expected an expedition base camp to look like." She didn't add that it was about what she had expected from an outfit of misfits and probable incompetents.

"Right now we're resting up for the next stage. We've been exploring the Suleiman Peninsula for three ship-months. Still plenty of work to be done here—species classification, detailed geological study—stuff like that. That can wait for the scientific teams, maybe years from now. We do the first-in surveys, mapping, rough study; especially we're here to find out what's dangerous."

"We're the expendable ones," she said.

"Now you're catching on. Anyway, to get back to your question, the next stage in our routine is breakfast. It's not much, but you get appetite suppressants to keep you from suffering too badly."

"I guess this is the part of the great adventure they didn't tell us about in school. Where do we eat?"

"If you're up to it, I'll show you."

"Fine. I didn't get much sleep flying down here but now I'm too jittery to sleep anyway." She clipped her medkit and comm unit onto her belt and followed Colin. The only acknowledgements she got from the other team members were a few grunts and nods. It looked as if Colin had represented the epitome of outgoing friendliness in this group.

They walked to a shanty that served the purpose of supply room-cum-mess hall. Breakfast was not served, it was issued. A bored-looking woman handed Dierdre a packet wrapped in thin plastic and pointed to an ID unit. Dierdre pressed her thumb against the unit's plate, acknowledging receipt of rations. They drew large tumblers of weak tea from a bulky, transparent bladder.

"Do they ration this, too?" she asked.

"Fluids are about the only thing that's not rationed," Colin said. "In fact, they encourage us to drink as much as we can hold. There's no sense dying of dehydration when we can drink the water here. So far, we haven't found any parasites or microorganisms that can harm us, but we sterilize it just in case."

She unwrapped the food packet, exposing a sickly-gray bar of concentrate the size of her hand. Resignedly, she bit into it. It had the consistency of a stiff paste and tasted of salt, sugar, vitamin and soy protein powder. She choked the mouthful down with the aid of some tea and made a disgusted face. "We've been in space for almost two centuries. At home, our synthesizers can make wood pulp taste like bouillabaise. Why do we have to eat this stuff?"

"Synthesizers need too much energy. The best they can do down here is primitive recycling. Next year we'll have decent chow. That's what they keep saying, anyway. Of course, the field expeditions will be the last to get it."

"I guess I could've stayed home if I'd wanted to live easy." She managed to eat half of the bar, then gave it up and stuffed the remainder in a pocket for later. Standing, she brushed crumbs from her coverall. "Could we go into the woods a little way? I've never seen a wild environment before this."

He got up. "Sure. It's safe as long as we stay near the camp. We have to sign out first." She followed him to the HQ shack where he logged them out, giving their planned route and approximate time of return. "If we don't log back in within an hour of that time," he told her, "the unit raises hell and the rescue parties go out. If they find you, they can make you wish they hadn't."

"I heard that nobody likes rescue parties." She

followed him from the HQ shack toward the mess shack, where they could fill their portable water bladders.

"That doesn't quite describe it. I got caught by a carnivorous plant once. It couldn't eat me, but it held me immobilized with a tentacle for about six hours. The search party found me and cut me loose, but for weeks they acted like it was all my fault, as if I'd planned it so they could lose some rest. I guess we'll get that way too, if we're down here long enough."

As they walked toward the forest margin, he ducked into the Team Red barracks to inform Forrest of their hike. When they proceeded, Dierdre found that she had to restrain herself to copy Colin's leisurely pace.

As they neared the woodline, Dierdre felt an intimidation she hoped Colin wouldn't notice. It looked dark in there, and it was crawling with *uncontrolled* life. It was all indescribably alien.

"Scary, isn't it?" Colin said.

"Not at all," she protested.

"You don't fool me. Everybody who's come down from orbit is scared the first time they confront a wild environment. I thought I'd go into convulsions the first time I walked under the trees. And that was right outside a big planetside base."

"Well, maybe it's a *little* bit scary." She felt sure he was exaggerating to spare her feelings, but she appreciated the gesture.

Once they were beneath the branches of the first trees, she lost the irrational terror she had felt. It seemed peaceful. Better yet, it was a good deal cooler. In contrast to the previous night, the quiet was positively vacuumlike. That made sense, when she thought about it. Nocturnal animals would naturally depend more on sound. She began to wish she had taken more biology classes.

"Is it safe to touch things?" she asked.

"Sure, as long as you don't grab an animal. Sometimes they resent handling."

She stooped and picked up a handful of dirt. Holding it to her nose, she inhaled its loamy aroma. "It smells just like the soil back in the biocontrol labs."

"Dirt seems to smell like dirt everyplace. There are probably differences, but human noses aren't very acute. Down at the bacterial level, it's likely that life forms are pretty similar. Come over this way, I'll show you something you've never seen before."

"I've never seen *any* of this before." She followed him down a gentle slope. Somewhere ahead, through a screen of dense growth, she could hear a strange, continuous sound. It awoke feelings she could only describe as ancestral. They pushed through the growth and there before them was a stream tumbling over a rocky bed. The sound was subtly different from any she had heard in a holographic reproduction, and here she could smell the damp streambed and feel the spray from where the rocks churned up a fine mist.

"It's beautiful!" She squatted on a damp rock and dipped her hand in the flow. The stream was perhaps five meters wide, not at all intimidating, unlike the ocean. She looked up at the sky, gleaming blue through a gap in the trees.

"I think I'm going to like this place," she said.

THREE

The boats didn't look strong enough to paddle across a swimming pool, much less to take to the open ocean. They consisted of a thin polymer fabric stretched over a metal-tube frame. They were ballasted with slabs of rock cut to fit the bilge and powered by solar-charged storage batteries. They were not fast, but they were cheap and efficient. Each was ten meters by three, without decking or overhead cover. All comm and navigation equipment was in weathertight modules.

"What if it rains?" Dierdre wanted to know.

"Get wet and like it," said Govinda Murphy. She was a wiry, nervous woman who rarely stopped moving.

"Team Red, climb aboard," Forrest shouted. Boat One was tied at the end of a spindly pier made of native wood, and metal struts scavenged from earlier building projects. It shook and swayed, seeming ready to collapse at any moment, as the team filed along it.

Dierdre was among the last to board. She tossed her duffel to Colin, who stored it amidships. Happily, she managed to scramble aboard without stumbling. When the whole team was aboard, the boat held thirteen explorers and their gear. Three other boats waited at the dock. Teams Blue, White and Gold would leave the next day.

As the sun broke over the horizon, Forrest addressed his team, the morning breeze ruffling his tawny beard. "Everybody listen close so I don't have to say this twice. Nobody sits on the gunnels while we're at sea. If you have to puke, do it over the leeward side. Got that? All right, cast off."

"Real inspiring oration, there," Dierdre whispered to Colin. "What's the leeward side?"

"That's the side where the wind's blowing away from you."

The silent engine started and the boat backed away from the pier, then reversed and nosed its way toward the entrance of the little lagoon. It hit open water just as the sun rose fully. In the open water, the gentle rocking of the craft turned to a more violent pitching, which smoothed out as they picked up speed.

To her relief, Dierdre found that she rather liked the motion of the boat. She had taken anti-nausea pills and was a bit groggy from their effects. It was another new experience, being tossed about amid a totally hostile environment. She looked over the side, hoping to see sea life, but the water was virtually opaque.

After about two hours, they sighted the island. Several of the team members hung queasily over the sides, but Dierdre felt fine. She stared eagerly at the island and was startled when a red-headed young man named Gaston pointed behind them.

"Look there!" he shouted.

They all looked back and saw a huge, humped form break the surface a hundred meters away. It was grayish and unbelievably big. With a hiss, a pillar of spray shot from an orifice, straight up for twenty meters. Beyond it, two other forms rose and did likewise. Then all three sank beneath the water.

"What was that?" Dierdre's heart was pounding.

The formerly benevolent ocean had turned hostile. It was full of monsters.

Forrest shrugged. "We see lots of things from a distance. All sorts of sea life's been observed from orbit, some of it bigger than those things. We've called those 'whales' for lack of a better term. They only show up near this archipelago. Nobody's figured out what keeps the oceanic life confined to specific areas. It's completely different from the way the Earth ecosystem worked."

"Do they ever get violent?" she asked.

"Not yet. Nobody's had a close look at them yet. They don't come closer to boats than those we just saw. So far."

Within an hour, they were a few hundred meters offshore. The southern tip of the island, where they were to land, appeared to be heavily wooded nearly to the waterline. It was girded with a narrow strip of sandy beach. A half-kilometer northward, on the eastern side of the tip, was a narrow inlet which had been chosen as the landing site. Wave action around the island was relatively mild, and in the little bay it was minimal. The boat nosed through the tiny breakers at its slowest speed and, with a gentle nudge, grounded.

"There," Forrest said, "jump smartly and nobody has to get wet feet. All ashore!"

Two bulky men named Sims and Okamura jumped ashore first. They carried beam rifles and trotted up the beach to the treeline, scanning alertly. While they stood guard, the others tossed gear onto the beach and jumped out onto the sand.

Dierdre knew that jumping was the ultimate test of accomplishment in a full-grav environment. She managed hers creditably, only getting one foot slightly wet. She picked up her duffel bag and trudged up the beach to the spot where everything was being stacked. Then she helped the others unload and carry the other gear. The vehicles would not arrive for several days. By the end of the task, the sun was at zenith and she was sweating profusely, but the island seemed to be marginally cooler than the mainland.

"Let's break," Forrest said. "We're going to be here a long time, so there's no sense anybody dropping from the heat and making more work for me."

Gratefully, Dierdre sat on her duffel. She took out a set of high-resolution magnifiers and scanned the inland prospect. For about a half-kilometer, the land sloped gently upward from the beach, then, abruptly, a line of cliffs formed a barrier as far as she could see. Lush, primeval growth hung over the edge of the cliffs; intensely green plants draped like carpets and hanging down in streamers, waving slowly in a breeze she could not feel. Aside from the green of the vegetation and the tan of the cliffs, there was little color. She could see no flowers.

She was about to turn the viewer off when she saw movement at the top of the cliff. Something long and serpentine poked out from the brush, swaying from side to side. She checked the distance reading at the bottom of her viewscreen. Then she checked it again. At this distance and magnification, the thing had to be really huge. She clicked in a higher magnification, but the thing was already withdrawing. She had an impression of a small head at the end of an absurdly long neck, then it was gone.

"I see something!" she said, excitedly. "At the top of those cliffs, thirty-five degrees."

Forrest and several others snatched up viewers and looked. "I don't see anything," the team leader said.

"It pulled back just as I called out. Big, really big. It looked like some kind of reptile, like a giant snake or something."

Forrest snorted disgustedly and set his viewer down. "First-time jitters. The whales spooked you and now you're seeing land animals."

"I saw it," she protested, her temper rising. "I don't just hallucinate." The others were staring at her, but she was too angry to feel embarrassed.

Forrest sat back down and took a drink from his bladder. "You'll notice that you saw something familiar. A reptile. That's not the sort of thing you see here. It's always totally unexpected."

"I didn't say it was a reptile! I said it was *like* a reptile. It's different!"

He wasn't impressed. "We'll know soon enough. We check out those cliffs tomorrow."

She felt as if her face were flaming. That made it even worse. It was always like this, when people treated her like some sort of aberrant child. Working hard, as always, she calmed herself. *It's up there, I saw it*, she told herself. *I'll make him eat every word.*

For the rest of the day, they sorted out their gear and erected temporary shelters. Dierdre merely unrolled her sleeping bag with its integral tent. Already, she felt alienated from the others. Social interaction had never been her strongest talent, and any sign of condescension could drive her into a rage. Since condescension was the natural attitude of the higher-ranking in any hierarchy, she had been in some sort of trouble most of her life. She knew that her temper was her worst enemy here. She had to guard against it, even if that meant keeping apart from the rest.

That night, she lay on her back, staring at the starscape overhead, her tent withdrawn for the moment. The two detailed for the first watch were down the beach somewhere, sitting near a tiny fire. She could hear their voices. There was no moon, but the densely packed stars cast a dim light. She had always seen the stars from space, and here they seemed oddly hazy, the result of atmospheric diffusion.

She saw a flickering overhead, and at first thought it was another effect of the rippling atmosphere, but it was something else. She lost it for several minutes, almost thought she had imagined it, then saw it again almost directly overhead. A shape blotted out a small section of stars. Something was *flying* up there.

She groped until her hand found her backpack, took out the viewer. She aimed it upward, turned to nightview. The stars bloomed like the bright suns they were, then dimmed as she set the viewer for a lower-altitude scan. She found it almost immediately. Against the dim background, the shape was ghostly-white from its own radiated heat. So faint was the white that she knew it had a low body temperature. She had no referent to judge its size, and the viewer wasn't able to gather enough data to give her a scale. It looked to be human-size, perhaps a bit smaller.

Whatever it was, it had a narrow body, a long tail between stubby hind legs, a wedge-shaped head on a fairly long neck, and wings. The wings seemed to take the place of forelegs, and they were vaguely batlike. But she was sure that no bat ever soared like that. The wings seemed to be of a thin, taut-stretched membrane, capable of subtle adjustment for riding the thermals.

In the faint ambient light, she could make out little else. After a few minutes, the creature soared away toward the cliffs. Dierdre put the viewer away. She was not about to make a fool of herself twice in the same day. She turned over and went to sleep.

Toward dawn Okamura woke her. "Time for your watch, Jamail."

"Okay," she said, sitting up and yawning, but he had already turned away, heading for his sack and an hour or two of sleep before everyone had to roll out. Still yawning, she stumbled toward the faint glow of the driftwood fire. It was little more than coals now. Her partner for the last watch of the evening was already there; a big, athletic woman named Hannie Meersma. The woman seemed open and friendly, but Dierdre found her intimidating. Hannie was tall and blond where Dierdre was small and dark. She was heavy-breasted and broad-hipped, but Dierdre had seen her sparring the day before, practicing some sort of esoteric hand-to-hand combat technique, and she was as quick and strong as any of the men. In one especially rough bout, she had knocked the hulking Sims unconscious. Dierdre suspected genetic engineering somewhere in the woman's background.

"You look half asleep," Hannie said. "Here, take some of this." She passed a bladder that was warming by the fire and Dierdre caught a whiff of its fragrant steam.

"Real coffee!"

"It's the one thing they don't stint on for field expeditions. The food and working conditions make morale low enough. Without coffee, it'd plummet through the magma."

Dierdre took the bladder and drank. The first swallow of coffee was like nectar. She had never been a coffee addict, but then she'd seldom been called upon to get up so early, either.

"The sentries have all reported it's been fairly quiet all night," Hannie said, "so we can assume we've entered a different ecosystem from the mainland. The nocturnal animals raised hell all night there."

"I noticed. I've heard a few noises tonight, though; distant honks and hisses, and something kept buzzing by my ears with a high-pitched hum, almost subliminal."

"You, too. I heard the same thing, thought maybe it was my imagination." Hannie pulled up a trouser leg and picked at a scab on her muscular calf. "And something bit me. I wish they'd learn that it's futile. I probably poisoned whatever it was."

Tiny creatures hopped around in the sand, some of them jumping suicidally into the fire. They hissed and popped when they struck the coals. Dierdre found it very unpleasant.

"That's awful," she said.

Hannie shrugged. "It's their choice, nobody's making them do it."

Two hours later, everybody was up, seemingly without the early-morning grouchiness that had prevailed back at the base camp. Now there was the subdued excitement of breaking new ground. They drank coffee and munched on food bars, talking a little too loudly.

"Assignments," Forrest called. "I'll lead A team. Here's our order of march: Sims and Okamura take point, then me. I go solo because we have an odd number this trip. Everybody else pairs up. After me, Colin and Jamail, then Hannie and Govinda. Team B: Gaston and Schubert go first, then Ping and Lefevre. Angus and Fumiyo take drag. This morning, we check out the cliffs. Both teams travel together until we reach the base, then we split up. Team A goes north, Team B, south. We keep going until 0300, then turn back, rendezvous at our splitup point, and return here before dark. Use your comm units for essential information, not for conversation. Any questions?"

"We may have trouble using our comm units for anything," Schubert said. He was Team Red's communications specialist. "I ran a comm check last night when I was on guard. Orbital reports hellatious sunspot activity, screwing up communications bad. Not the sophisticated ship-to-ship stuff, but this obsolete radio equipment we have planetside is going to be all but useless for a while. We may be able to keep contact here on the island, but comm with the mainland's going to be spotty. As for contacting main base or orbital, forget it."

"Hell," Govinda said, "what if we have a real emergency here? We'll be isolated!"

"None of that," Forrest snapped. "We haven't run into anything we couldn't handle so far; there's no reason to think it'll happen just because we can't call in help. You were looking for adventure when you signed up for this, weren't you? Remote communication is a fairly recent luxury for explorers. Just think of yourselves as Columbus or something, or the early space explorers."

"Wait a minute," said Ping, a delicate-looking young man with Southeast Asian features, "they had radio commo."

"Sure," Forrest said. "They could call out all they liked, but nobody could come get them, no matter how much trouble they were in. Imagine how frustrating *that* would be. Okay, everybody load up the gear you're taking. We move out in five minutes."

With discussion over, there was a brief, orderly bustle as boots were tightened, belts and packs were slung, canteens topped up and forgotten items were scrounged out of duffle bags. In five minutes, they were on the march.

The path Forrest chose paralleled a stream. Far ahead, above the scrubby trees, they could see a gorge where the stream cut through the cliffs. They were not under noise discipline, but there was little talking along the way. After a few hundred meters in the stifling heat, they had little breath to waste on idle chatter. There was no true trail, and they picked their way through the brush, where it seemed thinnest. Since time was not crucial, it was policy not to use machetes or other trail-clearing tools, since they could not be sure what chemicals might be released.

The trees seemed to be stunted, as might be expected on the narrow coastal shelf, where the only soil was a thin layer washed down over the millennia from the cliffs above. There were some troublesome vines, but most of the monotonously dark-green vegetation was no impediment. The rough, broken ground caused a good deal of stumbling and cursing. The growth was predominantly of two sorts: shrublike trees with twisted, woody trunks and spiky leaves, and, nearest to the water, a tall plant with a corrugated stem that looked like a bundle of reeds. It all looked strange but also disturbingly familiar. Dierdre couldn't put her finger on it, but there was something wrong with the vegetation. Then she knew what it was: the stuff just wasn't *alien* enough.

There was a sudden stinging sensation on the side of her neck and, without thought, she slapped it. She glanced at her palm and saw the squashed remnants of a minute creature with threadlike legs and a smear of red. She showed it to Colin.

"Look, this thing had red blood."

Colin examined it. "I think that's your blood."

She shook her head. "Nothing here should be adapted to drilling humans for blood. It's probably looking for something else entirely."

He slapped at something on his cheek. "They home on us like they were born to the trade."

Forrest called a break near the base of the cliffs. He looked decidedly preoccupied, unlike the businesslike persona he had shown earlier in the morning. Dierdre decided to risk another rebuff and walked to where he was sitting on a rocky outcrop.

"Boss, I don't want you to think I'm hallucinating or anything, but there's something weird about the insect life here."

He nodded abstractedly, studying inflamed welts on the backs of his hands. "I noticed. I told you my field was biology, didn't I?"

"You did."

"Well, there's something here that just doesn't compute." He turned and raised his voice. "Listen. I want samples of the insect equivalents that're crawling and buzzing around here. I know that's not a first-in team's job, but this may be important. I want samples to send back to the mainland with the first return boat. Be careful when you handle them; some of them bite and sting. Make sure you have antitoxins in your medkits and keep them handy."

"We were told nothing here—" somebody said.

"I know what we were told," Forrest cut in. "But

we have to keep an open mind. We may finally have come to someplace where the local life is similar enough to ours to make us edible. That could mean vulnerable to their poisons. It might just mean susceptible to their diseases, too."

"We're supposed to be immune to everything," said Angus. He was a geology and planetology specialist from Avalon, slow-moving but observant. The pickhammer at his belt was the badge of his trade.

"Sure," Forrest said, "but lots of people have died making assumptions like that. From here on, we go on the assumption that this is a potentially inimical environment. You've all had the classes, you know there's no reason why we can't be harmed by microbes evolved in an ecosystem only roughly analogous to Earth's. Everybody worries about big animals eating us, but microscopic ones invading our systems are a lot more likely. They can, theoretically, do a great deal of damage before the differences in metabolic chemistry kill them off. No telling what toxins we might have to absorb."

Govinda chimed in: "The big stuff, even the bugs we can watch out for. What can we do about the microbes?"

They watched Forrest attentively as he considered the question. "I guess there's always prayer, and our broad-spectrum vaccinations. Other than that, use lots of disinfectant on cuts and bites, make double sure about sterilizing water, and try not to breathe too much. Okay, people, break's over. Team B head south, we'll go north. Comm check in thirty minutes."

Packs were reshouldered and the teams split up. The trek along the base of the cliffs was even rougher than that paralleling the stream. Loose soil and scree made the footing treacherous, and Dierdre found this stage especially arduous, since the lopsided mode of progress put unfamiliar stress on her ankles.

After a half hour, Forrest tried a comm check. The other team's report was grainy but understandable.

It did not bode well for the future, though. The voice over the comm should have been as clear as if the other speaker had actually been present, even though the intervening distance was more than a hundred kilometers. They went another fifty meters and came upon something amazing.

Sims and Okamura were just out of sight ahead. Okamura's low whistle alerted them that the trail-breakers had stopped. "Hey, c'mere and looka this," Okamura called.

They found the men standing in the midst of a gray-white cage. Dierdre's mind did a flipflop adjustment of scale and she realized that it was a skeleton. The bones stretched for an amazing distance, tapering into neck and tail vertebrae, the partially-smashed ribcage arching higher than Sims's head. A smallish lump at one end, half buried in mossy soil, was the thing's skull.

"Hot damn!" Colin said. He began to scramble over the bones, checking out joints and muscle attachments while Forrest took a careful visual record with his shoulder-mounted unit. The others just stood and gawked.

Dierdre walked along the neck vertebrae until she reached the skull. It was small for so large an animal, and it wasn't the solid lump of bone she had expected. It seemed to be composed of rather delicate struts and buttresses. The bone had deteriorated more than the more massive ones, but she could see that the thing had had two eyes, and its jaws were lined with flat, peglike teeth.

"Colin," Forrest called, "isn't paleontology one of your fields?"

"More like a hobby," Colin answered, his voice a little shaky. "I never figured it'd be much use where we were going."

"Any idea what this might be?"

"Yeah, but I'm damned if I'm going to be the first to say it. They say, in the old days, skippers lost their ships for reporting sea serpents, and pilots got grounded for reporting flying saucers. I'm not about to earn a psych rating by speculating on what I'm pretty sure this is."

"Hey, Boss!" Dierdre said, triumphantly. "Remember that hallucination I had yesterday?"

"Okay, I take it back. You satisfied?" He continued taking his visual.

"No. Call the other team and tell them . . ."

"Back!" Sims barked. Something was making a lot of rustling and crunching noise at the top of the cliff. "There's something big up there! Everybody get back to the brushline."

Sims and Okamura stayed by the skeleton, kneeling, their beam rifles trained on the spot where they could see trees and brush shaking. Forrest stood behind them, leaning back, his recorder trained likewise. The other four made a hasty retreat to the brush. They gaped upward, where something huge and grayish was nearing the edge.

The cliff was about twenty meters high at this point, made up mostly of soft sandstone. Some of the overhanging vines dangled to no more than six or seven meters from their level. As the animal neared the edge, it started a minor landslide of loose rock and soil. Small creatures, startled, flew upward from the trees.

"Here he comes!" Okamura shouted excitedly.

"No shooting," Forrest ordered. "We're here for information, not trophies."

Dierdre was a little annoyed at his calmness. She suppressed a grudging admiration. She was still mad at him.

Abruptly, a head thrust through the brush. Dierdre gasped. She had been expecting something like the serpent-necked thing she had seen the day before, but this was entirely different. The head was immense, with a parrot beak surmounted by a short, upcurving horn. Above the bone-hooded eyes, two longer horns thrust forward. Behind the horns, a wide, semicircular frill spread over its back with incongruous elegance. Despite the size and the bizarre appearance, the most striking thing was the color: the horns were bright red, the beak mostly electric blue and the frill was startlingly patterned in red and yellow. What they could see of the body appeared to be slate-gray.

Its lower jaw worked methodically, gradually reducing a hanging mouthful of rough brush to swallowable pulp. The explorers all held their breath, but the thing made no sign of noticing them. The rhythmic crunching of its meal was the only noise. The last of the brush disappeared and the jaws stopped working. Now they could hear a low, continuous rumble; the sound of the beast's formidable digestive apparatus. After a last scan, its tiny eyes still showing no indication of noticing them, the head withdrew. The sounds of its leisurely regression faded away.

"Can I say it now?" Colin asked, shakily.

"I'll say it and take the risk of a psych rating," Forrest answered. "That thing was a dinosaur. A real, Earth-type dinosaur. I think it was a triceratops. Right, Colin?"

"Looked like it. That family had a lot of members, but that looked like the classic triceratops. The bones could be those of a diplodocus, but that'd take more detailed study."

"You're talking an impossibility," Hannie said. "This has to be some sort of parallel evolution."

"It's about as likely," Forrest said, "that we'd run into human beings speaking English. Evolution shouldn't be *that* parallel. Something big and vaguely reptilian, yeah, maybe. But not one of the classics like a triceratops."

"Or a stegosaurus," said Govinda, helpfully. "If we see a stegosaurus, we'll know for sure we're onto something weird."

Forrest was about to say something sarcastic

when his comm unit beeped. "Talk to me," he said.

"Ray!" It was Fumiyo, Team B's leader. "Something just flew over us! You won't believe this, but it looks just like one of those pterodactyls or pteranodons or whatever the hell they were in Paleo class!"

"Wait'll you see what we just saw," he answered. "Bring Team B back to the splitup point right away. We'll rendezvous there. Things have taken a radical change."

"I saw one of those flying lizards last night," Dierdre said. "With my viewer."

"Then why didn't you say . . ." Forrest stopped himself. "Oh, yeah, well. . . . Come on, people, we're heading back."

Two hours later they were back at their beach camp, everybody looking subdued. They ran holos of the creatures they had seen. The flying reptile had a pale underside, but its back was yellow and the head a brilliant green. The back of the head was graced with a finlike crest.

"As I recall our comparative zoology classes," Fumiyo said, "bright colors aren't characteristic of very large animals, back on Earth. Drab colors or camouflage were the norm. Why is that triceratops's face so gaudy?"

"Maybe it's a sexual display," Colin said, "like some birds. Dinosaurs are supposed to be closely related to birds."

"This is all sort of dodging the major question, isn't it?" Dierdre said. "Shouldn't we be wondering just what the hell *dinosaurs*, for God's sake, are doing on a planet a good many light years from their place of origin, millions of years after their supposed extinction?"

"I'll confess that the question crossed my mind," Forrest said. "Unfortunately, we suffer from a severe lack of data."

"So what do we do?" Fumiyo asked.

"What do we do? We're explorers, aren't we? So we explore."

"You mean," Govinda said, slowly raising an arm and pointing to the top of the plateau, "we go up *there*, where all the dinosaurs and stuff are?"

"Sure," Forrest said, "why not?"

"We're out of touch with the mainland and the orbitals," Schubert pointed out.

"Remember what I said this morning? About how, if you're going to explore, you have to take risks? Besides, this may be the best thing that could have happened to us."

Everyone looked puzzled, but Dierdre thought she could see what he was getting at. "You mean, why should we share the glory?"

For the first time, he looked at her with approval. "Right. Listen, people, if we report what we've seen, what's going to happen? This is probably the most important discovery since Derek Kuroda found the Rhea Objects years ago. It may be the key to how this screwy planet works. Do you think an exploration this important would be left to *us*?" He looked around, saw expressions of dismay, then anger. "That's right. The glamor boys would descend on this place like locusts, with their tame newsies in tow. We'd be hustled off to some new godforsaken hellhole to explore while they made sure nobody remembered we were the first here. I say, let's go in there and do a complete survey, gather all the data we can and when it's all in we shoot the whole thing straight up to Avalon, bypassing the Survey bureaucracy entirely."

"We could be jailed for that," Hannie said.

"Let's blame it on the sunspot activity," Schubert suggested. "Say we couldn't get anything out and transmitted directly to Avalon in desperation."

"What about Kurz and the other teams?" someone asked. "They'll be along in a few days."

"Kurz will love it, when I explain things to him,"

Forrest insisted. "We'll meet them as they land and clue them in. After all, he's the expedition leader, so it's his name that'll be attached to it. He's just like the rest of us; none of us may ever have a chance at a coup this big. Even if we all get sacked, so what? The publicity from this discovery will make us all famous, if we handle it right."

Dierdre could see right away that he had struck just the right note. The others first looked apprehensive, then skeptical, then, finally, enthusiastic. They had been virtually resigned to a career of dead-end positions on obscure expeditions. Trouble with the authorities had been an inevitability rather than a danger. The prospect of a big payoff made up for a great deal of risk.

"Hell, yes, let's go!" said Okamura. He already wasn't afraid of much.

"Yeah!" Govinda said, her usual jitters transformed to aggressiveness.

"Let's do it," Hannie said, almost placidly. Her calm acceptance of the proposition seemed to decide the others. One by one, they signalled assent.

"Great," Forrest said. "We rest up for the rest of today. Tommorrow morning, we hit those cliffs. Now that we know there are large carnivores here that're fully equipped to eat us, I'm doubling the guard. While there's light, I want you to gather plenty of firewood. We want *big* fires tonight."

"We want regular overhead scans," Govinda said. "Those flying dragons spook me."

Forrest turned to Colin. "How about it? What size of prey did those things go for?"

"From what was known at the time the Island Worlds left Sol, about the largest they could manage was a good-sized fish. Maybe they could pick up something the size of a small child, but that's about the maximum."

"That's a relief," Govinda said.

"Hold it," Colin cautioned. "That's just what was

known. It takes specialized conditions to become fossilized, and the flying reptiles were rarer than most. Just when the paleontologists thought they'd found the biggest one, somebody'd discover an unknown species twice as large. We just don't know how big they got. You find a lot of fossils of a particular dinosaur, it usually means there were a lot of them, herd animals like the triceratops, or maybe they just lived around the right type of mud that's ideal for fossilization. There may have been thousands of species that never were discovered."

"Okay, we watch the sky, just in case," Forrest ordered. "And nobody leaves the camp in groups of less than four. Damn, I wish they'd let us have more beam rifles. Okay, nobody goes out of sight of the camp unless Sims or Okamura goes along with a beamer." He pointed at the two men in question. "If one of you goes out with a mission, the other stays with the camp. Clear?" The two security men nodded stolidly.

When everyone was settled in for the evening around a rather large fire, Dierdre decided to bring up the most vexing subject once more. "How did they get here?" She didn't have to elaborate; everyone knew what she referred to. To her surprise, Steve Forrest wasn't annoyed at the question.

"It's too soon to draw any conclusions," he said, "but let's look at what little we know. Some years ago, Derek Kuroda found the Rhea Objects. They were of alien origin, and it was by studying them that Sieglinde Kornfeld-Taggart developed the star drive that brought us here. Nobody knows how old those alien power packs were when Kuroda found them. They might have been left behind an hour before he found them, or they might have been millions of years old.

"What they meant, without question, was that aliens had visited the Sol system. It could be that they took samples and brought them back here."

"But," Fumiyo interjected, "nobody's found any alien artifacts in this system."

"How do we know that?" Dierdre said. "We don't know what to look for. The effort's been intense, but we've only covered the tiniest part of this system, and we could be looking at alien artifacts without knowing it."

"They might've left here millions of years ago," Colin pointed out. "All traces of their works might have disappeared. The animal life is self-reproducing. If the environment's remained the same, there'd be no need for the dinosaurs to die out or evolve into something else. They might have changed in small ways, but they'd already gone through millions of years of evolution. Life forms like that tend to remain stable until radical environmental change comes along."

"Could this be the aliens' home system?" Schubert wondered.

"I think we'd see more sign of it if it were," Forrest said. "It might be a world-sized lab, maybe a zoo. Whoever they were, they did things in a big way. We can't even be sure that these are the same aliens. Earth might have been visited many times since life appeared there."

The little group stared into the fire, intimidated by the image of such power and such a span of time. Even for people accustomed to crossing the vast reaches of space, it was awe-inspiring. It meant that humans had taken only the first, faltering steps along a path trodden long ago by beings of unimaginable knowledge and power.

"What bothers me most," Colin said, "is the idea that maybe they might still be around."

FOUR

It was just past sunrise when they reached the base of the cliffs. Forrest had chosen a spot near where they had seen the triceratops because the cliffs dipped lower there than at other spots they had surveyed. Fumiyo's party of the day before gawked at the enormous skeleton while a party of four made a short recon farther up the cliffline. Within the hour, they returned.

"Great scaling site, Boss," Okamura reported. "It'll be an easy climb even for the newbys."

The spot they had found was a notch in the cliff cut by a small stream. The base of the notch was no more than ten meters above them and trailing vines dangled within easy reach.

"Govinda, Dierdre," Forrest called, "you two are the smallest. Climb those vines and anchor us some lines up there. Don't go farther in than it takes to find a good anchor point."

"Hot damn!" Govinda said, almost hopping with excitement.

Dierdre's stomach fluttered as she pulled on her gloves. "Anybody got any good first words for when we get to the top?" she asked, nervously.

"Just keep your eyes on your surroundings," Forrest said. "If you want memorable first words, we can make some up later. That's what everybody does anyway."

Each woman grabbed a handful of the vines, braced her feet against the cliff face, and pulled as hard as she could. If they were going to fall, it would be best to do it while they were still close to the ground. The vines held. They began to climb.

Before she had climbed five meters, Dierdre's arms and shoulders began to scream at her. It had started out so easily that the sudden fatigue came as a shock. She bit her lower lip and forged on. In moments, her stomach muscles began to give out. There were still three meters to go. Govinda, with more experience, was almost at the top. Well, so much for being first. Making progress by inches, Dierdre continued her climb. She was determined not to fail in front of Forrest and the others.

It hadn't *looked* like a difficult climb, not from below. Dark spots began to form before her eyes. She was losing feeling in her hands.

"Just another half meter, Jamail," Govinda called from above. "C'mon!"

Gasping and sick in her stomach, Dierdre inched upward. She was sure she would fall when a hand grabbed the back of her collar and hauled upward. With a final surge of strength, Dierdre scrambled over the crumbly, vine-matted edge of the drop-off and sprawled on her belly in the sweet-smelling foliage next to the tiny stream.

"That wasn't so rough, was it?" Govinda said. She looked as fresh as if she had walked up the cliff.

"Piece of cake," Dierdre gasped, stomach heaving, sure she would faint. Gradually, her distress subsided. "I'm going to have to practice this climbing business."

"You'll get lots of opportunity. Can you get on your feet? We have to find a big rock or tree or something, and damn if I'm going in there alone."

Shakily, Dierdre stood. Everything seemed to be in working order. "Let's go."

Cautiously, pushing their way through the dense foliage lining the stream, they tried to look in every direction at once. Tiny creatures ran along the branches of bushes and small trees, too swift to see clearly. Insects buzzed loudly, but the repellant that Schubert had concocted from his aid kit seemed to be working.

"Was that a snake?" Govinda said, pointing at a movement in the underbrush.

"I didn't see it. At least none of those monsters have been here lately. This growth hasn't been trampled or chewed up in a long time. Years, maybe," she added, hopefully.

"Here's a good one." Govinda pointed to a tree nearly a half-meter in thickness, its gnarled roots gripping the steep side of the ravine. They looped a rope around the trunk and went back to the edge, tossing the rest of the line over.

"Come on up!" Govinda called.

First to ascend were Sims and Okamura, their beam rifles slung across their backs. As soon as they were up, they took up positions a dozen meters into the brush, keeping watch overhead and inland. Forrest came next, followed by the others. The team leader scanned the surroundings, muttering constantly into his recorder unit. With the rope, the climb was far easier and the last of the team was atop the cliff within ten minutes.

Dierdre had not experienced such excitement in her life, not even on her first solo flight. The air here seemed to crackle with life and danger. A chilling thought struck her: it would be easy to die here. Then another thought: so what?

"Let's move out," Forrest called. "Up onto the plateau, single file, two-meter intervals. Sims, you go first, I go next. Okamura, take rear guard. Go."

Slowly, they made their way up the steep bank.

The growth was dense, and Sims had to grunt and heave to force his way through, taking the easiest route he could find, quartering the slope rather than trying to climb straight up. Dierdre, still tired from her climb, took a position near the rear so that the trail would be well broken by the time she got to it.

The climb to the plateau took only a few minutes. They found themselves standing among tall trees that formed cathedral-like arches overhead. There was dense underbrush in places, but huge tunnels drilled through it forming long, intersecting corridors.

"Damn," Forrest said. "Now that's what I call a game trail." He inspected one, its tangled roof fully five meters from the forest floor. The floor itself was bare dirt in the tunnels, mossy loam everywhere else.

Colin stooped to study the ground. "This is packed too hard to take footprints. When we get to softer ground, we'll see plenty of them."

"Here's something," Hannie called. A few paces from the path, she had found a footprint impressed in the soft loam. It was at least forty centimeters wide, with toe and claw impressions. Everyone gaped at it.

"The broad ones like this," Colin said, "will be mostly herbivores. The ones to watch out for will have tracks like big birds, with long toes and not much footpad. Some will leave nothing but toe impressions."

"I'd just as soon not meet a tyrannosaur," Hannie said.

Colin shook his head. "A predator that size probably wouldn't even notice you. There were smaller ones a lot more dangerous. Small by dinosaur standards, that is. There was a real horror called a deinonychus. About man-sized, and they travelled in packs. Their hind feet each had a gut hook about half as long as your forearm. There were probably a lot of others never discovered."

"That's enough gawking," Forrest said. "We'll see plenty of tracks before long, and the animals that make them, too. Keep close, keep low and try not to attract attention. Pretend this is a war and we're moving through enemy territory. Until we know more about the habits of these creatures, we'll assume that they attack motion, smell, anything. Try to keep out of sight and keep downwind of the big ones. Don't forget to scan overhead." He thought for a moment. "And don't assume that just because an animal is a vegetarian that it can't be mean. Back on Earth, rhinos and bulls and elephants could be plenty rough when they felt provoked. We're intruders here, so act accordingly. Okay, let's move out, same way as before."

They reshouldered packs and weapons and began to trek inland, away from the cliffs. Dierdre found herself looking and listening harder than she ever had in her life. Her skin was sensitive to the slightest change in the wind and she sniffed the air for any significant smell. It was amazing to have all her senses and faculties engaged at once and she realized that most people go through life half-dead to the world around them. She wondered if this was part of the appeal that so many people found in war, this atavistic sense of hunting and being hunted at the same time.

It was oddly quiet in the forest. The loudest noise was the clicking and buzzing of insects. They saw no large animals, but once they startled a family of brightly-striped dinosaurs that had been sleeping in the shade. Everyone jumped at the burst of motion, then laughed nervously as they saw that the reptiles stood no more than knee-high. The little creatures stood on two legs with long tails, serpent-like necks and tiny heads. They fled in panic, tails high, into the forest.

"I wonder what they taste like," Sims said.

"We'd all like some decent food," Forrest said.

"But the rules clearly state that explorer teams are not to kill anything unless they're attacked."

"Do they say," Govinda asked, "that you can't eat it after it's attacked and you've killed it?"

Forrest thought a moment. "No, I guess not. Nobody'd thought we'd ever run into edible animal life down here. But, hell, you've lived on tank-raised seafood and synthetic meat all your lives. Do you really think you could butcher an animal for food?"

"I'm a biologist," Fumiyo said. "Biologists don't butcher animals, they dissect them. Hell, yes, I could cut one up and eat it. The stuff we've been eating the last few months would turn Buddha into a cannibal."

"Get your minds off your stomachs and back on your surroundings," the team leader ordered. "It's still morning. Let's push on."

Dierdre wondered if they were reverting to primitives in the primordial surroundings. She had never seriously considered killing a live animal and eating it. She felt she should be revolted at the thought. Instead, it made her mouth water.

The ground began to slope downward, and just before noon they came to a broad swamp. The trees thinned and for a while it looked as if they had been still on solid ground, but the grasses beneath their feet began to squish. Forrest held up his hand, signalling a stop. They had come to the edge of the treeline and beyond was a field of reeds. Here and there they could catch a glimpse of water. In the distance they could see large, slow-moving animals wading in the shallows.

"It looks peaceful, if primitive," Schubert said.

Just before them was a tangle of fallen logs, their roots undoubtedly rotted by rising waters from the swamp, all of them felled in a storm so that they lay with their tops in the same direction, their bark bumpy and scaly. The explorers started when one of the "logs" detached itself and glided into the water, parting reeds as it went until it disappeared.

"Colin," Forrest called, "can you identify it?"

"I think it was some sort of crocodilian. They were around at the same time as the dinosaurs. I'd say that that one was more than ten meters long, bigger than the surviving crocs. We'd better stay well back from the water. Crocodilians move fast when they're hunting and it'd be almost on top of you before you could see or hear it."

"You heard him," Forrest said. "We stay well within the trees, not where the growth is dense. We want to be able to see what's coming."

"Hey, look at that!" someone said, pointing. A hundred meters away, one of the flying reptiles was plunging toward a patch of open water. Just before it hit the surface, the broad wings warped downward, braking the fall. The elongated head darted out on its serpentine neck and then jerked back in a spray of water, clutching something silver and wriggling between the rows of back-curving teeth. With a flapping of leathery wings, the pterodactyl flew inland toward a range of steep hills just visible in the distance.

"Damn!" Govinda said. "That was beautiful!" It was amazing to see the animal world in action. Even for those who had been on earlier expeditions, it was impossible to respond to alien wildlife as to this scene from the past of their own planet. Even the best of the educational holos could never deliver the feeling of actually witnessing the real thing.

Keeping within the treeline, they sought a way around the swamp. Once, they tiptoed around a small herd of triceratops. The immense beasts paid them no heed, continuing placidly if noisily to munch the grass and brush. About half of the adult specimens lacked the brilliant coloration of the animal they had seen the day before. The immature members of the herd were likewise drab.

At noon Forrest called a halt and they sat in a wide circle with guards posted well away from the main group. He ordered Schubert to try a comm check.

"Absolutely no contact at all," Schubert reported happily. "We're getting nothing but static."

"Great. Let's hope it stays that way for a few days. I want to get a good look at this place. We need to find something really significant before we report in."

"Significant!" Fumiyo said. "What could be more significant than what we've found already?"

"What we've seen so far," Forrest waved an arm to take in their surroundings, "is tantalizing. We have some idea of what we're seeing. We still don't know how, when, who or why."

Dierdre put down the pine cone she had been studying. "You want to find signs of the aliens who did this? Artifacts?"

He nodded. "Or the aliens themselves. They could still be here, you know."

"That would definitely get our names in the history books," said Gaston, a dark, squat man from Avalon. "First contact. We've been talking about it for years."

"But are we the ones to handle it?" Fumiyo wanted to know.

"I can't think of anybody better," Forrest said. "Do you think our superiors are any smarter than we are? Hell, no. They just have seniority. When it comes to first contact, nobody has any experience, so that's not even a factor."

Everybody seemed to think that made sense. If their judgement was questionable, they had no lack of self-confidence and healthy egotism.

Something had been bothering Dierdre for most of the day, but she hadn't been able to sort it out from a host of other confused impressions. Now it resurfaced and she realized what it was.

"Hey, boss, I just thought of something. Those bugs that've been eating on us act like they like warm blood, but we've seen nothing here but reptiles. Did mosquitoes and dinosaurs coexist?"

Forrest cocked an eyebrow at Colin.

"Hard to say. People still argue over whether dinosaurs were cold-blooded or not. In any case, there were mammals around through most of the dinosaur period—little ones, like rats. Whether there were enough of them to support swarms of blood-sucking parasites, I don't know. Maybe nobody does. Insects rarely leave fossils behind."

"Parasites," somebody repeated. The very idea was horrifying. Generations spent in the controlled environments of the asteroid colonies had eliminated any tolerance for such horrors of the natural world.

"Weren't there all kinds of horrible diseases you could get just from being dunked in contaminated water?" someone asked.

"Forget that," Govinda said. "If we all have to stop washing on this expedition, I'm gonna swim back to the base camp."

"Let's keep our worries to a minimum," Forrest cautioned. "I don't think there were any diseases you could get that way that'd kill you very fast. If somebody comes down with something, we can probably evacuate them. Same procedure as dealing with serious injury."

"How come," Angus said, "all those heroic explorer stories we were raised on never said anything about the bugs and the diseases?"

"They did, if you go back far enough. In Magellan's day, you could expect at least fifty percent dead from disease or accident on a typical voyage. For a really big, round-the-world expedition, they could send out five ships. If one ship made it back, with half a crew and a cargo of spices, they figured it'd been a successful voyage."

"I guess that's okay for the Dark Ages," Hannie said. "Being gobbled up by a dinosaur is one thing, but dysentery is so *undignified.* Galloping diarrhea until you hemorrhage. That's no way for an explorer to die."

Sims tossed a pine cone at her. "If you wanted it easy, you could've stayed at home."

"Enough talk and relaxation," Forrest ordered. "Let's be on our way. I want everybody to be on the lookout for . . ." He hesitated. "For something different, out of place. I know that everything here looks exotic and new, but if you find something that really looks like it doesn't belong here, that's not a part of the natural landscape, *that* may be tangible evidence of the aliens."

"I think we get your drift, boss," Dierdre said, reshouldering her pack.

"Good. Jamail, you lead off, right behind Okamura."

Dierdre stepped out, smiling inwardly. She decided that being given the secondary point position was a sign that she was now accepted as a full-fledged explorer. She had, she decided complacently, acquitted herself rather well so far.

They continued to skirt the swamp and by late afternoon they came to a small lagoon where the water growth was less dense. A family of huge reptiles grazed on bottom growth, scooping up great, messy wads of muck and greenery, chewing it slowly in their wide, ducklike beaks. They paid no attention to the explorers, who were no more than fifty meters away.

"No gawking," Forrest said, "we'll see plenty more." Everybody gawked anyway, Forrest included. This was the closest they had come to any of the bigger specimens. These were mottled green-gray-brown, although it wasn't clear how much of that was hide and how much was mud.

"They don't seem too impressed with us," someone said.

"Would you be?" Colin asked.

By late afternoon they were not only physically exhausted but emotionally wrung out. It had been the longest, most exciting day of any of their young lives. The sights had been incredible and eventually even Forrest's no-gawking litany subsided to an occasional muttered "buncha damned tourists." The hint of omnipresent danger added to the strain, as did the knowledge that they were in willful violation of the regs. They were anxious to see everything, but nobody gave Forrest an argument when he decided to call it quits for the day.

They found a favorable campsite on high ground with a good field of view in all directions. They had discovered in the course of the day that the bloodsucking pests favored the low, swampy areas. In the final hour of daylight they gathered enough firewood to last the night. There were to be no after-dark separations from the group.

Dierdre tossed down her last load of wood and collapsed atop her pack. "I've gotta have some sack time or I'm gonna die right here!" she announced.

"You don't get to die until you've stood watch, Jamail," Forrest told her. He consulted his roster. "Which, in your case, will be 0300 to 0400, along with Lefevre."

"I might've known. The deadest part of the night." She unwrapped a ration bar and bit into it. She was so exhausted that it almost tasted good. "Well, knowing what's all around us should keep me awake."

She finished the concentrate, choking it down with chemical-tasting water. She unrolled her sleeping bag and sprawled on top of it, not even bothering to take off her boots. She told herself that, in a few minutes, when she worked up the energy, she would take her boots off and crawl into the bag.

The next thing she felt was someone shaking her shoulder. For a moment she thought she would need to use her hands to force her eyelids apart. They parted gummily and she saw Govinda leaning over her. "What's the matter?"

"Nothing's the matter," Govinda yawned. "It's time

for your watch. There's a bucket of water over by the fire. Go splash some on your face."

"It can't be 0300 yet." She squinted at her watch. "On the other hand, maybe it is. What's it been like?" She sat, stretching the kinks out of her back. Her neck only seemed to turn in one direction.

"Real quiet. I guess these reptiles are solar-powered. Once I heard some snorting and honking off in the distance, but that was all. Lotta bugs, though. Don't sit too close to the fire. They like it."

Govinda stumbled off to her bed and Dierdre took a few lurching steps toward the fire. Immediately, she knew that she had made a major mistake by leaving her boots on. Her feet were almost numb, but what little she could feel was pain. In fact, she was sore all over. Standing by the water bucket, she checked her body out, one part at a time. Yes, it all hurt, every bit of it. She splashed water into her face and felt marginally less awful.

Lefevre squatted by the fire, tossing a few more sticks onto it. In the intensified firelight she saw his teeth flash in a grin. "Hurting, huh?"

"Do you people just like to see suffering, or what?"

"Everybody has to learn. I have to admit this has been a hell of an initiation for a newby, though. Better sit down and get your boots off. Keep your feet raised so they won't swell too much."

That seemed like a good idea. She checked the ground for bugs and sat. Then she found she couldn't get her boots off. Her feet were too swollen. She gritted her teeth, but she was determined not to cry. This was getting to be too much.

Lefevre got up and walked over to her. He grabbed her by the calf of one leg, took her boot in his other hand and yanked it off in one violent motion, peeling her sock off and dropping it on top of the boot. He repeated the procedure with the other boot.

The air felt cool and soothing on her feet. "Thanks."

He sat down by her. "Here, put your feet in my lap."

She studied him suspiciously. He was tall and knobby, dark with an ugly-handsome face. Was he making some sort of pass at her?

He seemed to read her thoughts. "Forget it. Govinda'd skin me. I have a secondary degree in physical therapy. You'd better let me work on these if you don't want to be walking around like a cripple tomorrow."

"Okay." She held out her left foot and he started with her toes. At first she thought she would scream with the pain, but that faded quickly. After twenty minutes, she decided that this was something she could really get used to. Lucky Govinda.

"I didn't know you two were attached."

"She hasn't talked to me in a week. She gets that way sometimes. She's still assertive about her prior claim, though." He did something absolutely fabulous with her achilles tendon.

"Don't worry. She'll make up next time she feels the need of a massage."

"That's the way it usually works out. I figure another day or two. Hard climbing usually brings her around." He got up. "Well, I better get to the other side of the fire. It's not a good idea to stay bunched up."

She was reluctant to reclaim her feet. "I really appreciate this." They felt almost normal. She had just added something new to the already lengthy list of qualities she wanted in a man. If he was this good with feet, what must the rest feel like?

She rested her chin on her knees and listened to the night around her. As Govinda had said, it was quiet. She could hear little above the faint crackling of the fire. Maybe the old cold-blood theorists were right and the dinosaurs needed sunlight to get started. She could sympathize with that. At least it might mean that they were safe after dark. These optimistic thoughts were interrupted when an enormous beetle walked across her bare foot. She gasped and jerked, sending it tumbling. Upended, its legs waving feebly in the air, it looked more comical than menacing. She decided it was probably not dangerous and flipped it over with a stick. It waddled unconcernedly away, apparently attracted by the fire. The thing was almost as big as her hand. She wondered how large the insects got around here. Just as she was feeling better about the reptiles, too.

These thoughts on the wildlife started her brooding on the aliens. They must have had power and technology that made the human variety seem Stone Age by comparison. They had made, she was convinced, actually *made* this planet, or at least redesigned it for their own purposes. Only that could explain its geological absurdities. They had populated it with what she was now sure were the fauna of hundreds of planets, the only requirement being compatibility with an Earth-type atmosphere.

And why? As a lab or zoo, most likely. Humans would do exactly the same thing if they had the power. The big question, as she saw it, was not why the aliens had done this, but what had happened to them. Where were they? How did all this keep functioning smoothly in their absence? It seemed to her unbelievable that such a mishmash of environments could remain stable over a great length of time. Something prevented volcanic and seismic and atmospheric activity from altering the balance of environmental conditions. Yet, so far, nobody had discovered any mechanism that accounted for it.

She got her second shock of the night when something swooped into the firelight from overhead. It darted about confusedly, striking at the ground, its narrow head lancing forward on a long, thin neck. It moved too quickly for her to fix details but she had an impression of batlike wings, tiny teeth and enormous eyes that reflected the firelight like lamps. It was no larger than a pigeon. She had seen holos of pigeons. After a few seconds, it darted away.

"What was that?" she said.

"Another flying reptile," Lefevre answered. "This one adapted for night flying. Did you see those eyes? I think it was confused by the firelight, maybe mistook moving shadows on the ground for small animals."

"I guess they don't all need sunlight to operate. That one I saw two nights ago was a nocturnal flyer. It was a lot bigger, though. I got the impression that little thing had feathers. Did you see any?"

"Didn't get a close enough look. There must've been a lot of transitional forms that didn't leave fossils behind."

Another mystery. At least thinking about them helped pass the time, and let her forget her aches and pains. Before she knew it, it was time to wake up her relief. If she was lucky, she might get another whole hour of sleep before Forrest rousted them out for another day of slogging.

FIVE

By midafternoon of the second day on the plateau, Dierdre had had enough of dinosaurs. She was willing to put adventure on hold and let breathtaking scientific discoveries take a break for a while. What she really wanted was a bath. They were now several days from the base camp on the mainland, and she had never gone so long without a bath before. She was sweaty and itchy and her whole body felt gummy. She hated to think that she smelled like the others.

"I've decided how I'm going to make my fortune," she told Colin during a break. "I'll go into gene-splice research and design a microorganism that eats sweat and body oil and excretes perfume as a byproduct."

"I think it was tried once, back on Earth. The cosmetics cartel bought up the patents, destroyed the data and had the scientists executed."

"Isn't it always that way? What do you think are the chances of getting a bath around here? There are plenty of small streams and pools. By myself, I mean. I'm not quite ready to be as casual as the rest of these nature-lovers. There are some things I still prefer to do in private."

"It wouldn't hurt to ask, I guess, but not just now.

Wait till later in the day, when he's too tired to argue. Right now he's too impatient to stop, plus he's afraid that if he lets one of us get killed, it'll look bad on his record."

"He's all heart. Okay, I'll wait until he looks exhausted and punchy."

The rest of the afternoon they spent making a detailed record of the ground they traversed. They had become so used to the huge reptiles that they began to take greater notice of the smaller ones. Perched on a bush, somebody spotted a tiny creature that was neither reptile nor bird, but some sort of transitional form. Its neck and head were scaly, but its back and paddlelike wings had definite, though crude-looking, feathers. Its flat tail was likewise edged with feathers. It blinked at them fearlessly as they crowded around and recorded it. Finally, it flapped away in what was not quite flight, but more of an extended jump. Dierdre found a dropped feather and stored it in a specimen envelope.

Colin chuckled. "The Earth paleontologists are going to have a fit, if word of this ever reaches them. A bunch of amateurs light years away from them have come up with more hard data on primitive Earth life than generations of specialists back home. This sure beats chipping matrix away from fossils."

Forrest called a halt as they climbed into a range of low hills. They were near a rushing stream and had a panoramic vista of the plain below.

"We're not going to find a better spot than this today," he announced, dropping his pack. They began setting up camp, taking more care than the previous day. There had been repeated rain showers since morning, so the tents went up and clothing was hung out to dry.

While foraging for firewood, Dierdre came across the perfect site: a shallow pool formed where a giant boulder blocked a tiny stream. While topping up her canteen, she checked the temperature. It was pleasantly cool, just what she needed after the days of tropical heat.

She found Forrest going over the holos they had recorded that day. They were fascinating even with the low-grade reproduction equipment they had. He was looking gaunt and hollow-eyed, so she decided now was as good a time as any.

"Hey, Boss, I just found a good site for a quick bath. How about it? It's close, just uphill a few dozen meters. You can hear me holler if I get into trouble."

"Everybody will be going up there in a while," he said, not looking up from his holos, "you can wait."

"I need privacy," she insisted.

He looked up, annoyed. "What is it, some sort of religious thing?"

"Yeah, something like that."

"Oh, all right, but take Okamura with you. He can stay close by but out of sight."

"I can live with that." It was a better compromise than she would have expected. She liked Okamura better than Sims, who was always breathing down her neck.

"Be back before the light gets too dim. We're going to set out lights tonight and record some of the nocturnal life."

"Right, Boss." She ran to her pack and scrounged out a towel, soap and clean clothes. She found Okamura sitting with his back against a tree, his beam rifle propped next to him. He sighed and got to his feet when she told him Forrest's instructions, faintly amused by her insistence on privacy.

"You think you have anything other women don't have?" he said as they trudged uphill.

"What I have I prefer to keep to myself or carefully chosen companions. I don't know any of you that well."

He chuckled. "Well, everybody to his own . . . my God, look at that!" He pointed to the plain below. An immense reptile, far larger than any they had seen so far, had sauntered from the forest to browse on the tops of trees. It was built like a giraffe, but was far more massive. "How big can these things get?"

"Colin says there were some really huge ones that're only known from a couple of bones. There has to be an upper limit somewhere. The square-cube law applies to these things, too." She examined the cake of soap. "Does this stuff really work in cold water?"

"It's about the only thing we have that performs as advertised. Just lather up and rinse it off. Is that your swimming hole?" He pointed at the glinting pool in a depression at the base of a granite cliff. A narrow game path led from the ridge they stood on down to the stream, running along the base of the cliff.

"That's it. You stay up here and watch the pretty dinosaurs. I won't be long."

" 'Kay," he said, sitting down. "Yell if anything starts chewing on you. Look, there's more of them." Below, knobby heads perched atop long necks loomed above the trees.

"Looks like the rest of the family's coming in for dinner. I'll be back in a few minutes." Towel over shoulder, she walked down the path, footsore but elated at the prospect of a bath. The nearer edge of the pool was marshy, muddy and full of weeds. The opposite side looked more promising, rocky and probably deeper. She followed the path along the base of the cliff, which towered to her left. Midway, the path curved to the left, where the cliff curved inward, forming an oddly regular U-shaped wall. At the inner curve was a crevice leading into the stone. Thinking it could be the lair of something awful, she cut across the base of the "U" and continued to the rocks on the far side.

She sat on a flat-topped boulder of appropriate height and pulled off her boots and socks, trying not to breathe through her nose in the process. Then she stood and peeled off her sweat-stiff clothes. The soap cake had an embedded cord, and she immediately found out why. It was trickier getting into the deep water than she would have expected. The bottom was extremely irregular and rocks kept turning under her feet. She hung the soap around her neck and proceeded, using her hands on convenient boulders to keep from falling.

The center of the pool had a gravel bottom and the water came to just below her breasts. It was perfect. She began scrubbing industriously, ducking her head under and lathering her black hair until it squeaked. Then she just let herself soak for a few minutes, deciding that moments like this might make an explorer's life bearable, after all.

Eventually, she forced herself to get out of the water. Standing by the pile of her discarded clothes, she toweled off, noting that the soap had, indeed, left no sticky residue in spite of the tepid and no doubt mineral-laden water.

Sitting on her flat rock, she began to wring out her hair. Her dense, dark thatch always seemed to hold several liters. Twisting vigorously, both hands full of damp locks, she noticed something. There was a very odd regularity about the cave-crevice in the equally odd and regular indentation at the base of the cliff. She knew that water action could have made the symmetrical notch in the cliff face, but the cave entrance was just too centrally located, and too regularly rectangular. Even stranger was a pile of stones in front of the entrance. They looked almost like steps.

She knew it had to be an illusion, but she had to investigate.

Quickly, she dressed, revelling in the feel of clean clothes. She wrapped the malodorous bundle of worn clothes in her towel, shook her hair across her shoulders to air-dry, and went to check out the cave.

Close up, the impression of regularity was even

stronger. The thing just didn't look natural. The opening was about a meter from the level of the path. It was approximately man-height. Gingerly, she climbed the "steps" and stopped just outside the entrance. It was awfully dark in there.

Dierdre set down her bundle, braced a hand against the side of the entrance, and leaned inside, ready to bolt at the first evidence of a tenant. She couldn't make out much. The lowering sun was behind her, but the light couldn't penetrate far. The tunnel within had a fairly level floor and an arched roof. All the surfaces she could see were rough enough that they just could be natural, but she felt that they weren't. She sniffed the air. It was faintly musty, but carried no animal scent she could detect. Surely, she thought, the lair of a predator would reek. She had no experience to confirm such a thing, but it just seemed sensible.

She had discovered all she was going to without going in. She thought of calling Okamura down. It would be comforting to have his beam rifle handy, in case of emergency. But he would insist on reporting the find to Forrest before going in. She knew that she was about to make the kind of foolish mistake that had always gotten her into trouble before. She stepped inside.

Three steps in, she stopped and waited for her eyes to adjust to the interior dimness. She could see that the tunnel went into the hill for about thirty meters before taking a turn to the right that cut off further view. Just a little bit farther, she thought, then I'll go back.

Halfway to the turn, she realized that the pearly light inside couldn't all be coming through the entrance. It was too pale to be reflected sunlight, even reflected through dust. It was pale, and it seemed to come from all directions at once. It was just possible that it was some sort of natural phosphorescence or bioluminescence, but she didn't think so.

The oppressive heat and humidity were gone and it was comfortably cool. She didn't know whether that was natural or not. Maybe caves were always like that. She had never been in one before. Then she came to the righthand curve and unhooked the power torch from her belt, only to find that she didn't need it. She stood in a chamber where the ambient light was noticeably brighter than in the tunnel. Also, this chamber was definitely, unequivocally, artificial.

Her scalp tingled and her stomach lurched. She wasn't sure whether what her heart was doing was a genuine flutter or just beating rapidly, but it was doing something irregular. This had happened only once before in human history, when Derek Kuroda had discovered the Rhea Objects. She had discovered genuine alien artifacts. It looked as if the whole cave was an alien artifact. The chamber in which she stood was roughly cubical, with a domed roof. Whoever had made it apparently felt no need for smooth surfaces or sharp angles, but the regular dimensions ruled out natural formation. One wall had been cut to form a tier of shelves, and another was studded with pegs, as if to hang equipment on. Then there were the discs.

There were two of them, on the opposite wall, about shoulder height and a meter apart. In a half-daze, she walked across the small room for a closer look. The discs were set in holes in the stone wall, about ten centimeters in depth. They were, she estimated, about twenty centimeters in diameter, and they looked metallic. Each had a vertical ridge across its diameter.

Barely daring to breathe, Dierdre flexed her fingers, itching to touch the discs, to evaluate their feel and texture. She wanted to learn everything she could about them before reporting back. It was dangerous, she knew. These things might carry some deadly charge.

What would old Derek do in a case like this? she wondered. He had found two objects on Rhea. He had turned in one, as the law at that time had required. He took the other one, lied through his teeth about it, and turned it over to Sieglinde Kornfeld-Taggart. As a result, the nearby stars of the galaxy had been made accessible to human beings without need for multi-generation ships.

Admit it, she thought, you want all the glory. Well, why not? Wasn't that what they were all here for? There would be plenty of glory to spread around. She just wanted the first and biggest chunk of it. It might also get her killed, but you never got something for nothing.

She reached out and touched the righthand disc. It felt cool and metallic. The ridge seemed to be designed for gripping. There was no tingle of energy but then, she thought, there wouldn't be if she touched a terminal of a powerful electrical generator. Not until she touched the other terminal.

She pushed against the disc. There was no give. She hadn't really expected it to. The design of the thing suggested a dial, something meant to be turned. She took a deep breath and twisted. No give to the left. It turned easily to the right, moved ninety degrees and then stopped. Nothing happened. She turned it back and removed her hand.

With her left hand, she touched the other disc. This one turned only to the left. The design implied, she thought, that the dials were meant to be grasped and turned simultaneously. Already, she was able to make an informed inference about the aliens. The Rhea Objects had given no idea about the appearance or dimensions of the aliens. It seemed now that they were probably roughly man-sized and they had an arm span, or tentacle or whatever span, about like the human norm. Unless they were meant to be turned by two individuals, which threw her theory into the trash.

She heard a voice in the distance, someone calling her name. Okamura. If she was going to do something to make her name immortal, even if it killed her, she had to do it fast. Still holding the lefthand disc, she gritted her teeth and grabbed the one to the right. She was still alive. So far, so good. She forced herself to keep her eyes open as she turned both dials simultaneously.

There was a sudden . . . what? Something like a bolt of lightning hitting nearby, only she had never experienced lightning. She had a sense of great power discharging, but there was no real sound, no sense of impact, no smell of ozone. Still, something had happened.

The wall before her looked unchanged, but something *felt* different. She released the discs and turned. She saw that the chamber was altered. Instead of the shelved wall and the pegged wall, she saw another small chamber with two discs in its far wall. It wasn't the only one, either. There were half a dozen others opening at various angles off what now seemed to be a foyer. It was weirdly disorienting. Had her turning the controls caused all these to open up? How was that possible? The chamber now seemed five or six times as big as when she had entered.

She spotted the exit to the tunnel outside and decided it was time to report back to the expedition. Besides, she was terrified and wanted out. As she stepped away, she realized that this place had become a confusing maze. She put her hat, by now rather battered, on the floor beneath the discs she had just turned. It wouldn't do to lead the others back and then not be able to remember which controls she had tampered with.

She went into the tunnel and turned left. It felt much colder than before, but she figured she was just shivering from fear.

She hurried briskly toward the entrance, then slowed when she realized that there was no Jurassic or Cretaceous or whatever flora outside, but brilliant whiteness, tinged with red. Slowly, awe-struck, she stepped outside. An icy wind blew through her thin, tropical clothes as if she were naked. She could feel crystals forming in her still-damp hair, in her nostrils. It was cold such as she had never experienced. Whiteness not only carpeted the ground, it blew through the air. Bits of something even colder than the ambient air struck her exposed face and hands.

Her first instinct was to get back into the cave, out of this wind. She told herself that explorers should be made of sterner stuff. She would analyze her surroundings for at least a minute.

She knew what the flying white stuff had to be. It was snow. She had seen innumerable holos of it, but nothing had prepared her for what it felt like. It wasn't much like the frost that formed inside refrigeration units, as she had always assumed. She was confused, but she thought she was doing pretty well just to hold onto her sanity. What the *hell* had just happened?

That chamber back there was some sort of transporter, but where had it transported her to? This looked like an arctic region, but was she still on the same planet? Off in the distance, she could just make out huge forms moving. More dinosaurs? In this cold? Then she saw that they were shaggy, covered with long, coarse hair. Mammoths or wooly rhinos or something, she wasn't going to hang around to find out. Arms wrapped around herself for warmth, she retreated into the cave to think things through. With her back against the tunnel wall, she studied the plumes of steam emerging from her mouth and nose while she pondered.

She had just undergone some form of matter transmission. For years, it had been possible to transmit electromagnetic signals instantaneously. Sieglinde Kornfeld had cracked the superluminal barrier about the time Dierdre was born. Ever since, Sieglinde and a thousand other scientists had tried to apply the new technology to transmitting matter, without success. Until now. Dierdre was certain that the alien device had transported her to . . . somewhere. Instantaneously? Had to be. Her hair was still damp. And even if she was still on the same planet, she was far, far from the tropics.

Could she get back? Was she hopelessly lost somewhere in an alien transportation net? It didn't even bear thinking about. All she could do was go back to the device and repeat the same sequence of actions that had brought her here. At least she'd had the foresight to mark the terminal at which she had arrived. She had to get back *now*. She was scared and she was freezing.

Halfway back to the transporter room, she stopped. Even if she got back, they might not believe her. Sure, they'd follow her to the cave and everyone would agree that she'd discovered an alien artifact, but who would believe her story about matter transmission? They'd want to turn the discovery over to the authorities, who might study it for years before trying it out. For all that time, her story would be questioned and she would live under a cloud of suspicion. The thought was intolerable. What could she do? What kind of evidence would be convincing?

She strode back to the entrance. With both hands, she began to scoop snow together into a big ball. The stuff on top didn't seem to want to stick, but beneath the surface she found snow that packed efficiently, just as she had seen in holos. She wondered how fast it would melt in the tropics. Probably fast, so she kept packing it until she had a mass as big as her head.

Back at the transporter chamber, she put her hat back on and was struck by another quandary. How could she use both hands on the controls and hold onto her snowball? She didn't want to stick it into her shirt. She was already too cold. Feeling ridiculous, she clenched it between her knees. She might be going to some totally alien place, but there was no sense in delaying. Teeth gritted, she grasped the discs and twisted them back to the vertical.

There was the same lightning-strike sensation and she was in another chamber. The snowball was still between her knees. So far, so good. It was much warmer. Best of all, she could breathe the air. She turned around, retrieving her snowball. The chamber had only the single set of controls. The shelves and pegs were there, the tunnel outside curved away to the left.

"Jamail!" She could have fainted with relief. It was Okamura, calling for her. She ran to the cave entrance, then almost did faint. After the arctic cold, the tropic heat almost dropped her in her tracks. Okamura caught her just as she stumbled through the cave entrance, her head swimming.

"God, Jamail, I thought something'd caught you and dragged you inside! What the hell've you been doing in there?"

"Sorry, Okamura. I didn't mean to scare you. We need to get back to the camp, fast!"

"I know. It'll be dark soon. what's that?" He bent forward and studied her burden. "Did you find *ice* in there?"

"Better than that!" She laughed, then shut herself off as she recognized a hysterical note. "Let's go." She picked up her bundle of laundry with her free hand and they hurried back.

Forrest looked up from his notes as they came back into camp. He was frowning, naturally enough. "It's about time. I told you . . ."

"Catch," she said, tossing the snowball. Instinctively, Forrest caught it. His face was puzzled at first, then blank. When the reality of the cold struck him he dropped it as if it had been red-hot.

"What the hell . . . what's this?" He picked it back up, brushing off the dirt and leaf-mold.

"It's a snowball. Never seen one before?"

"She went into a cave back there, Steve," Okamura said. "When she came out, she was carrying that."

Forrest stared at her, his face grim and pale. "You'd better do some fast talking."

"First call everybody together so they can all hear it and handle my snowball before it melts. I don't want anybody calling me a liar."

Forrest bellowed for everybody to gather around and then, in a lower voice: "You sure are sensitive. Well, since you can defy the laws of nature, I guess you ought to be." When all were gathered, the snowball was passed from hand to hand amid much exclamation of wonder and disbelief.

"I never thought I'd see dinosaurs," Lefevre said, "but a snowball in the tropics is about as good."

"Talk, Jamail," Forrest ordered.

She was surprised at how brief a time it took to tell what had happened. There really wasn't much, any more than there had been much to relate when Derek Kuroda had literally stubbed his toe on the first Rhea Object. It was just that the discovery itself was epoch-making.

"You found an alien machine," Forrest said, aghast, "and you *operated* it?"

"Well, yes. Just sort of an experiment."

"So you could be first," he said through gritted teeth. "So you could have all the glory."

"Sure. So it might've killed me. So what? I was willing to take the risk."

"It might have killed *you*? Did it occur to you that it might have been a weapon system? That it might have been the self-destruct control of this whole planet?"

"No," she confessed, "I never thought of that."

"Never thought of it!" He sputtered. "This is the most flagrant violation of regulation since . . . since . . ." Words failed him.

"Oh, can it, Steve," Govinda cut in. "What've we

all been doing since we saw our first big lizard? If Dierdre wasn't an insubordinate troublemaker she wouldn't be here with the rest of us. I think she did just great!"

"Right!" said Hannie, enthusiastically. "I want to try her gadget next!" Everybody else clamored in protest, demanding to go next by right of age, seniority or other pretext.

"Shut up, everybody," said Forrest. "Nobody's leaving this camp until daylight, and that's it." He contemplated the now swiftly-melting remnant of a snowball. "We don't even know whether the transporter leads to another spot on this planet or to another solar system entirely. Jamail, did you see anything besides snow and furry animals?"

"It was cold. I couldn't hang around."

"Any idea what time of day it was?" he asked.

"There was a lot of red in the sky. I didn't check my compass to see what direction I was facing. It was either evening or morning. I guess the sun was about the same angle as from here now."

"It'll be easy enough to find out whether it's on this planet," Schubert said. "Just send somebody through with commo equipment. If we get signals from the orbitals, we're here."

"Has anybody considered," Fumiyo said, "that it could be this planet but at a different *time*?"

"No!" Forrest protested. "One impossibility at a time. I'm willing to consider instantaneous matter transmission. People have been working on that for most of my life. I don't even want to think about time travel!"

Tired though they were, nobody slept a great deal that night. Everybody wanted to talk about the new discovery. Most of them came by to congratulate Dierdre on her initiative, gall, or good luck, depending upon how they perceived it. She swore she wouldn't let it go to her head, but it was refreshing to have peer approval, even admiration. Except from Forrest, who was still angry with her.

At first light they had a hurried breakfast, packed up and shifted camp to the ridge above the little pool. Before he would allow anyone to go inside the cave, Forrest made a complete record of the surrounding area.

"All right, now we go in," he said. "Everyone gets a look at the alien gadget, then out again. Nobody touches it until we've made a detailed study and record of the tunnel and the transporter chamber. Meanwhile, you can all relax out here, clean up, wash your clothes, you know the drill. When we report this find, this place is going to be swarming, so you want to look pretty for the newsies. Schubert, what's commo status?"

"Still bad, but it's clearing up. I'd say we'll be able to reach the orbitals by this evening, tomorrow at the latest."

"Start trying to make commo with Kurz. He should be on the beach with the rest by now. If you can get him, tell him to home on our signal, that it's super urgent and no more than that."

"You got it, Boss."

"Okay, it looks cramped in there. Dierdre, you lead the way. Single file going in, no more than four of us in that chamber at a time. Let's go." They trooped inside. Everybody spoke in low tones, as if the aliens might be somewhere nearby, listening. For all they knew, that could actually be the case. Everyone made appropriately awed noises in the transporter chamber, although it was agreed that the whole thing looked disappointingly plain. There was nothing to suggest an alien technology except for Dierdre's singular experience.

Forrest shooed them all out except for Fumiyo, and the two set about recording the tunnel and chamber in great detail. The rest were soaking in the pool within minutes. Dierdre went to the gravelly channel where the backed-up water made its way around the blocking boulder. There she began to learn the art of hand-laundering her clothes. She soaped, trampled, wrung out and beat her clothes against the boulder, just as she had seen Indian village women doing in old holos.

Govinda, still dripping, joined her and dumped a pack of clothes into the stream. "We live in space for generations, we travel between solar systems, and we end up doing our laundry just like in the Stone Age. Do you think maybe we took a wrong turn someplace?"

"If we'd wanted it easy," Dierdre intoned the inevitable formula, "we could've stayed at home." She found that wringing out clothes was rougher than she had thought. The water softened the skin of her palms and fingers and twisting the rough cloth raised blisters. "I have to admit, this sort of thing takes a lot of the romance out of it."

"Yeah." Govinda ran her fingers through her short, yellow hair. She was rail-thin, with adolescent bumps for breasts. Her movements were quick and birdlike, but she was tireless on the march and could carry an amazing weight for so small a woman. "If someone can figure out how your gadget works, it might make this a whole lot easier. We could still have the fun of doing the exploring, but we'll have instant access to the facilities in space: comfortable beds, decent food, laundry service . . ."

"Forget it," Hannie said, climbing imposingly nude from the pool behind them. "I like it as it is. If it gets to be that easy, any fool can be an explorer." Her hair was dark from the water, and she spread it over her bulky shoulders to dry.

"You're probably right," Dierdre said. The woman was like some throwback out of a prehistoric Teutonic forest. She had to weigh as much as Dierdre and Govinda put together. "It wouldn't be bad to have *occasional* access, though. Most of the people I studied with couldn't stand this life, even if they got to sleep in an Avalon luxury inn every night."

Hannie's big, white teeth flashed in a broad grin. "I won't argue with that. I'll bet most of our prison guards couldn't stand much of this." Dierdre wasn't about to ask what that meant.

Sims began to emerge from the pool. "Hey, mind if I join . . ."

Hannie's fist caught him squarely in the sternum, pitching him back to land in the water with a mighty splash. "This is woman talk. Space out."

"What I'm hoping," Dierdre said, ignoring the interruption, "is that what the aliens left behind is some sort of interstellar transport system. Think of it!" She grew enthusiastic as she warmed to the subject. "Right now, with our best drive system and human life expectancy nearing the two-century mark, you can't reasonably expect to visit more than ten or fifteen systems in your lifetime. Less than that if you're going to do in-depth exploring when you get there. So much is wasted in transit time. With an instantaneous transport, we could visit dozens, maybe hundreds!"

"Don't get your hopes up," Govinda cautioned. "Lots of people thought the Rhea Objects would give us superluminal travel, but they didn't. Superluminal commo, sure, but only for electromagnetic signals, not matter."

"Besides," Hannie added, "we're pretty sure the aliens used ships. Sieglinde was positive the Rhea Objects were power packs for a space vessel."

"Maybe the receiver terminal has to go ahead first, through conventional space," Dierdre hazarded.

"Then why wasn't one ever found in Sol System?" Govinda asked.

"We never explored much of that system," Dierdre said. "Hell, there was lots of *Earth* that never got explored. A facility as small as that one in there could be lost for thousands of years near a major city.

Out in the other planets, the moons, the Belt, it could stay lost for millions of years." It was, she thought, a hell of a conversation for three wet people to be having while pounding laundry on flat rocks.

"We keep talking like there's just one race of aliens," Hannie pointed out. "Maybe the ones who made the transporter aren't even connected with the ones that left the Rhea Objects behind."

"Yeah!' Govinda said. "Wouldn't that be great? I mean, the philosophical implications get bigger all the time! Maybe the galaxy's crawling with intelligent life! If that's the case, how long before we run into it?"

"It might already have happened," Dierdre said. "The Delta Pav expedition was just one of dozens. I'd like for us to be the first, naturally."

"Damn!" Hannie said, resting her chin on her knuckles in the classic *Le Penseur* pose. "I hadn't thought of that. There's Einsteinian time-dilation complications here. When we finally get together again and compare notes, how are we going to figure out who was first to do *anything*? Beyond a solely local basis, I mean, like exploring this planet."

It was, Dierdre thought, a typical explorer's worry. Pure knowledge be damned, everybody wanted to be *first*. "We do have superluminal commo," she said.

"That's no good," Govinda said. "Some of the expeditions went out before it was perfected, and others refused to use it because they wanted to cut ties totally. Besides, even when you're talking to someone over SL commo, elapsed subjective time since the last communication can vary tremendously."

"Not much sense speculating," Hannie sighed. "The big brains will be down here soon. They'll shove us aside, confer, study. Maybe in a couple of years we'll hear their tentative conclusions."

"Sure," Dierdre said, slapping her pants against a rock. "But I *like* to speculate."

By midafternoon, Forrest was ready to experiment with the transporter. "I'll go first," he said. Fumiyo, Schubert, Dierdre and Lefevre were in the transporter room. Others crowded the hall outside. "I'll stay long enough to confirm if it's the same arctic location Jamail went to, then I come right back. If I don't return, absolutely *nobody* follows me. From what Jamail says, it's not a dangerous environment, so a rescue attempt would be pointless. If I don't return, it'll mean I ended up somewhere else."

He wiped his sweaty palms on the seat of his coverall, not bothering to hide his nervousness. Teeth clenched, he grasped the controls and turned them.

Dierdre stood next to Fumiyo, who had mini holo recorders spotted around the chamber to record the event. They all stared hard, but nobody could really describe what happened next. There was no flashy display, no lightning and thunder. He did not blink out of view suddenly, nor did he slowly fade. The watchers felt as if they had been momentarily distracted, and when they took notice, he was gone.

"Did anyone see anything?" Fumiyo asked.

"I don't think human perceptions are set up for this phenomenon," Lefevre said. "I felt a sort of subliminal twinge."

"It was what I felt when I went through," Dierdre said, "only much fainter."

Schubert studied his sound equipment. "There was no noise, not even subsonic."

"No sound of displaced air," Fumiyo mused. "That means his body was replaced by exactly the same volume of air. It's going to be interesting going over our atmospheric data. I hope it's sensitive enough to tell us if there was a change of atmospheric chemistry."

They waited nervously for what seemed like an hour but was actually no more than ten minutes. Then, to their unutterable relief, Forrest reappeared as quietly as he had gone, a light dusting of snow on his hat and shoulders. He turned around with a broad grin. "Just like Jamail described it!" He turned to her. "Dierdre, did you scoop up your snowball to the right of the tunnel entrance?"

She thought for a second. "Yeah,"

"The indentation's still there. The snow hasn't filled it yet."

Word was passed to the people in the tunnel and they could hear cheering.

"I'm going back now," Forrest said. "Jamail, you come next, then Schubert, then Fumiyo. Nobody else until we return. When I've left, wait one minute between transmissions so I can get out of the way. Surely these things must be set up so two people can't solidify in the same spot, but why take chances."

"Schubert has our only heavy commo equipment," Fumiyo said. "Otherwise we have only our belt sets. Do we dare risk it?"

"Kurz should be here by tomorrow afternoon, and it's not doing us much good with the sunspot activity, anyway. Besides, I need it for an experiment. Let's get going." He turned around and was gone.

Dierdre waited for a minute and followed. She was ready this time. She had put on two of everything and wore gloves. She had even brought along an extra undershirt to tie around her ears, if they should start to freeze. There was the now-familiar shock, then she was in the multiple transporter chamber with Forrest. She noticed that he had marked their terminal with a red grease pencil.

In a few minutes the other two were in the room as well. They conferred briefly and it was agreed that everybody felt fine and they had all experienced identical sensations. They went to the tunnel entrance and admired the snow for a while, then Dierdre and Fumiyo did a scan with their viewers while the two men set up the commo equipment.

Dierdre found that her scanner saw right through the snow. There were a number of large animals downhill, their massive bodies throwing out a heat signature like so many beacons. The hair covering and infrared viewing combined to make the contours of the beasts fuzzy, but Dierdre was pretty sure she could make out prehensile trunks at the larger ends.

"Now," Forrest said, "see if you can pick up the orbitals."

Schubert fiddled with his controls. "Still getting static from the sunspots, but the orbitals are up there."

"So we're still on the same planet," Fumiyo said.

"And we're still in the same time zone judging from the sun's direction from the meridian. Also, this is summer time in the north and the sun is visible in the Arctic but not in the Antartic. So, we must've moved straight north. If this static will just clear up, I can get an exact fix on our position. Ray, you want me to try to raise an orbital?"

"No! Not till Kurz and the others are here. We need to talk it over and work out our tactics. Besides, I've figured a way we can get immediate attention, but we'll need two heavy transmitters to do it, and tomorrow the sunspot activity will be a lot less."

"Shouldn't we do some exploring around here?" Fumiyo asked.

"Just the immediate area, to make sure we're safe. Jamail, go back and bring Colin and Sims up. Colin won't feel the cold in that body suit of his, and Sims used to be an ice miner. They can go out a short distance and take a look."

Dierdre went back, used to the process by now. Everyone clamored to be next but she named Forrest's choices and told the rest what they had learned. Excitement was running high. When she had guided the other two to the snowy tunnel mouth, Forrest gave Colin their best high-magnification, high-resolution viewer.

"Get a look at those animals, but don't go too far. This snow could turn heavy. Report in every ten minutes with your comm set. Remember, we're in completely unknown territory again," he told Sims and Colin.

"You don't have to tell me." Colin was gazing through the viewer at the big animals below. "Unless I miss my guess, those things are mammoths. The ice ages produced some really fearsome predators . . . sabertooths, dire wolves, cave bears, Felis Atrox . . ."

"Felis Atrox?" Dierdre asked, hugging herself.

"That's right. It means 'atrocious cat' and that about describes it. Like an African lion, only twice as big with a head three times as big. Ice age predators weren't as big as the ones in the dinosaur age, but they were plenty big enough and they were *much* smarter."

"Then keep your finger on your trigger, Sims," Forrest advised. "You two get going, but be back within one hour. I don't want you to freeze."

Sims shrugged. "Feels like home to me."

"You were dressed for it at home," Colin told him. "Come on."

As time passed, Forrest sent people back to warm up while others passed through. Dierdre spent much of the time in the ice-age transporter room, making sure that nobody touched the other controls. When Colin and Sims returned, the party adjourned to the transporter room where it wasn't so cold. Despite his previous bravado, Sims' teeth were chattering.

"They're mammoths, all right," Colin reported. "And there are lots of others, as well. This place looks bleak, but it's swarming with animal life, like the African veldt used to be. Our situation here is almost identical to the other transporter site: we're in foothills above a big plain, with mountains beyond the hills. The mammoths seem to like the hills, and we saw some wooly rhinos, too. Out on the plain below there are huge mixed herds, mostly some kind of long-horned bison, but there are things like clumsy giraffes, too."

"Predators?" Forrest asked.

Colin nodded. "Plenty. It seems the bison cows are dropping calves. Nothing draws mammalian predators like the smell of blood, babies and placentas. There must be a thousand wolves circling the herd looking for easy pickings. Big ones."

Dierdre shuddered. Raw nature wasn't as nice as the child-oriented holos she had loved in her younger days. "I guess everybody had better stick close, huh?"

"What I'm wondering," Sims said, "is why none of the animals are using these tunnels as dens. They're both wide open, but we haven't found a trace of animal life except what the wind's blown in. What's keeping them out?"

"Good question, but one we're not likely to answer. All right, you two go back and thaw out, and send up anybody who hasn't been through yet. Dierdre, how about you?"

"I'm fine." Actually, she was cold, but it was no more miserable than the tropic heat. She didn't want to miss a minute of this.

At the end of the day, she helped Forrest and Fumiyo pack up their equipment and they made their way tiredly back to the other cave, now so jaded that they barely thought of the exotic process that was transporting them unknown thousands of kilometers. Govinda was on duty in the other chamber. When the last were through, Forrest said, "We're shutting this place down for the night. Nobody reenters until morning, and only with my permission."

Govinda wasn't paying attention. She was watching the tunnel outside. "Boss, there's some kind of commotion outside."

"Uh-oh," Forrest said. "Come on, let's go assess the damage."

They found the camp in an uproar. Everyone was gathered around something that lay on the ground. Dierdre felt a sense of dread. Had someone been hurt? Killed?

"I had to shoot it!" Okamura said to anyone who would listen. "It was self-defense!"

"Damn right," Ping confirmed. "It was going to eat us!"

"What happened?" Forrest demanded. On the ground lay a reptile bulkier than a large man. Its body was similar to a tyrannosaur's but its head looked more like a crocodile's. Its forelimbs were stubby but thick, and ended in large talons tipped with sickle-shaped, four-inch claws.

"Ping and Angus and me went out for firewood, just over that way," Okamura pointed over the ridge to the left. "Not more than five hundred meters downhill. We were in a clearing, and this thing came right up off the ground and charged down on us. It must've been lying flat on its belly in plain view, but you can see how it's camouflaged. I saw nothing but claws and teeth and I opened fire when it wasn't ten meters away."

"That's how it happened, Boss," Angus affirmed.

Forrest squatted by the thing. Its belly was pale, but the back was mottled gray, green and brown, a perfect match for the forest floor. At the back of the head was a circular hole.

"If it was charging at you," Forrest said, "how come the hole's at the back of the head?"

"Uh-uh," Okamura said, squatting by the head. "That's where the beam came out." He tugged the ghastly, long-toothed jaws apart. "*This* is where I shot it." There was a neat hole burned in the roof of the thing's mouth.

"Good shooting, Oke," said Hannie, "especially in such a stressful situation."

"Sounds like justifiable reptilocide to me," Forrest said. "I think an autopsy is in order."

"Let me at that thing," Fumiyo said, flipping open a laser scalpel with the panache of an old-time hoodlum displaying a switchblade. "Just get a holo recorder on it and stand back."

In practice, it took the efforts of several people to get the monster dissected. To their horror, it was still twitching. Most of the team watched with a kind of morbid fascination.

At one point, Fumiyo reached into its thorax and emerged with something bloody and quivering. "I think this is a primitive four-chambered heart. So some of them *were* warm-blooded, after a fashion." She dropped the heart into a specimen bag that would preserve it for several weeks. With the efficiency of a trained technician, she extracted other organs, snippets of brain and muscle tissue, nerves, blood vessels, and other bodily pieces. Few of the others could watch when she extracted the eyes. By the time it was fully dark, she finished up under a floodlight, a neat pile of specimen bags at her feet.

"Let's see, anything else?" she asked.

"For one thing," Forrest said, "you need a bath." Fumiyo looked like a battle casualty.

"Well, that's about it for the innards. We can dry the hide, and bones will keep. What do we do with all this?" She waved at the litter of disjointed limbs, ribs and skinned tail. "Leave it for the scavengers?"

"I'll show you what we do with it," said Hannie, grabbing up a meaty haunch and hauling it to the fire. She had whittled a green stick to a point and she skewered the joint on it, then suspended it over a bed of coals, supported by a pair of forked sticks she had foresightfully erected an hour before.

"That's disgusting!" someone said.

Hannie smiled. "Nobody's forcing you to share."

The others watched queasily until the first wave of scent reached them. Then it seemed that everybody was whittling sticks and snatching up hunks of meat. Packs were opened and they tried to find anything that could be used for seasoning, but all they could come up with was powdered salt tablets from their medkits.

"How do we know when it's done?" Dierdre asked

Hannie. She was embarrassed at the way she was salivating.

"We'll just have to keep testing," Hannie said, thumbing the edge of her knife.

In the end, it turned out that seasoning was unnecessary. The smoke bestowed savor and their own appetites and flavor-starved taste buds did the rest. They all ate until they felt utterly, atavistically, caveman satisfied.

"I'm gonna pay for this in some future life," Ping said, gnawing the last shreds from a rib, "but it's worth it."

"As good as any synthetic I ever ate," Forrest said. "Sort of like a cross between lobster and poultry. Any idea what it was, Colin?"

Colin shook his head, licking his fingertips. "It's nothing I ever saw. Probably some unknown species."

"We'll have to give it a fitting name," Dierdre said. "Deliciosaurus or something like that." She felt guilty and replete. It was wonderful. Whatever else she could say about her brief time as an explorer, it certainly hadn't been dull or without its rewards. What was next?

They spent the morning getting holo recordings of the big mammalian fauna, staying within a kilometer of the tunnel. The cold was cruel, but they were willing to suffer for the experience. Here the party stayed close together, with both beamer-wielders flanking.

Despite their size and their upcurving tusks, Dierdre found the mammoths endearingly comical and friendly-looking. She knew better than to let this sentimental judgement affect her behavior. She had taken enough foolish risks and knew that trying to pet a mammoth would be one too many. It was tempting, though, especially when she saw several fuzzy infants peeking shyly from beneath their mother's belly fur.

"I wonder how they taste?" someone said.

"Cut that out!" Forrest declared. "One carnivorous orgy per expedition is enough. Besides, we still have some lizard meat left from yesterday. Now we're going to go get some views of those rhinos. We stay more than a hundred meters from them, though. The African variety were almost blind, but we don't assume that these are. The African type would sometimes charge an intruder on sight, and we *definitely* assume that these will."

They found the wooly rhinos to be more aesthetically pleasing than the holos they had all seen of the hairless African and Indian rhinos. The sloping, brutish heads were the same, but the flowing reddish fur waved gracefully as the animals moved, and the extremely long nose horns were slender and elegant.

Returning to the transporter, they passed by a rock overhang. Like everything else, it was covered with snow. Someone gasped.

"Freeze, everybody," Forrest said, in a calm voice. "All right, who saw something?"

It was Govinda who had gasped. "Everybody look up and to the right, real slow. That big bump on top of the rock isn't part of the rock."

They all looked. Dierdre felt the hair on her scalp stiffen. An enormous cat lay on the overhanging rock, regarding them with lambent yellow eyes. A broad ruff of white fur gave the face something of a tiger's shape, but the muzzle was wider. The wideness was accentuated by a pair of outsized canine teeth, easily eight inches long. The cat lay half-curled on its side, head erect, and only its thick, fluffy tail moving, swatting the snow that lay on the rock.

"Get pictures," Forrest said quietly. "Nobody run, and get good pictures. It doesn't look threatening; probably it's eaten recently."

"It's beautiful!" Fumiyo said. "But I didn't expect they'd be white."

"Adapted for snow," Colin said, holoing steadily. "It may be a different color in summer. Besides, this isn't a *smilodon*, the one you always see pictures of. Its shoulders aren't bulky enough. But it's a relative."

"It has stripes," Dierdre noted. "They're faint, but you can just make them out. I had a longhair back home marked something like that."

"This isn't your average puddy-tat," Forrest said. "Now I want everybody to resume moving uphill, very slowly, thinking brave thoughts so it doesn't figure out how scared we are. Keep the beamers trained on it, but don't shoot unless it attacks. If we kill something this pretty, we'll never explain it to the people back home."

They made it back without incident, only to be met by another menace when they were back at the tropical cave camp. Kurz and the other two teams had arrived. The instant they showed, Kurz began a high-decibel butt-chewing, taking them all in but with special emphasis on Forrest. "I have never experienced such asinine, such insufferably foolish and insubordinate . . ." They all sat on the ground and Dierdre tuned him out until he ran out of steam, as she knew he would. They could all hear the false note in his voice. The ass-chewing was purely *pro forma*. Like Team Red (it had been a while since she had thought of herself as part of Team Red), Kurz and the others had been utterly stunned by the dinosaurs all around them.

When Kurz paused for breath, Forrest began to tell him about the transporter. "You what!?" Kurz yelled in a strangled scream. Gradually, the commander's choler subsided and the two sat down for a tête-a-tête.

Dierdre's head felt congested. These sudden changes from arctic conditions to tropic were doing none of them any good. Someone lanky ambled over to her and sat down. "Sounds like you been real busy, hon."

Dierdre smiled. "Hello, Barbara. It's good to see you." The other woman looked different out of her jungle-girl garb. To Dierdre's surprise, Barbara carried a beam rifle, and it was a heavier-duty model than those borne by Sims and Okamura. The short, coppery hair was the same, though, as was the lazy smile and friendly manner.

"My, my, don't you look salty for a girl barely off the shuttle. Made one of the big epoch-making discoveries, too, I hear."

"I don't know whether it means eternal fame or jail, though," Dierdre admitted.

"That's the choice more often than not, as I understand it." She ran her fingers through her short, wiry hair. "They say old Francis Drake went all the way around Terra, shot up a bunch of Spanish ships, looted some towns, and when he got home he didn't know whether Queen Elizabeth would knight him or behead him. Been out of touch all that time, you see, just like you here. It all depended on English-Spanish relations when he got back. Well, it looks like your fate's gonna depend on how they're feeling up there. I'll be pulling for you."

"Thanks. It's good to know somebody's on my side."

"Fact is, I think the holos you've got will make you instant celebrities, all of you. Survey won't be happy, but they won't dare touch you. God! I never thought I'd see *dinosaurs*! Aren't they something?"

"They are," Dierdre confirmed. "But today, we saw a sabertooth! There's something about a mammal that's even more impressive, maybe because it's a relative."

"A sabertooth? You mean one of the big cats? Let me see."

Dierdre called Colin over and he began to run the day's holos. People from the other team began to crowd around. They had overdosed on dinosaurs and were fascinated by the Ice Age fauna.

"Mammoths!" somebody said. "How come we never had luck like that?"

"You don't live right," said Ping. "It takes many lifetimes of virtuous behavior to earn rewards like this." Even Kurz's exhausted people laughed.

"Tell me that from jail, Ping," said a squat, black man who had a Bantu accent. They laughed louder.

"It true you people been living on dinosaur meat?" asked a skinny blonde.

"Haven't eaten anything else since we saw 'em," said Sims. "What've you people been eating? Concentrates? That's about what I'd expect. Hell, we go out and kill our own. Some of these civilized types cook theirs, but not me. Eat it raw, I say, and don't bother to bleed the carcass. Why, yesterday I started chewing on a stegosaur's tail, and by the time the signal reached his brain, I'd . . ."

"Somebody shut him up," Forrest yelled. "We've got some important decisions to make."

"Maybe you do, Forrest," shouted a woman of Hannie's general build and attitude. Dierdre decided there must be some place that bred this type. "What I need is a bath."

"Och, and is that no the Lord's truth!" said Bela Szini. "The pond's that way, lassie, and I'll lend ye ma soap, if ye've no brought yerr own." He came to sit by Dierdre. "We're all proud o' ye, lass, don't mind what Kurz says. Gall such as ye have is a rare gift, and if ye go to prison, we'll keep in regular contact."

"That's good to know. But Barbara gives me odds that I'll beat the charge, whatever the charge may be."

When she turned in for the night, Dierdre finally allowed herself to contemplate what she had accomplished. For all she knew, she had totally ruined her career as a planetside explorer. On the other hand, short as that career had been, it had been eventful. It appeared that she had been the first to do something unique in human history. She tried to remember the names of people who had scored unquestioned firsts in human exploration: Columbus, well, there was some question about that; Magellan, Peary, Orville Wright, or was it Wilbur? Gagarin, Armstrong, then a whole raft of them as space had opened up, and landings on new bodies had become common occurrences. Derek Kuroda, the first to discover an unquestioned alien artifact. And now, she thought smugly, Dierdre Jamail; first human being to travel by matter transmission. She wondered how many generations of schoolchildren would be forced to memorize her name. Even if they jailed her, at least she would have that. With that thought, she went to sleep.

SIX

Late the next day, Dierdre watched as Derek Kuroda himself arrived. She had heard of him all her life, so it was a surprise to see how young he looked in person. Of course she knew that he was barely middle-aged and modern medicine kept even the elderly looking relatively young; still, it seemed that a hero of a previous generation should be more venerable.

Kuroda stepped from his shuttle, closely followed by his wife, Antigone Ciano. After them followed a gaggle of scientists and bureaucrats, practically tripping over one another in their haste to get at the new discovery.

"Where is it?" Kuroda said, without preamble. He wore his red hair long, in the fashion prevalent when he made his famous discovery. Dierdre guessed that he did that so that people would be sure to recognize him from his old holos. She had more reason than most to know that explorers share a streak of vanity.

"It's cramped in there, sir," Kurz said. "We'll have to take you in a few at a time."

"I want a look at this thing and then I am taking charge. All of you are off of this expedition as of now. You bypassed me and the whole Survey structure to make this discovery public. You violated every rule in the bylaws."

"There is precedent," Kurz said blandly.

Kuroda's face turned fiery red. "Where's the discoverer?"

Dierdre stepped forward with a fluttery stomach. "I found it."

"Congratulations," Kuroda said. "And tried it out, I understand. Consider yourself under arrest. I ought to arrest the lot of you."

Dierdre's trepidation vanished and she could actually feel the anger climbing her spine. "Hey, don't blame us for sunspot activity, Mr. Kuroda! That's what put us out of touch. If we bent a few rules, it's because we heard all about you when we were kids and we admired your methods so much."

"Tell him, Jamail!" someone said. There was applause and encouragement from behind her.

Antigone laid a hand on Kuroda's arm. "Calm down, love. You should never chew out armed people."

"Take me to see this thing," Kuroda said, tightly.

Dierdre, still seething, felt someone take her arm. "Come along with me, dear," Antigone said. They walked a little behind the others.

"Am I really under arrest?" Dierdre half-whispered. "Hell, I don't even know how to *act* arrested!"

"Oh, that's just Derek being dramatic. He has no authority to arrest anybody. There are others who can and will, but you're already a big media heroine, so don't worry. You won't need a defense counselor, you'll need an agent to handle all the holo contracts that'll be coming your way."

Dierdre found it a little hard to imagine all those people up there talking about her. She didn't feel any different. "It's still not fair! He's taken Steve and Kurz and the rest of us off our own expedition!"

Antigone smiled. "They'll be reinstated before we come back down this hill. Derek loves conspiracy. He and Forrest and Kurz will be deep in some plot before long. Your judgement was questionable, but since you decided to run an outlaw expedition, you played it brilliantly. One thing Island Worlders always admire is gall."

As they neared the cave, Antigone took Dierdre's arm again and pushed to the front. "The discoverer gets to guide us in," she proclaimed. "Even I have that much holo savvy. Get your recorders going."

"Let me brush my hair first," Dierdre whispered.

"Forget it," Antigone advised. "We can doctor the holos later."

Shoulders back, hoping she looked heroic, Dierdre led them in. She began some memorable words, but they choked in her throat when she turned into the transport chamber and saw a woman standing with her back turned, studying the controls. She was small, with short, blonde hair.

"Who're you?" Kurz said. "This woman isn't with my team. We posted guards around this site."

"It wouldn't have done any good," Kuroda said. "Hello, Aunt Sieglinde."

"Hello, Derek." The woman turned around and Dierdre studied her. So this was the legendary Sieglinde Kornfeld-Taggart. It seemed to be Dierdre's day for meeting celebrities. Only fitting, she thought, since she now seemed to be something of a celebrity herself.

"How did you get in here, Dr. Kornfeld?" Kurz demanded.

"I can usually go where I want to." She turned to Kuroda and his party. "Get your recordings and touch nothing. There's very little to see in any case. Then everybody assemble outside. I need to address the exploration teams before the Survey brass arrives and starts to mess things up."

"Bossy, isn't she?" Dierdre whispered.

Sieglinde looked at her. "You're Jamail, aren't you?"

"That's right. And I don't see what's the big mystery about how you got in here. You must've landed at the ice-age end of this thing and come through."

Sieglinde gave her an oddly pitying look. "No, I've been reckless in the past, but never suicidal."

Dierdre didn't understand what the words meant, but they filled her with terrible dread. This woman, acknowledged to be one of history's greatest geniuses, had deduced something about the transporter that the rest of them had missed.

The newcomers all had a look at the alien device and agreed that there was, indeed, very little to see. They filed out and assembled near the mouth of the cave. Last out was Sieglinde.

"We don't have much time," she said baldly, "so listen. I'm Sieglinde Kornfeld-Taggart. You've heard of me. I want everybody who's gone through the transporter to step forward." All of Team Red stepped out. She looked appalled. "So many! God, what a pack of young idiots! All muscles and glands and not two rational brain cells among the lot."

"Aren't you being a little rough, Sieglinde?" said Kuroda, with a seeming 180-degree rotation of attitude. "After all, this was a pretty ballsy—"

She ignored him. "Did any of you stop to speculate on how this thing does what it does?"

"Actually," Kurz said, "we were sort of hoping that you could explain that."

"I'll find out, never fear," she promised, "but I've already come up with some speculations and you'd better hope that the most likely one is wrong."

"Uh-oh," Forrest said. "What's that?"

"Are you familiar with wave-pattern theory?" They all looked at one another and shrugged.

"It's twentieth-century stuff, early twentieth at that. Schroedinger and de Broglie established that matter has wave nature. This thing may read the wave-patterns of your body, clothes and all, encode the data and transmit it through indeterminate n-space instantaneously, just as I've been doing with message data for years. The receiver reads the data and reconstructs the matter. In this case, your bodies. But get this: if this theory is correct, your body is *destroyed*, then reassembled from data. Your memories are intact, because they are part of the electrochemical structure of your brain. All of it has wave pattern, so it all gets transported, conditionally."

They digested that for a while, then: "Wait a minute." It was Dierdre who caught the implications first. "Do you mean that we're not the originals? We died the first time we went through the transmitter, and now we're just replicas with the same memories?"

"It's a possibility," Sieglinde said. The protests were loud and in some cases jeering, but suddenly everyone was terribly uneasy.

"But, Dr. Kornfeld," Ping said, "wouldn't we know?"

She shook her head. "No. How could you?"

"What did you mean by 'conditionally?' " Forrest asked.

"I meant we have no way of knowing whether this apparatus is one hundred percent efficient. For all we know, you weren't reassembled with everything in place, including your minds. Although I have my doubts whether they were much good to begin with. It never occurred to you, huh?"

"They can't all be great geniuses, Sieglinde," Antigone said.

"They could at least behave like high-grade morons." She gestured toward Dierdre. "Jamail here at least has some excuse. She found an alien artifact and decided it was worth staking her life to find out what it did. Stupid, but understandable when you consider that these young fools are all gloryhounds."

Thanks a lot, thought a chastened and now thoroughly frightened Dierdre.

"Dr. Kornfeld," said Sims, "we figured the aliens used it, so why not us? Whatever else they were, they were pretty intelligent. Would they have used it if it wasn't safe?"

"Maybe they only used it to transport materials. Maybe they used it themselves, but they were hive creatures and individual identity didn't matter. Maybe they were already electronic intelligences. Maybe they just didn't care. And we don't know how old these things are or how much deterioration they might have suffered."

"But aren't we all just the sum of our memories?" Fumiyo asked, desperation in her voice. "As long as those are intact—"

"They may not be," Sieglinde shot back. "Even if they are, so what? I wouldn't want to die right now even if I knew that a copy of me would be made, complete with all my memories."

"All right, Sieglinde," Kuroda said, "you've got them all good and scared. I don't think anybody's going to be tempted to use these things again until we thoroughly understand them."

"Good. Who's been through the most times?"

Everyone pointed at Dierdre. "Uh, I guess that's right. I made seven transits."

"Then you may already be a fourteenth-generation copy of the original Jamail. You just may be getting a little fuzzy around the edges. You stick close to me. If the worst has happened, then you've suffered the most damage. In fact," she turned back to Kuroda, "I want all these people who've used the transporter under my charge. I'll be setting up a lab here, and another at the Pleistocene end. They can be my lab assistants for the duration. I want access denied to everyone else without my express permission."

"Dr. Kornfeld!" said one of the scientists. "May I remind you that you are not a part of Survey and have no position or authority whatsoever?"

"I have more prestige than anybody since Isaac Newton. Do you think anyone in our scientific community would seriously dispute this with me?"

"Some will try," Antigone said, "but it won't do them any good."

"Wait a minute," Kurz protested. "Forrest and his people are part of my team and we haven't finished our preliminary—"

"Yes you have," Kuroda broke in. "Right now our biggest, most thorough planetside exploration so far is being readied. In a few days, this archipelago will be swarming from one end to the other with detail teams. It'll be mapped, holographed and studied more thoroughly than Earth ever was. You people just stay camped here until we can figure out what to do with you. I'll do what I can to keep us all out of trouble, but I'm not making any promises." He turned and headed back toward his shuttle.

"Derek," Sieglinde called, "where are you going?"

"I'm going to play tourist and find some dinosaurs while I have the chance. Do you think I'd miss an opportunity like this?"

Over the next few days, the first-in team had plenty to do. To their great chagrin, it had nothing to do with exploring. Sieglinde put them to work assembling her lab, which was flown in in sections and put together on the spot. The sections were bonded together while Sieglinde supervised the transport of her instruments. When not on construction detail, they were clearing landing areas for Sieglind's shuttle craft as well as for Survey's. Since she wanted as few people on-site as possible, they had to do nearly everything.

There were compensations. Being at the center of the priority-one project, they got first call on the best equipment, prefab accomodations, and rations brought down directly from orbit. They were no longer part of a shoestring operation.

In the evenings, when they were not too exhausted to speak, they talked endlessly of their unique condition, coming to no coherent conclusions in the process.

"What it comes down to," Colin insisted, "is the question, 'what constitutes *us*?' If all our memories are there, the sum of our life experiences, then we're still us, right?"

"I don't think the *me-ness* of me is changed any," Govinda said. "But then, I guess I wouldn't know."

"If memory's all that counts," Dierdre said, "then we're all dying all the time, because we keep adding new memories and forgetting older ones, so we're different people from day to day."

"The philosophical implications are mind-boggling," Colin agreed.

"If you think the philosophers are gonna have a field day," Govinda said, "wait'll the religious types get hold of it. Poor old LeFevre's worried sick because he thinks maybe his soul didn't make it through the transporter. He's been pestering Sieglinde, asking her whether a soul has a wave pattern."

"Maybe Dierdre here has fourteen funerals coming," Colin pointed out. "Think your family can afford it?"

"As if we didn't have enough to worry about," she said.

When the lab was finished, Sieglinde put them through a rigorous testing program. She had accessed all their medical records and put Fumiyo in charge of her medical lab. She set up an instant communication system linking all the top physicians, hospitals and medical research facilities within the Delta Pavonis system. When the medical data were in, she began personal interviews.

"How about it, Doc," Dierdre said as she entered Sieglinde's office, "are we us?"

"Sit down. Everything checks out so far, but then I didn't expect any radical physical change. Personality is something else." The room was dim. Sieglinde's face was faintly lit by her screen, from which she was reading something. "Why couldn't you have been a paragon? Your record's so bad it's going to be difficult to spot any deterioration."

Dierdre leaned back in her chair, luxuriating in

the building's air conditioning. "If you think my record's bad, wait till you get to Hannie's. She tells me she was a violent criminal before some doctor at Ciano Clinic got her brain chemistry sorted out."

"Yes, she's going to be an interesting case. Have you spoken with your family?"

"Yes. My mother's worried and my father says it's just like me to find an utterly new and unique kind of trouble to get into."

Sieglinde gave her one of her infrequent smiles. "I'll speak to them later. Also to some of your classmates."

"They'll say I'm different, all right. I'm not the school kid they remember." She leaned forward and rested her elbows on her knees. "Do you really think you're going to learn anything that way?"

"No, I really don't trust that sort of subjective data. It's just that there's little else to go on."

"You know what, Doc? Unless you find real physical evidence of imperfect transmission or reassembly or whatever, I don't think we're ever going to know. If we can't even agree on what constitutes a human being, how can we tell if there's been change?"

Sirglinde looked at her with new appraisal. "You've grown a bit less superficial than when I first met you. You're less experience-centered and more into the nature of things."

"I hadn't thought about it, but I suppose you're right. The thought that I may have killed myself fourteen times is sobering."

"Don't despair just yet. I have a suspicion that you're still the same person."

"I hope you can back that up. If the transporter works the way you think, I'm remade from a different set of elementary particles each time my wave-pattern is replicated, right?"

"Yes, but elementary particles don't have self-identity. Even without going through anything as exotic as a transporter, your body is constantly replacing old material with new. It isn't instantaneous, but there probably isn't an elementary particle in my body that was there a couple of years ago. Does that mean I'm not who I was? It happens over and over again throughout everyone's life."

"Keep telling me that. I need it."

"I'm kicking around another concept as well. It may require a whole new category combining physics and the life sciences even to explore, but I feel"—uncharacteristically, she paused, her usual relentless confidence faltering,—"I hate to use a word like 'feel', but the breakthrough discoveries usually involve as much intuition as conscious deduction."

"Go right ahead," Dierdre said avidly. "I promise not to pick at your logic."

"All right, that's fair. I feel that the fact the transmission is instantaneous has something to do with it. The time element here, or rather the lack of it, may be essential. Whatever is happening in this process takes place within this universe and, while there's a displacement of matter, there is no measurable instant of time when your consciousness mind does *not* exist. Do you follow me?"

Dierdre nodded so hard she almost sprained her neck. "Right! No time lapse, no new me, just the old me in a different place!"

"Mind you, I'm way out on a theoretical limb here. It's too new and untested even to call a theory, but my intuitive hypotheses have proven out before, more often than not."

"I admit I'm not exactly objective, but it sounds great to me. I'll buy it for lack of anything more hopeful."

"Enough of that." Sieglinde leaned back, her eyes half-shut, and for once Dierdre could see how tired she was. It occurred to her that, despite appearances, Sieglinde had to be close to a hundred, not a terribly advanced age as things were now, but nobody that age should be expected to put in the kind of hours Sieglinde did. Her eyes opened wide and she was back to normal. "Tomorrow I begin testing inside the cave. I want you to be my personal assistant. Report to the cave mouth at 0600 tomorrow."

"You're the boss," Dierdre said happily, looking forward to a break from construction work. She stood. "Can I tell the others about this new theory of yours?"

"As long as you emphasize that it's highly tentative. And I'm not going to make any public comment on it until I have more evidence. The media types have no patience with anything tentative. Tell them your wildest speculations and they'll report it as gospel. I've fallen into that trap before and came out looking like a fool. Now run along."

Dierdre ran out, her spirits rising for the first time in many days.

"It looks like rock, but it isn't." They were going over the floor, sides and roof of the tunnel.

"How can you tell?" Dierdre asked. If there was one planetary feature Island Worlders knew about, it was rock. Living and working in hollowed-out asteroids made them connoisseurs.

"The chemistry isn't right. Molecular structure indicates a metamorphic rock formed under high pressure, but crystalline structure indicates extreme low-pressure formation. It's rock of a sort, but it isn't natural."

"I can't say I'm really surprised. I guess we could make artificial rock if we needed it. We already know the aliens were way ahead of us in applied science."

Sieglinde held one of her devices within a centimeter of one of the walls, near the roof, and swept it slowly from right to left. "Correct. What I'm really interested in is what's behind these walls. The instrumentation has to be here someplace. Here and in the transport chamber. I have a minor mystery to solve here in the tunnel, and a great big one in the chamber."

"I'd say there are a lot more than two mysteries," Dierdre said. She had her bush shirt off and wore just her thin singlet above her belt. In the tunnel she was safe from sun and biting insects, and she intended to be comfortable. Her dense, black hair was pulled back into a ponytail and she was sweating slightly as she lugged a case of Sieglinde's instruments. Most of them were of Sieglinde's own design and manufacture. They were small and compact, but there seemed to be about a thousand of them in the case.

"Lots. But I'm going to tackle the easiest one first. To wit: why do no animals come in this cave, which would make an ideal den?"

"Hell, Sims asked that question on the first trip we all took together, and he has as much imagination as a turnip. We figured some sort of force shield."

"Why doesn't it keep us out?"

"Body chemistry, maybe?" Dierdre hazarded.

"Unlikely. Those creatures out there are genetically Earth animals. Their internal chemistry is identical to ours."

Sieglinde stuck the instrument she had been using back into the case and took out another and began to scan the ceiling. Dierdre pondered the problem for a while.

"Listen, Doc," she said at length, "how about we try this: let's catch an animal from nearby. One of the primitive mammals we've seen might be best: it'll be easier to read its reaction. That's an Earth animal born here. Have some others sent over from the mainland. We're now pretty sure they're from other planets, too. Have a cat brought down from the orbitals. That's a nonintelligent Earth animal that's not from these islands. See if they'll come in here. If they won't, see what happens when we carry them in."

Sieglinde looked at her for a while. "What an elegant idea. What would you conclude if all of them, including the cat, are repelled by the cave?"

"That maybe the shield is specific for something other than species or chemistry or origin. Maybe it's intelligence."

"If they can remote-read intelligence, I'll give up and admit they're smarter than me. But your experiment's a good one. I'll see you get credit for it when I publish my study. It would be perfect if we also had some alien animals from a different planet, but we'll go with what we've got. Go back to the lab and send for what we need, on my authority. Tell Forrest to detail some people to find a few local animals. All animals to be delivered as soon as possible. We can't use them right away. First they'll have to get over the panic of capture and transportation. Tell the orbitals to send some rats and rabbits, too. Cats are temperamental, so we'll need a wider sampling. Go."

Dierdre dashed out. That was what she liked about Sieglinde. No stalling or hesitation. Plus, she would instantly delegate authority to her most junior assistant. Dierdre found that it was fun to boss around the higher-ups. She wondered if that meant she was lacking in potential for genuine leadership positions, since she got such a kick out of pretending like this.

The first person she ran into was Forrest. She told him what they needed and he nodded glumly. After their brief moment of glory, things had settled down to boring routine. "Sure, I'll send a few people out. Hell, I might take charge myself. There's not enough for us to do here. We should be out exploring."

"Don't despair, you're not going to die of old age here. This is just until Sieglinde's through with us. When this is over, we'll have it made. Even if Survey won't have us, there are plenty of independent outfits that will. I've had dozens of offers."

Forrest scratched in his beard, which needed trimming. "So've I. But damn it, I wanted to make Survey my career."

"Be patient, they'll come around. Look at Derek Kuroda. He's been in trouble more times than he can count, but they always get over it and give him an important position."

"That's because they have so much trouble keeping their best people. Everyone wants to go independent after a while."

"Then maybe Survey isn't such a great career," she said, exasperated. "What do you want? Glory or security? To go up the ladder in Survey you have to be a team player. As it happens, most of us in this nine-ball outfit aren't made to be team players."

"Eight-ball," he corrected. "The expression was eight-ball."

"Just one digit off. Nobody remembers where it comes from, anyway. Don't go all pedantic on me. If . . ." She broke off as a formation of three shuttles shrieked overhead, carrying Survey detail teams engaged in exploring every square millimeter of the archipelago. The sky had been full of them for days. They both looked up enviously. Dierdre sighed. "Yeah," she admitted, "I wish I was out combing the boonies, too. Come on, let's see what kind of nonlethal wildlife we can scare up."

Three days later they had their menagerie assembled. There were a dozen creatures brought in from various parts of the planet, some vaguely crustacean, insectile or reptilian, but most with no Terrestrial equivalents. Team Red had brought in a couple of very small dinosaurs, a feathered lizard-bird, and three primitive, opossum-like mammals. From the ships, there were white rats, rabbits, monkeys and cats. Survey had insisted on using only animals guaranteed sterile, in case any got loose in the ecosystem.

Besides Team Red, there were a number of scientists from Survey; others had come down from orbit for the occasion. A sizable holo crew was in place, both to record the occasion and to transmit it live to the various scientists, institutions and interested individuals. After the initial furor, public interest had waned, and now most laymen awaited official word on the new marvel.

Sieglinde emerged from the cave, trailed by a couple of assistants. These had arrived the day before with several decidedly odd-looking remote handlers. These were spindly robot devices, rolling on four spoked wheels. At the front of each was a pedestal topped with swiveling holo sensors and recorders. Just below the sensor case, each had a pair of jointed, telescoping arms which terminated, ridiculously, in a pair of plastic-fleshed hands so realistic they might have been cut from a cadaver. Between the wheels was slung a simple, woven-wire basket. They looked nothing at all like the sleek robot servitors used in space and at the better-equipped ground facilities. They looked cobbled together from spare parts for a specific purpose, which was exactly the case.

As usual, Sieglinde began without preamble. "In order to enconomize on time and resources, we're embarking on several simultaneous experiments. These little buggers with the ghastly-looking hands," she gestured to the uncomplaining robots, "will make the transition from this cave to its ice-age analogue as many times as necessary. That's why the hands. We know that human hands will work on the controls, so why change a winning combination?"

She pointed to the mini-zoo before the cave. "Before, during and after the transitions, we will be conducting the Jamail Experiment, named for Miss Jamail, who dreamed it up." Dierdre beamed with pride, while some of her peers glowered enviously. "The point of this experiment will be to determine why the local animals seem never to have entered these caves. Something keeps them out, and I've a suspicion that when we find out what it is, we'll also learn what keeps the various creatures that inhabit this planet confined to their specific habitats when there are no visible barriers."

"Dr. Kornfeld," said a tall, shaven-headed man in

a Ciano Institute coverall, "if you haven't yet heard, the oceanographic team has just turned in its preliminary report. It seems that the invisible barriers hold true for the oceans as well. You know those creatures we've been calling whales? They really *are* whales. We've found many species that've been extinct on Earth for more than a century. They migrate along a strip of ocean to the west of this archipelago. Their area runs north and south for thousands of kilometers. They don't seem to cross over to the eastern side of the island, where big seagoing dinosaurs have been found. The oceanic reptiles apparently are not migratory."

"Thank you, Dr. Mahler. It's more evidence, if we need it, that this whole planet is a vast artifact, a zoo-laboratory consisting of artificial rather than natural environments in order to maintain what seem to be incredibly stable ecologies."

A science reporter for one of the holo networks spoke up. "The robots are designed to carry things. What will they be taking through?"

"First, they'll just go through unloaded, to determine that the hands work and that they remain functional after transition. Then, they'll take computers through. These will be running detailed, very complicated programs in synch with other computers on planet and in orbit. If there are imperfections in the transmission process, they should show up instantly as discrepancies in the programs. After that, we'll send animals through. Unlike our daring explorers here, we can dissect the animals."

"Will you be sending humans through?" the reporter asked.

"Absolutely not! Not until we know more about how this thing works. We've had plenty of well-meaning but suicidal volunteers, but since we already have Team Red, we've no need of them."

"After the first transmissions from here," she went on, "my assistants at the other end will send robots through the transporters in the ice-age chamber. There are six besides the one that connects with this cage. Those robots will be equipped with high-powered transmitters to allow us to locate their transporter sites. They are programmed to wait for instructions from orbit. If none are received, they are to record their surroundings for several minutes, then seek to return the way they came."

"That's quite a slate of experiments," the reporter commented.

"They'll keep us busy today."

The reporter looked stunned. "Today! Most scientists would spend months on any one of these experiments. You plan to carry them all out at once?"

"I expect to die sometime in this century," she said. "Before that happens, I want to find out about this thing. Now, if there are no further questions, let's be about it." Without waiting to see if there were any further questions, she returned to the cave, followed by the technicians and robots.

"She sure doesn't mess around once she gets started," Govinda said admiringly.

"She does things in a big way," Dierdre agreed. "Who's handling things up at the cold end?"

"Derek Kuroda," Forrest answered. "Survey insists on asserting authority over the project. Sieglinde agreed to pretend they're in charge if they'd make Derek her nominal superior."

"Very slick," Dierdre commented.

Sieglinde's voice came over their comm units. "Start bringing them in, in the order I gave you."

One at a time, the animals were carried to the cave entrance. Without exception, the animals of planetary origin refused to go in. None could be enticed to enter, and those carried into the entrance reacted with utter panic, even the usually phlegmatic reptiles.

"Okay," said Forrest after the last of the planetary creatures had been tried, "they won't go in. Take them back to the lab and let them calm down. We'll try the animals from the orbitals now. Jamail, try a cat."

Dierdre took a fat feline from a cage and carried it to the cave entrance. The cat was striped light and dark orange and seemed happy to be free of the cage. After a few days of depression, it had grown resigned to full gravity. Gingerly, wary of its claws, Dierdre set the cat down and went inside. She crouched on one knee and held out a hand.

"Come on, Tiger, come on in." Unhesitantly, the cat walked in and rubbed its face against her hand, purring. She looked up, grinning. "It's looking like chemistry, after all."

None of the offworld Earth animals seemed uneasy in the cave. All went smoothly until Ping picked up a rabbit and tried to bring it inside. As he stepped into the threshold of the cave, he ran into something, rebounded from it, and collapsed on his back with blood running from his nose. The rabbit scampered off with Colin and Okamura in pursuit.

Fumiyo pronounced Ping sound but stunned. "What hit me?" he asked when he came to a minute later.

"Looked like you ran into an invisible wall," Forrest said. "Let's get a look at the holos."

Sieglinde came out as soon as they reported the incident. She said nothing as the holo was run several times, showing the event from different angles. Ping had walked into something as solid as steel but completely undetectable. She pointed to the time readout that flashed independently of the holographic image.

"Just what I thought. It happened when we were sending one of the robots through. The cave seals solid during transmission."

Dierdre thought of all the times she had walked over the threshold. "But what if somebody'd been standing right in the doorway when you did that? They might've been cut in two!"

"Find out," Sieglinde said. "Put something in the doorway next time we send a robot through." She returned to the cave.

At her next signal, they put an empty cage in the entrance. At the moment of transportation there was no sound or visual display, but the cage was firmly shoved out.

"The barrier seems to be elastic in nature," Fumiyo said.

"Or else very selective," Forrest amended. "Let's try an animal next. Jamail, try your cat again. Get him to flop down across the threshold. He doesn't look like he needs much encouragement to take it easy."

"Sorry, Tiger," she said to the cat. "It looks like you're going to suffer for science." She didn't think it likely that the cat would be harmed. Whatever other qualities the aliens had, they didn't seem inclined to cause wanton injury. She set the cat down and scratched beneath its chin. It lay down on one side and stretched, purring. A few moments later it was scooted out, jumping to its feet, spitting with indignation.

In late afternoon Sieglinde came out. "Secure the animals and let's go to the lab. Derek will start sending his robots through the other transporters in ten minutes."

In the lab, Sieglinde took her chair. The rest stood. A few moments later, Derek was among them. The image was incredibly realistic, but lifetimes of experience allowed them to pick up on the minute discrepancies that told them this was a holographic image.

"They've all gone through," Derek said, a little nervously. "Orbital communication should be reporting in a few minutes, if everything goes well.

After a half-minute of silence, an amplified voice boomed through the lab, causing nearly everyone to jump, a result of fatigue and overstressed nerves.

"Planetside Transporter Project, this is OrbitCom. We have your No. 1 robot triangulated. It's smack in the middle of North Continent, western hemisphere. Here's the image." A holographic scan appeared on one of the lab walls. It showed a cave like the two they had seen already. At least two more transporters were visible. Everyone cheered.

"Here comes No. 2," the voice continued, "South Continent, western hemisphere, just below the equator." This time the reaction was more subdued, as the caves were beginning to get familiar. This one showed one other transporter.

"Nothing at all from No. 3," said OrbitCom. "Here's No. 4. Not much of an image, for the excellent reason that it's under water, off the shore of the big inland sea."

"Now aren't you glad you didn't try those other transporters?" Sieglinde said.

"Still nothing from Three, Five or Six," OrbitCom said. "Hold it, we're getting something from Five, but real weak. Damn! No wonder! It's right under the North Polar icecap, about a hundred-fifty meters down in the ice. We're gonna need to do some enhancement on this signal before we can construct a decent holo. Be patient. They've all been signalled to stay where they are."

The lab buzzed with conversation for the next five minutes. All talk ceased when OrbitCom broke in once more. "We've spotted Three! No wonder we missed its signal, it's on the big moon!" This time the lab erupted in pandemonium, with much hopping and backslapping.

"It transports across space!" Sieglinde said, bouncing in her chair like a little girl. Almost instantly, she restored her usual, impassive demeanor. Moments later, there was a commotion in Derek's lab in the ice age transporter cave. Sieglinde tapped her console and suddenly they all seemed to be standing in the other lab, surrounded by a total-environment holo image. A group of technicians were clustered around one of the transporter terminals.

"Six's back!" one called. Then: "Ow! It's cold!" They could see the spindly robot now. It was frosted with white crystals.

"Check the instruments," Derek said. "I want to know why we didn't get a signal."

"Maybe it went to the *south* pole," Dierdre said. "Too far under the ice for the signal to make it out."

"I get minus 250 Celsius," called a technician. "That's colder than planetary ice should get. It's also bollixed up our instruments. Most of them aren't designed for cold like that. We're not gonna get any usable holos off this one."

"Derek," Sieglinde said, "arrange for some cold-shielded instruments to be sent down and send them through tomorrow."

"Right."

"And don't give up yet. These transmitters are subluminal. We may hear something yet."

"We've got an image from Five now," said OrbitCom. Derek's lab faded and they had a one-wall view of what robot Five was looking at. The view panned continuously from left to right and back again as the robot scanned. It was a huge, cavernous room, featureless except for the discs inset into the walls. Other tunnels and chambers opened off this one at intervals. They viewed for several seconds in speechless astonishment.

"Look at the transporters!" said the reporter in a strangled voice. "*Hundreds* of them!"

"Sims!" Sieglinde's voice was a whipcrack. "You're an ice miner, aren't you?"

"Right, Doc."

"Take my shuttle and get up to that site. "I'm giving you top priority. Commandeer whatever you need; personnel, vehicles, equipment. Dig down to that place and inform me the instant you've found a way in. Nobody to enter until I get there. Go!"

Sims ran out of the lab. They heard his voice dwindling with distance. "Damn, I just *love* this!"

Sieglinde rubbed her face and sighed. "Busy day, people, and we're in for another one tomorrow. Let's adjourn and get something to eat." They were about to leave when another transmission came over Sieglinde's priority channel. The man who appeared in holographic image was stocky, blond-haired with ruddy cheeks. He wore explorer's clothes suitable for a temperate climate.

"Dr. Kornfeld, I'm Pavel Minsky, head of Detail Survey Team Odysseus. We're about five hundred klicks south of the ice age transporter site, and about fifteen hundred meters lower altitude. We're on a big peninsula, where the climate's temperate, courtesy of a warm ocean current. Fauna's mostly middle Pleistocene, not quite as spectacular as in the ice age area, but a lot more abundant. Today, my Team Green recorded something you should see."

Sieglinde shrugged off her weariness. "Let's see it, Pavel."

They got a view of a grassy clearing edged by a dense forest. Butterflys and flowers added color to a predominantly green scene. A small herd of deerlike animals with wonderfully baroque antlers wandered across the field of view. Some of them, males apparently, even had small, forked antlers sprouting from their snouts near the nose.

"Fred Turner, Team Green leader," said a voice. "We were recording these curlyhorns early this afternoon when we encountered these other guys. They were so quiet and careful we didn't even notice them at first. Look closely to the right of the clearing, just within the treeline."

It was dark beneath the trees, but they began to make out small forms moving cautiously. There was something faintly disturbing in the way they moved, a careful deliberation that was unlike the manner of the animal life they had seen so far.

"Monkeys?" Sieglinde said. "Apes? I can't quite make them out."

"That's what we thought at first. When we got back to camp we did some enhancement. Look at this."

The point of view abruptly zoomed in and the enhancement program dispelled the darkness beneath the branches, revealing the curious creatures as if in full daylight. There was a collective gasp. They were small, about a meter in height, covered with short, coarse brown hair. The faces were apelike, with low foreheads and protruding, near-chinless jaws. But the bright, black eyes were intelligent. They had no tails and they stood upright. They seemed unafraid, but intensely curious. There were a dozen visible, some of them females with infants.

"Hominids!" Sieglinde said.

"That's what they are. We haven't yet identified them with any of the known fossil types, but we've only been at it a few hours. Probably won't know for sure until we get skeletons or at least teeth to study. We haven't chased them or molested them in any way, just gone about our business. If they want to make contact, fine, but as I understand it there's no rush about this."

Pavel broke in. "I've ordered no more shuttle flights over this area. From now on they land at the coast and haul our supplies in."

"Good work, Pavel," Sieglinde said. "Good work, Team Green. When word of this gets out, you may get unauthorized intruders. Remember, you're the law in your area. Don't hesitate to open fire if anyone tries to molest these creatures."

"Already got guards in place," Pavel said. "They're our find, just like the transporters are Kurz's Team Red's. We're taking a proprietary interest, you might say. Out."

Finally, they retired to eat and talk over the day's events.

"Sooner or later," Forrest insisted, "We've got to find really huge transporters. They got those dinosaurs here somehow."

"Maybe they brought them in as babies and reared them here," Fumiyo pointed out. "Maybe even as eggs or fertilized embryos. They could transport hundreds of thousands that way in a container the size of a backpack. Our ships have potential cattle herds stored away by the millions, along with enough other livestock to populate a planet. We didn't bring them across space full grown."

"Who can guess how far they developed this wave technology," Dierdre said. "Maybe all they really needed was the data, and the actual transport wasn't necessary." Conversation continued in this vein until Sieglinde rapped on the table.

"So far you're agreeing with each other too much. Try another angle, it might improve your minds. Everybody is going under the assumption that this is a sort of zoo, where the aliens collected specimens of life from all over the galaxy."

"That fits with the evidence. It seems the most likely inference," Forrest said.

"Because we're zoo-building creatures and we assume they behaved like us. Let's look at it another way. Suppose this is a biological lab where new life forms are developed and distributed to other planets, using the transporters."

Dierdre was first to catch the implications. "Including the hominids?"

"Including the hominids."

"Aw, come on, Doc," Ping protested. "Our kind of life originated on Earth. The fossil record's there." Most of the team agreed.

Sieglinde shook her head. "You reject the idea because it's our received wisdom that our life originated on our planet. Once, it was heresy to suggest that there was life anywhere else. When we got here, we knew for sure that there was other organic life. We still don't know how it originates, whether it develops on the individual planets, or gets around through interstellar space somehow. And the Earth fossil record is still full of unexplained holes. This could be an explanation. The aliens seeded Earth with species they'd developed. Those species lived there for hundreds of thousands, even millions of years, long enough to leave plenty of fossils. Then the aliens sent in new species they'd brewed up, maybe even arranged for periodic mass extinctions to make room for the new animals. That would answer a lot of questions, wouldn't it?"

They pondered that for a minute. "Hey, Doc," Forrest said, "do you really believe that?"

She looked at him pityingly. "Hell, no! It's just a possibility I'm playing with. Do you people only think about things you already *believe*? You're not scientists. You might as well be theologians."

"Lighten up, Doc," Dierdre said. "We're almost as brilliant as you, we're just a little slower, that's all."

Sieglinde leaned back and laughed. "We're all suffering from data overload. Go get some sleep."

They trudged off to their beds, but it turned out that the day's marvels were not yet over. In the middle of the night they were awakened by the voice of OrbitCom booming over their communication system. Robot Six had returned. It had broadcast from Copernicus, a Mars-sized moon orbiting Baal, a multiringed gas giant far out toward the edge of the system. The robot had arrived at its destination, had beamed its transmission and, having received no orders to the contrary, had obeyed its programming and returned, arriving in Derek Kuroda's lab six hours ahead of its own transmission.

SEVEN

Sieglinde punched her console and lines of incomprehensible symbols scrolled upward from the set, too fast for anybody else in the lab to read, even if they had been able to comprehend the personal symbology she had invented for her work. Only the most advanced physicists and mathematicians, many of them her own students, had ever mastered it. To the team members and technicians in the room, it might as well have been Sanskrit.

"We've got discrepancies here," she said. "Serious ones. Everything complex we've sent through the offworld transporters; computers and animals especially, have arrived at the other end with glitches in their electronic or electrochemical structure. The defects from specimens sent out to this planet's larger moon were just barely detectable, even with my best instruments. Those from Copernicus were far more serious. I think that the transporter's reliability is directly linked to distance of transmission."

"You say serious, Doc," Forrest said. "How serious?"

She frowned. "Any glitch at all seems catastrophic to me, but I'll concede that my passion for order and perfection leads to exaggeration. Let's say that you'd have to be careful sending a computer through while it was handling anything important. With self-correcting systems, you'd be unlikely to have trouble, though, as long as it was adjusted to deal with this sort of failure."

She ran some holos of the experimental animals. "As for the animals, their behavior is mainly instinct-driven and so far we've observed no definite behavioral discrepancies. The differences have shown up in electrochemical activity. Their brains are too primitive to be greatly affected by the changes. Anything with more complex mental faculties, though, would be at risk.

"We now have little reason to believe that the humans who went through were altered. Planetary transportation is probably safe, although I still consider the risk foolish at this point. At most, you're sparing yourself a few hours and a little discomfort. Transportation across space, though, should not be attempted by humans at this time. It wouldn't be you that showed up at the other end. The complex wave patterns of the human brain require extreme subtlety and precision to record and transmit. The very slightest imprecision would result in someone very different from you being reassembled."

"Sieglinde," Derek asked, "do you think this glitch is actually an inevitable function of distance between transporters, or could it be deterioration from age? Such evidence as we have indicates that some of these transporters have been in place for millions of years."

"Or maybe," Forrest hazarded, "a design flaw? Maybe these aliens weren't as godlike as we've come to imagine them."

Dierdre thought that was a perceptive comment. She had some questions of her own, but she liked the way Forrest had hit on that. She also thought his curly blond beard framed his jaw nicely. She shoved the thought aside. She prided herself on how long she could nurse a grudge, and she still resented the patronizing way he had treated her when she first joined the team.

"The age is still problematical," Sieglinde said. "We really have no data to go on. My own personal vessel, for instance, is almost a hundred years old. Someone discovering it drifting in space, abandoned, could read the date of manufacture on the builder's plaque, but probably only the hull dates from that time. The aliens could be keeping these devices maintained.

"As for Steve's comment"—she shook her head, not in discouragement but in wonder—"I'm just beginning to get an idea how they've accomplished this, and it's so complex that I'm amazed they could send a potted turnip through and have it still alive on the other side. As for their intelligence, they may well have been more intelligent than we are. One thing we do know is that humans are the dumbest creatures capable of developing technology, so they couldn't have been *less* intelligent. On the other hand, they may just have had more time to work in."

"Doc," Dierdre said, "you mentioned when we first surveyed the cave that there were two mysteries about the cave and one about the transporter room that you needed to figure out. We've pretty well settled the one about the animal barrier. What are the other two?"

"One is minor: why do the caves stay so clean? I found that even windblown trash, leaves, feathers, dust and such don't settle for long. Snow doesn't drift in in the ice age cave. Some force gently pushes everything out after a few days. I now think it's a variant use of the force field that Ping smacked his nose on. I haven't had time to figure it out yet, but it's simple compared to the transporter.

"The other is more perplexing. How does the transporter chamber contain all that energy? The area surrounding the object to be transported contains the energy from the—what shall we call it?—*disin-*

corporated body and stores it for the instant prior to transportation, and does the same at the other end while the wave pattern is interpreted and reincorporated. To give you an idea of what this means, the energy of a body massing 100 kilograms, when converted to pure energy, would yield about the explosive force of a couple of hundred megatons of TNT."

They winced slightly at the thought of the sort of forces they had so blithely meddled with.

"As to the aliens themselves," she went on, "we're still dealing in guesswork. The few inferences we can draw are all conditional. From the size of the transporter chambers they were roughly human-sized and had hands of some sort. *If* the users on this planet were its originators. They might have been servant creatures, or robots. And we can be pretty sure that they were willing to deal with time in great big chunks."

"Maybe they had a different perception of time," Dierdre suggested.

"Elaborate on that," Sieglinde said.

Dierdre waved her hands, slightly embarrassed. "It's just something I've been thinking about. I did a paper on it in my ephebe year."

"I read it," Sieglinde said, "continue."

Dierdre never failed to be amazed at Sieglinde's thoroughness. "Well, the human conception of time is totally subjective, and its rhythms and intervals are all determined by the specialized, localized circumstances peculiar to Earth: rotation of the planet, night and day, lunar cycles, tidal cycles, seasonal changes, the orbit of the planet and so forth. Even under the local conditions of Earth there were creatures with life cycles far briefer than humans, and a few that were longer. It would be unreasonable to expect aliens even to approximate our conception of time.

"Even aside from human perception of time, which is faulty to begin with, it gets really elastic when we get away from the home system. We all know that quasi-luminal travel slows down the rate of the passage of time for the traveller when measured against that for the person who does not travel." Nobody had to question what she meant. She wasn't addressing a group of dummies.

"Now, this can mean several things in relation to our putative aliens. They may just have tremendously long lives, in which case spans of time unthinkable to us become reasonable. Or they might have been hive-creatures and shared a group mind, in which the mortality of individual bodies means less than the formation and death of our bodily cells."

Dierdre sat back and took a deep breath. She wasn't used to talking this long. Arguing, yes, but not lecturing. "That's just considering the possibilities of organic life. Electronic intelligences might not consider time a factor at all."

"Super-computers?" Derek queried.

"Something like that. Something as far beyond our computers as they are ahead of a primitive calculator. It's not unthinkable. We went from calculators to sophisticated computers in less than a century."

Sieglinde nodded. "And if they're self-correcting, not relying on organic electrochemical brain action, they might be able to use the transporters across interstellar distances without risk. It's a good thought. I suspect they were made of matter, though. It's what the transporters were designed to handle."

"But, that's just the first part of this chain of thought," Dierdre persisted.

"Then finish it," Sieglinde urged.

"Well, I was thinking about different *per*ceptions of time that might separate us from the aliens, but what about differing *con*ceptions?"

Everyone else looked puzzled at this, but Sieglinde smiled as if it had been just what she had expected to hear. "You're onto something. Go ahead."

"We're born, we live and we die and everything in

between is experienced along a linear time-line. Maybe they could experience time in a different way."

"You mean time travel?" Derek said.

"It's one possibility. It's been thought impossible for centuries beyond the sub-atomic level, but that doesn't mean anything. These aliens licked the speed of light limitation, so maybe they mastered time travel as well.

"Actually, though, I wasn't planning to go that far. What I was thinking was, maybe they could experience time not as a continuous line, but as discrete segments along the line, chosen perhaps at will. We have some slight capability that way. Our conscious minds don't really experience the passage of time while we're asleep or comatose, only our bodies. Maybe they could step outside the timestream. That way, even with a human lifetime, you could set up an experiment in evolution, then jump ahead a million years to see how it was making out."

"Where do they stay in the meantime?" Forrest asked.

"Ask her," Dierdre said, pointing at Sieglinde. "She's the physicist, I'm just a theorist."

"Very good," Sieglinde proclaimed. "Dierdre's taken my advice about freeing her speculations from conventional patterns of belief. As a matter of fact, I've been speculating along much the same lines. Of around thirty scenarios I've considered, her 'punctuated time frame' theory is one of the five I consider to be the most likely.

The others looked at her admiringly, impressed that she had been thinking along the same lines as the great Dr. Kornfeld. Dierdre was a little crestfallen, though. Not only had her theory not been original, but according to Sieglinde it only made it into the top five.

"As to where they would go in the interim," Sieglinde said, "I think it would be analogous to the state that matter enters prior to transmission through their transporters. They might be broken down into wave patterns, stored in an indeterminate n-time, and reincorporated after the proper passage of real time. As to how the time is determined and the retranslation effected, I have no idea. But if that's what they're doing, I'll find out."

Nobody doubted that she would do it. Dr. Kornfeld didn't go by anyone else's rules.

"Any news on the hominids?" Derek asked.

Fumiyo, who had been assigned to keep current on that subject, reported. "Teams in the environments consistent with human or proto-human life have begun special procedures to detect and observe hominids. Remote snoops, all but invisible, are being installed in favorable areas. Two more hominid species have been identified. Well, there's some disagreement on one of them. Many anthropologists and zoologists say it's really an ape; foot, leg and spinal structure not advanced enough to call homonid. The other, though, was spotted just yesterday. It's more advanced than the ones Minsky's Team Green found."

A holo appeared in the middle of the room. A single creature squatted by a waterhole, drinking from a cupped palm. It was not quite as hairy as the first specimens had been, with more bare skin showing on face, chest and hands. The skin itself was pale tan. The face still looked as much animal as human, but its angle was more nearly vertical. Most human of all were the hands and feet. The big toes were slightly separated from the others, but the arch and heel were pronounced. The hands, except for the thick hair that grew almost to the knuckles, would have passed muster in any card game.

Forrest whistled. "Getting close. Fumiyo, has anyone recorded definite speech? That'd be the clincher."

"Not yet. They're reluctant to pursue the band Team Green found, but listening devices have been placed. This one was a single individual, so we can't know until a group is observed. The other looked too primitive."

"Doc," Ping said, "what're we gonna *do* if we discover real, definite, no-fooling humans?"

"Rewrite a little history, I suspect. Actually, that will be a matter for the *Althing* to decide, not us. One thing, though, hominid or human, there won't be very many of them. The area suitable for primitive human habitation is too small. And, it's consistent with known Earth history. For millennia, protohuman and human numbers were minuscule. What's really going to stir things up is if we find that they originated here and were transported to Earth rather than vice versa." That thought had been on all their minds, an unwelcome complication of what was already complicated enough.

"How are the other probes making out?" Hannie asked. "Now that they know what to look for?" It was easy for them to forget that there were other Island Worlds out there, exploring other systems. Most of Team Red were too young to remember the Sol Orbit days, when they had all been concentrated around a single star. Delta Pavonis had been one of the nearer destinations, but a few stars had been reached earlier, a few more had checked in after the Avalonian arrival in the Delta Pavonis area, and many more would be travelling for years or decades before reaching their chosen stars.

"I haven't had time to keep track lately," Sieglinde said. "Derek?"

"Nothing much so far. The Alphans have been at their destination the longest, and our news took them completely by surprise." This was the expedition that had chosen the system nearest to Earth, Alpha Centauri, a two-star system with a third, more distant companion star, Proxima Centauri. The main star had been designated Alpha Prime and its fourth planet had proven to be amazingly Earthlike: slightly more massive than the motherworld, but with a larger radius; in consequence its surface gravity was very nearly Earth normal. It rotated every twenty-five hours and had a three hundred fourteen day year. The discoverers had named it, fittingly if unimaginatively, Terra Nova. The second star, commonly called Alpha Deuce, was separated from Prime by 23.6 astronomical units and appeared in the Terra Novan night sky as an intensely bright point of light, except during a brief time of year when it was too near the primary to be seen.

The planet had abundant flora and fauna, but nothing had been discovered that was as exotic as the dinosaurs and other anomalous life forms found at Delta Pavonis. All life forms discovered so far seemed to be of common origin and consistent with variations in the planetwide ecology, much as their Earth analogues had been.

"They've been there nearly two decades," Fumiyo pointed out. "Surely they'd have found anything bizarre if it was to be found."

"Not necessarily," Dierdre said. "Orbital surveillance only tells you so much. We've been here for years without detecting those great big dinosaurs, or the mammoths, or even the whales. Somebody's got to get up close to find some things. It took a shoestring operation like ours to stumble across them. The whole population of the Alpha Centauri expedition isn't as big as one old-time major city on Earth, and most of them stayed in space. Only the dumb and adventurous go down onto the planets. A planet's a big place for just a few thousand explorers to cover, even with two decades to do it in."

"They're combing the place for transporters now," Derek said. "There are some life forms that seem rather intelligent, but so far no sign of artifacts, culture or archaeological remains. Of course, that double-star setup makes for occasional catastrophic climate changes, which wouldn't be very conducive to the rise of civilization. Seismic activity's supposed to be pretty fierce as well. Otherwise, it sounds like a fine place. Better than this one, anyway."

"Tau Ceti?" Sieglinde asked.

"Another system like ours, or Earth's: four Jupiter-style gas giants, a few lifeless rocks of the Mars-Venus variety, and one Earth-type. The climatological situation is very benign in the temperate zones, but no intelligent life so far. They haven't been there as long as the Alpha Centauri expedition. They've found some puzzling remains—what look a little like wall foundations—but artifact status is uncertain. If they're alien or humanoid artifacts, they're incredibly ancient."

Sieglinde leaned back and pondered. "Quite aside from the mundanities of planetary exploration and the bizarre things we've discovered here, there's another anomaly that has my brain reeling."

"At least yours reels," Derek commented. "Mine went numb a couple of years back. What's troubling you now?"

"When we blasted out of solar orbit, three-quarters of the Island World expeditions chose nearby star systems that featured Sol-type primaries and definite evidence of planetary systems. We had no certainty of finding Earth-type planets at all, much less in any abundance. I'd have been happy and surprised to find one in five planetary systems. Now three of us have reached our destinations, and all three found usable Earth-type planets. It's far too small a sampling for statistical analysis, but it's also far too great a coincidence. The general distribution of planetary types has been about as expected—the bulk of matter tied up in a few gas giants, smaller rock balls and some asteroids. But an Earth-type takes an extremely delicate balance of mass, distance, elements and so forth. There has to be a tremendous amount of water, and the orbit has to maintain a distance throughout the year that allows the very narrow surface-temperature range at which water stays liquid except for ice caps and some atmospheric vapor. To top it all off, it's necessary to have a varying planetary axial tilt in order to maintain a mix of benign climates. In the great cosmic crapshoot, we've rolled too many naturals."

"Should that surprise us?" Dierdre asked. She waved her hands in an all-inclusive gesture, taking in the whole planet and a large part of the solar system. "Just look at this planet! We've known since we got here that there was something unnatural about it—the way it's divided up into climatic and ecological zones, the incredible diversity of life, all of it differing from one zone to another right down to their molecular structure. If our aliens can build a whole world as artificial as this one, what's to stop them from building an Earth or two in any solar system they come to?"

"Priority message coming through," Ping said. A moment later a voice from one of the orbitals filled the room.

"This is Survey news service. Today we've received further confirmation of the planetary lab theory. Dr. Krishna Srinivas of the Beowulf Island survey team reports that his team has discovered fauna seemingly related to that found on Alpha Centauri's Terra Nova."

"I don't know whether to cheer or be scared," Dierdre said.

"I've been scared since we got to this place," Sieglinde affirmed.

The meeting broke up. The next bombshell arrived a few months later, with the first report from Eta Cassiopeiae.

EIGHT

The newcomer arrived by shuttle early in the morning, while it was still cool. They had rolled dice to see who got the task of meeting him, being his escort and giving him his orientation. Dierdre had lost. There was a spaceport facility on the coast now. The scoutcraft would be bringing him in from there.

She heard the craft before she saw it, then the clumsy, boxy shape came into view over a range of low hills to the southeast. She remembered her first ride on such a craft. It seemed years ago, although it had been—what? She counted. Just under one Delta Pav year, about one point one Earth year. Things had changed considerably in that short time.

There was now an experimental agricultural station next to the landing field. The maize was coming along nicely, she noted. The plants were grown from original Earth seed, never adapted for offworld conditions. There were stations like this all over the archipelago, taking advantage of the Earth-type soil conditions to replenish the orbitals' precious supply of unaltered seed. The viability of gene-manipulated flora was always suspect, and a supply of control material was a necessary hedge against unforseen consequences.

Dierdre held on to her hat as the scoutcraft's rotors stirred up a minor tornado of grass, twigs and dust. Next to the main cargo door the crew had painted a tyrannosaur and the words "Dino Express." When the craft was settled, the door lowered and extruded its ramp. From inside, the cargomaster grinned and waved.

"G'morning, Dee!"

She waved back. "Good morning, Karl. What did you bring me?"

"Got some exotic instruments for the boss lady, six crates of wine from Avalon, this month's holo releases from Deryabar Studios and a brand-new superluminal commo specialist, still in his original wrapper."

"That last item's the one I was sent for. Send him out. The rest can go up the hill by robot cart."

"He'll be right out." Karl chuckled maliciously, which, when she thought about it later, should have given her some warning.

An apparition appeared at the top of the ramp, and Dierdre gaped as she had at her first dinosaur. He looked slightly older than herself, slightly taller, and far paler. He managed to look thin and flabby at the same time, and he descended the ramp on legs as wobbly as a drunk's. But it was not his obvious unsuitability to the climate that had her goggling. That was not uncommon among newcomers just down from the orbitals with no acclimatization training. No, it was his clothes.

For some reason, this one had not chosen to wear practical coveralls, nor yet the hokey safari-style getups generally favored by sightseeing asteroid-dwellers down for a visit. He was wearing this season's highest fashion, the sort of thing Avalonian socialites wore when being interviewed by those breathless holo reporters that Dierdre detested so much. His short jacket was brilliant scarlet, heavily embroidered with gold thread. An eruption of foamy lace cascaded from his throat, topped by a face as perfect as genetics and surgery could make it. His sky-blue tights terminated in pointed shoes with high, red-laquered heels. In ten-percent gravity, they would be elegant. Planetside, they made him teeter alarmingly. She forced herself not to stare at the ornate codpiece. It *had* to be padded. Heavily.

"I'm Dierdre Jamail," she said when he reached bottom. "I'm to show you around and take you to your quarters."

He managed a weak smile. Perspiration covered his face and dripped into the lace fall. "The famous discoverer? Charmed." He offered a soft hand. "I am Matthias Pflug. I'm here from the Martin Shaw Institute, superluminal department."

That, at least, was impressive. The Shaw Institute accepted only the top graduates each year. But it had to be somebody's idea of a joke, sending this one here.

"Dr. Kornfeld says I'm to see to your needs personally. There are all sorts of rumors going around concerning this mysterious mission of yours."

He took out a large handkerchief and mopped his face. "Is it always so hot here?"

Dierdre was perfectly comfortable in the early-morning coolness, but she remembered how it had felt her first morning here.

"This is as cool as it gets. We'd better get you indoors, where the atmosphere's controlled. Maybe you ought to ride. The cargo robot ought to be here soon."

"I think I can walk it," he said.

"Pardon me in advance for saying it," she said, as they trudged slowly uphill, "but you really aren't dressed for the climate." Or for much of anything else, she added mentally.

"This came up so quickly," he said, still mopping, "I didn't have time to get ready. And under no circumstances would I wear one of those Ernest Hemingway White Hunter outfits that've become all the rage." He stopped and pointed at a group of brown animals munching grass nearby. "Are those things dangerous?"

"Those are just calves," Dierdre assured him. "That's an agricultural station. We have sheep, too. Don't worry about the dinosaurs. They mostly avoid this place since we've moved in, although a really big pterosaur got away with a lamb a few days ago."

He studied the clear sky apprehensively. "I want to see the fauna, of course. Maybe from a shuttle."

"We'll find you something." She wondered who she could con into guiding this impossibility into the bush.

When they reached the now-sprawling lab complex and passed inside, he almost fainted from relief. "Air!" he said. "I'd almost forgotten what air was like. It's like breathing under water out there."

"You may not be cut out for this kind of life," she hazarded. Mouths dropped open as they passed people in the corridor. Others came out of offices and labs to stare. If one of the mysterious aliens had dropped into their midst it could not have been more out of place.

"You'll be staying here," Dierdre said, pushing aside a plastic curtain. The chamber was no more than four meters on a side, furnished with a cot, a chest and a hanging rack.

"Rather, ah, Spartan, isn't it?"

"It's better than sleeping on the ground with the bugs chewing you. We're outside most of the time. We only use our cells to sleep in and then we're usually so exhausted we don't pay much attention to the surroundings."

"I suppose asceticism has its own charm. Mortification of the flesh and all that. Thank you, Miss Jamail. Please tell Dr. Kornfeld that I would like to see her at her earliest convenience. Now, I think I had better lie down for a few minutes." He collapsed bonelessly onto the bunk.

Dierdre made sure he was still breathing, then went in search of Sieglinde, whom she found in the transporter chamber. "Doc, this guy is a joke. One of your enemies must've sent him, or maybe one of his."

"No, I asked for him personally. Former student of mine." She spoke without taking her attention from her instruments. Dierdre had always admired Sieglinde's ability to keep her attention on two things at once. It did make her speech rather abstracted, though. "Family's one of the big rich ones from the old days in the Belt. Self-designated aristocrats, very prominent socially."

"I never had any use for that sort," Dierdre said.

"They never had any for you either, I'll wager."

Dierdre winced. Sieglinde tolerated arrogance, but she had no liking for self-importance. She had an abnormal sensitivity for the difference between the two, and did not hesitate to let you know when you had crossed the line. She could make it hurt.

"Right. He says he wants to see you as soon as possible, but I'd let him rest a while."

"I've scheduled his presentation for 2030, right after dinner. Pass the word that nobody is to have too much wine or beer with dinner, I want everybody clear-headed for this."

"Got you. Are we in for another historic occasion?"

Sieglinde nodded, her fingers continuing to dance over her keyboard. "As important as the Rhea Objects, or this island, or your discovery of the transporters."

"*Sic transit gloria mundi*, huh? Or should it be *gloria cosmos*? No, that's mixing Latin and Greek. I never was good with Classical languages."

For the first time Sieglinde looked up and smiled. "Close enough, but don't worry. It's true we live in an age of marvels and the historic occasions are coming thick and fast. This may well prove to be one of the watershed periods of human history, as important as coming down out of the trees or learning to speak or going into space. But don't worry, you'll still be in the history books. Maybe not right up there with Columbus or Magellan, but at least equal to Lindbergh."

Dierdre grinned. "Great. Everybody remembers his name, even if they're not too sure what it was he did. Beats being forgotten."

"Good. You haven't lost your sense of humor. There're times when it's all you have to keep you going."

At the mess table, Dierdre's word about moderation drew some groans.

"Ahh, shut up," Forrest told the groaners. "A few months back a bladder of beer off a shuttle was the biggest luxury you could dream about. Now you're whining because the boss lady turns off the tap. What a bunch of orbies." This last was a word of opprobrium coined by the planetside personnel. It was short for "orbiters."

Down the table a vociferous argument was going on. "It *has* to be padded!" Okamura insisted. He turned to Dierdre. "You saw him closest, Dee. What's your verdict, padded or unpadded?"

"Padded," she said, assuredly.

"I don't know," Fumiyo said. "I knew a guy back at the Academy. He was skinny like that, but you should have seen his—"

"Crap," said Hannie, succinctly. She had just come in from a three-day jungle trek, guiding a team of paleontologists and holographers. She was still dressed in her filthy outback coverall. "I haven't laid eyes on this orby fashion plate yet, but there isn't one of them worth—"

"Assembly in the amphitheater in five minutes," said Sieglinde's voice over the intercom. "Move it."

The amphitheater was a holographic pit. It was

circular, with tiers of seats that could accomodate up to two hundred spectators. Besides Team Red, all the lab and support personnel were present, about half filling the room. Sieglinde expected to have a much larger facility, eventually.

Dierdre took a seat near the middle of the room. She picked one that was flanked by empty seats and was gratified when Forrest took the seat to her right. He had plenty to choose from. Hannie sat to her left and Dierdre leaned toward Forrest, not to make a play for him, but because Hannie had not had time to bathe before dinner and the summons to the amphitheater. The woman was overpowering in every possible way.

The lights in the seats dimmed while those in the pit brightened slightly. There was a gasp as Matthias Pflug walked into the center of the pit. Not only had he not changed into planetside clothes, he had added a short evening cape, a garment so spectacularly useless that anyone with pretensions to fashion just had to own one. Dierdre heard an especially loud gasp next to her but at that moment Pflug began to speak.

"Dr. Kornfeld has asked me to make a special trip here to bring you a presentation of the holographic record transmitted to us at the Shaw Institute through superluminal communication from the expedition to Eta Cassiopeiae. This transmission arrived mere hours ago. We have put considerable labor into reducing it to the form you shall see. Quite aside from the historical import of the events at Eta Cassiopeiae, this has been a momentous use of Dr. Kornfeld's superluminal communication technology." His voice and manner were far more assured now, and Dierdre realized that much of his earlier shakiness had been sheer fatigue. He had put in some long hours at this project. There was much raucous cheering at the praise for Sieglinde's technological marvel.

Dierdre felt a hand at her knee. Shudderingly, she

relaxed into her chair. At last, he was making his move. It was about time.

"This transmission," Pflug continued, "came on the narrow band used only by the Shaw Institute. The senders wanted to make sure that the news would be handled at this end by responsible people." Team Red felt the rebuke in his words. Some of them made rude noises. The hand slid along Dierdre's thigh. She vowed to herself not to fall into an attitude of abandoned acceptance for at least five minutes. Or until the holos started, at which time nobody would be able to see what was happening.

"What you are about to see is a condensation of several months of exploration on Eta Cassiopeiae's two Earthlike planets." There were shouts of disbelief. "Yes, I said two. The discoverers named them Atlantis and Xanadu. Dr. Kornfeld's wonderment at the frequency of Earthlike planets goes up a notch, eh?"

The fingers dug painfully into Dierdre's thigh. She winced. Was he a little kinky? Then she realized something: it was her *left* thigh. She looked over and saw Hannie's face, staring downward with an unreadable expression. Dierdre's mind went through a disorienting change of gears. Sure, Hannie was a little weird, but then, weren't they all? Sure, the two of them had been friends, after a fashion, but *this*? Then she noticed that the Amazon was not paying her the slightest attention. Hannie's eyes were glued to Matthias Pflug.

"Get ready for something even more bizarre. These two planets don't just orbit the primary, they orbit *each other*!" From the audience there were cries such as, "Scientific impossibility," and, "Oh, bullshit!"

"Scoff if you like," Pflug said, "but it's true. These two planets, Earthlike within a few hundred kilometers of diameter, are not the sole anomaly of the system. Other planets consist of a single, Mercury-like, lifeless rock, and three gas giants. A little different from the other systems so far, eh?"

Dierdre had to admit that Pflug had some style. It was a bit hard to concentrate, with Hannie's hand clamping down like a power tool. She took the woman's thick wrist in both hands and dug her thumbs into the nerve point on the small finger side, pressing as hard as she could.

"Ease off, Hannie! I only have one femoral artery in that leg, and you're destroying it!"

Hannie leaned close, the pressure causing her no apparent pain. "I want him!" she hissed.

"What? Him? Pflug? You can—" At first, all Dierdre could think about was that she had prayed to find someone to take the little fop off her hands. Now she realized that he might be worth something. "—You can take a flying leap. He's mine."

"Trade assignments with me!" Hannie urged.

"Why should I go out and sweat my tail off in the brush when I can pull a cushy assignment right here?" This was getting better all the time.

"Will you two shut up?" Forrest said out the side of his mouth.

"I know that a double-planet system like this has long been deemed impossible," Pflug continued. "However, I remind you that many astronomers right up to the twenty-first century considered Earth's Moon a theoretical impossibility, despite its obvious existence. There may still be much to learn about the dynamics of planetary formation. However, the anomaly of the double planets, Xanadu and Atlantis, proved to be the least of the surprises in store for them."

"I'll pull all your graveyard shift duties every night I'm on-site for the next month," Hannie offered.

"You're hardly ever here. Make it two months."

"Okay."

"Deal." The custom of shaking hands had been lost during the zero-gravity decades, but Hannie gave her a sloppy kiss on the ear.

"Shhh!" Forrest hissed.

"The first sequence you will see was made by the first-in team. Some of the voice-overs are theirs, some we added for purposes of clarification. We've dispensed with the usual first-off-the-shuttle and historic first words sequences and have gone forward several days into the preliminary exploration, when things really began to get interesting."

The room lights went out and the holo began. To all appearences, the viewers hung suspended at a viewpoint atop a high cliff overlooking a tremendous valley. The scene was one of breath-taking grandeur. The valley was intensely green, ringed by high, craggy cliffs. Plateaus and valley were carpeted with dense forest, and a broad river wound a lazy path through the valley, and in the distance they could see an immense waterfall where the river tumbled over the cliff wall and into the valley.

For a few minutes the extravagant beauty of the scene held them spellbound, then their trained explorer's eyes spotted something strange on the valley floor—oddly regular lines, some straight, others curved. Mostly they showed up as mere variations in the color of the vegetation, but there appeared to be some physical features as well.

"Xanadu preliminary survey, day five, 0930 hours, Team Leader Arthur Perlmutter reporting. Our assignment is to get a close look at the anomalous formations that seem to carpet the bottom of this river valley for hundreds of kilometers. They were spotted from orbit but are too covered with vegetation to tell much from above. This is the largest cluster of the formations, in the upper canyon of what is now officially the Alph River. We landed here atop the plateau at 0915 and are making a quick overall scan of this end of the valley. This afternoon, we begin exploration of the valley floor."

The scene jumped to one taken from ground level. Directly before them was a wall. It was covered with vegetation—huge trees with roots that snaked down to pry stones loose—but it was perfectly clear that the thing was no natural phenomenon. There was murmuring from the spectators. It was fascinating, but they were getting used to marvels. At first there was nothing to give scale to the scene, then they saw a file of explorers walking along the base of the wall. Each block was the height of a man and twice as long.

"They're everyplace!" said Perlmutter's excited voice. "This was once a huge city, although so far we've found no indication of who might've built it. We're looking for sculpture, writing, anything that might give an idea of what they were."

A sharp-faced man walked into the scene. A holographic label flashed over his head: "Nathan McIntyre, geologist."

"Nothing to prove tech level, Chief," McIntyre said. "It's too eroded and worn to show tool marks. Neolithic cultures have built on a scale this massive."

"But the size of the cities!" said Perlmutter's voice. The man himself was still invisible. "There must've been millions of inhabitants in this valley alone. Primitive agriculture couldn't have supported so many."

McIntyre shrugged. "We don't know what they were, so how do we know what sort of support they needed? Besides, all these ruins may not have been inhabited at the same time. Maybe they'd build one, wear out the soil in a few generations, then build another one fifty klicks away. Happened all the time, back on Earth. We need more data."

There followed a collage of exploration scenes. Apparently, there was no true excavation, but things were pried up from the dirt for examination. At one point the holo zeroed on a knot of excited explorers surrounding a grinning man. For the recorder's benefit he held out his find: A glasslike figurine of a bat-winged creature. A voiceover broke in: "This does not resemble any creature so far discovered, but we've only been at it for a short time. It could be extinct or mythological. Whatever it is, the medium is extremely hard, indicating relatively advanced technology or great patience to carve."

Abruptly, the scene changed to the inside of a scoutcraft. People were piling into the cargo bay through the main door, their attitude one of panic. Through the door could be seen a vista of the now-familiar greenery. Above, a holo label flashed: "Day 9, Alph River Valley Expedition. 1600 hrs."

"What the hell are they?" someone shouted.

"Never got a look at them," said McIntyre. He clutched his left arm, which was bleeding steadily from a wound in the biceps. A young girl began to treat the wound from her medkit.

"How's Perlmutter?" McIntyre demanded.

A man with a medical corps patch on his coverall came into the scene, holding out a bloodied stick. "He'll be OK, but look at what I just carved out of his butt."

Sound halted as the holo enlarged the object. It was a polished wooden stick painted in a delicate pattern. It terminated at one end in an elegantly shaped point of flaked stone. The other end bore three feathers, each differently hued.

"Obviously an arrow," said the voiceover. "Anthro specialists have pronounced the craftsmanship superb. Range and penetration analysis indicates a weapon of about twenty kilo draw weight, consistent with the hunting weapons of primitive Earth societies, far less powerful than the armor-piercing war bows of later Medieval cultures."

For the first time they saw Perlmutter. He was bent over an examination table while a medic made repairs behind him.

"We never saw them. Still haven't. We were checking out a big stone tank, some sort of cistern. While we were looking at it the arrows started coming in from the trees. We didn't realize at first that we were under attack. Damn things don't make any noise." He winced as the medic did something, then his face cleared as the wound was sprayed with an anaesthetic. "That's better. Anyway, I knew something was wrong when I got shot in my heroic backside. One hit Timoshenko's backpack and we knew we were in the middle of an Old West holo. I gave the order to evacuate and we hightailed it. Try running with an arrow in your butt sometime. They just keep on cutting. There were further casualties, but none serious. McIntyre's arm was the worst. We have ceased explorations until protective suits can be brought down."

The voiceover cut back in. "Other expeditions reported sporadic attacks in subsequent days, but there were no further casualties after armored suits were distributed. Only primitive weapons were encountered. Strict orders were given that there was to be no return fire and no pursuit. This is, after all, their planet. Holos failed to record anything but flitting shadows in the brush. No villages or campsites were located."

The scene shifted to a rolling plain in a zone less lushly vegetated than the previous ones. "On the twenty-third day," the voiceover continued, "the Mao Zedong Plain Exploration Unit made contact with non-hostile natives."

Six people in black protective coveralls and light helmets sat cross-legged on the ground. Before them was spread a blanket on which rested an assortment of items: mirrors, ornaments of metal and glass, paints. Point of view was from behind the explorers, who faced a treeline. Above one of them flashed a label: "Mustafa Lin, team leader."

A voice, apparently Lin's, took up the narration. "We'd seen their campfires the day before. The trade goods came down on the same shuttle as the protective gear, in hopes that the locals might be interested in the same sort of items that Earth pre-techs valued. It was a long wait, but they finally put in an appearance at 1635."

Abruptly, a group of figures appeared at the treeline. One detached from the group and strode forward without hesitation. In the holo pit, there was a collective gasp, then shouting. A single word predominated amid the babble: "human!"

The native walked up to the explorers, a long spear sloped over one shoulder. A few paces from them he stuck the spear into the ground by its pointed butt, then stepped up to the blanket of trade goods and stood staring at the explorers. His attitude was assured, almost arrogant, but he displayed no overt hostility.

The scene froze, and all elements aside from the native were eliminated. The image grew until it was three times life-size and began to rotate slowly, giving them all a detailed view. It was all the more detailed in that he wore no clothing whatever. The skin was yellowish, with an olive tinge, and much of it was covered with intricate designs, either tattooed or painted.

"Don't jump to conclusions," Pflug said. "He certainly looks human, but he belongs to no race ever seen by us, and it could be a case of parallel evolution."

"Oh, come on," said a voice Dierdre recognized as belonging to a lab technician named Greenberg, "he's circumcised! That's too damn parallel!"

"Nonetheless," Pflug said patiently, "we'll draw no conclusions before we have genetic material to examine. As of this transmission, they had not taken any. Friendly relations have to be established before you can properly ask for samples of bodily fluids and such. Might violate taboos, and there's no rush."

Eagerly, Dierdre examined the—she didn't know what word to use—Alien? He seemed too human for that. The nose was short and down-pointed, with wide, teardrop-shaped nostrils. The eyes were narrow but very long, the irises bright yellow. The lips were so thin as to be nearly nonexistent. The ears were large but lay almost flat against the skull. The hair was coarse and fiery red in color. It was dense on the top of the head, but the temples were either shaven or naturally hairless. The shoulders and the backs of the arms were also covered with hair. His build was sturdy and muscular, with little body fat. He wore ornaments of nonmetallic materials.

The holo brought in others from the group, expanded and rotated them in the same fashion. The women were similar to the men facially, but had far more everted lips. Their small, conical breasts were covered with short, silky hair except for the nipples, but they lacked the shoulder and arm hair of the men. The pubic delta was identical with that of the human female.

There were two children, one of each sex, who resembled their elders except for having hair only on their scalps.

Within the group the main individual differences were in hair color, which ranged from bright red to almost yellow, with only a slight reddish tinge. Size, build and facial features varied slightly, an oddity to the Island Worlders, accustomed to their own wildly diverse gene pool.

"If they *are* human," Pflug said, "the extraordinary homogeneity they display is consistent with the pre-technological societies on Earth, at the times when they had little infusion of new blood. Such people take on an inbred look."

The holo continued for several more minutes. The native examined the offered goods, but he made no show of eagerness. After a few minutes the holo stopped and the lights came up. Pflug resumed his lecture.

"Isn't he pretty?" Hannie said, none too quietly. Chuckles erupted from the nearby seats.

Either Pflug hadn't heard or was determined not to show it. "There is more, but you can study that at leisure. Other groups were recorded from a distance, some identical to the first group, others seeming to differ in minor details, probably racial. Keep in mind that only a small part of a single continent has been even slightly explored. Planetary population may run to multiple-millions. There is, however, no sign of industry, artificial illumination beyond fire, or even intensive agriculture. If any of these people are agricultural, it is only at subsistence level. Whether or not it was their ancestors who built the cities we don't yet know. The scene now shifts to the exploration on the twin planet, Atlantis, where the discoveries were rather more alarming."

The new holo's point of view was that from a low-flying scoutcraft. The gasp of surprise from the spectators was far more intense than that which had greeted the appearance of the "human." The scoutcraft was flying over the ruins of a city, and this time there was no doubt of the builder's tech level. Some of the ruins were hundreds of meters high.

"The whole planet's covered with them," said a voiceover. "You can't go down anywhere without finding these ruins. No signs of life at all, so far. Look at this." The scoutcraft slowly circled the stump of a high building, its topmost levels melted into slag. "The temperatures that caused this must have been extremely high."

The scene shifted to the ruins of a smaller city. In the center of a circle of flattened rubble stood the skeletal remains of a few small buildings. A different voice reported. "Damage here consistent with the toroid shock pattern of an airburst, probably nuclear in nature."

Another city, this one largely intact except for the ravages of time. "If this one was wiped out at the same time as the others," said another voiceover, "it must have been by chemical or biological agents. We can see no blast or heat damage."

The holo stopped and the lights came back up.

Pflug stepped back into the center of the pit. There was no chuckling now and he addressed a very subdued crowd. "There can of course be no surface exploration by humans until it is determined that no dangerous elements remain. Robot probes have taken carbon-14 readings and it seems that all the destruction occurred at once, approximately one thousand Earth years ago. Flora and fauna on the planet are present but sparse, apparently still recovering from the catastrophe."

Sieglinde joined him in the holo pit. "Concentrate on this, everyone. This is the fate we barely escaped on Earth. It's possible they were attacked by aliens, but all appearances indicate planetary suicide. Tell them about the space facilities, Matthias."

"The remains of extensive launch facilities were found in several locations. They indicate space technology of about early twenty-first century level, still chemical-powered. There are orbiting fragments of what were once large space stations. They must have visited Xanadu, but whether the natives are their descendants or true natives we can't know yet."

"Any remains of the inhabitants found yet?" Forrest asked.

"None lying in plain view. Exposed remains are rather unlikely after such a time span. There are bound to be some entombed somewhere, but that will take more detailed exploration. They don't seem to have gone in for monumental sculpture, so we're still in the dark about what they looked like. Entrance apertures of the surviving structures are consistent with human proportions."

"What's on everybody's mind, I'm sure," Sieglinde said, "is the question of whether 'our' aliens had anything to do with this. Were these unfortunate people one of their failed experiments?"

"We're now going over the data on the fauna studied on Xanadu. If there is any correspondence with any found here at Delta Pav, we'll know there was some sort of contact," Pflug said.

It gave them a lot to think about. A great deal to depress them, as well. However, it was not the knowledge of a planet stripped bare of life, somber as that was, that saddened them.

It was late. For the two hours since Pflug's presentation, they had sat in the lounge-cum-mess hall discussing the implications of the new revelations. Nothing much had been decided except that all the action seemed to be elsewhere just now. Other people were getting famous and the media had all but forgotten Team Red.

"It's not fair!" Okamura was saying. "They're out there discovering humans, *humans*, for God's sake! And even getting shot by them! And here we are being labtechs and nursemaiding VIPs on tour to see the big lizards." His disgust was palpable, and it was shared.

"Poor, unfortunate victims," said Greenberg, the technician, who didn't share their sense of outrage, "haven't made a history-changing, self-immortalizing discovery in—what?—almost a year, now? We're going to have to petition Survey to find you something equal to your talents and stature." The rest of the technicians and non-Team Red personnel made appreciative noises. Nobody loves a prima donna.

"There speaks the voice of envy," Forrest said. "You homebodies can't appreciate what it means to push into the unknown. You like it safe and secure." The banter was tired, almost ritualistic, and no one could work up much interest. They were all accustomed to trusting their lives to incredibly fragile artificial environments in the midst of the most unforgiving environment of all. The Survey psych examiners had determined that the explorer temperament was a matter of restlessness and curiosity, not courage.

All chatter stopped when Hannie came in. Eyes

bugged. Mouths dropped open. She had been out to the pool and was scrubbed within an inch of her life, but that was the least of the transformation. Her hair, unplaited for a change, hung in massive, glossy waves almost to her waist. She wore a clinging, one-piece jumpsuit that bared her back and shoulders and had a neckline plunging to the belt buckle in front. Most outrageous of all, somewhere she had found cosmetics. She walked to the table and sat demurely next to Dierdre.

"Not a word," she said. "A word from one of you and bones will break."

Dierdre wondered what it was, this mysterious combination of brain and gland chemistry that caused people, men especially, to take leave of their rational faculties. Nearly every day for months, these people had frolicked *au naturel* in the pool. After the first few weeks, Dierdre had overcome her self-consciousness enough to join in. All that time, Hannie had been no different from the other women, except for her size. Now, because she was partly covered with fabric and paint, the men couldn't take their eyes off her. They would claim, of course, that it was just because she looked different. They would be lying.

Then, there was the perfume. It was subtle, something she wouldn't have expected from Hannie, a woman whose usual tactic in any situation was to overwhelm with any resource she had available. Musk-based, most likely, just possibly containing one of the illegal pheromones. This would bear looking into.

After the impromptu session broke up, Dierdre and Hannie went out into a corridor, planning to casually run into Hannie's designated prey.

"The perfume," Dierdre said. "Got any more?"

Hannie wiped her sweaty palms on the snug seat of her coverall and extracted a tiny vial from a pocket hidden somewhere. She handed it to Dierdre. "Don't overdo it. Just a touch behind each ear and in your cleavage."

"The natural heat disperses the pheromones better that way?"

"No. Because that's where his face'll go first."

Dierdre eyed the vial dubiously. "That being the case, you should have put it in your belly button."

"I did. Where is he?" Hannie was getting over her nervousness and beginning to regain her huntress look. They couldn't find Pflug inside the lab, and decided it might look too deliberate to track him down in his room, so they went to see if he might be outside.

On the veranda, the humidity wrapped them like a warm, wet blanket. The field sloping down to the landing pad was floodlit, primarily so the caretakers could protect the animals and vegetation at the agricultural station from marauding local fauna. Three figures stood halfway down the slope, talking and gesturing, but too far away to hear.

"There he is," Dierdre said. "Looks like Sieglinde and Forrest are with him."

"Sure," Hannie said. "Wouldn't do to let him wander around all alone. Come on."

Surreptitiously, Dierdre dabbed the perfume in the recommended spots. She wondered if she ought to hedge her bets by finding some privacy and dabbing a few more spots. Then she decided that, by the time they were down to that, they would be past the perfume stage.

The three looked up when the two women approached. Sieglinde was showing them something on one of the instruments she had designed. Like so many of them, it looked like a plain sheet of transparent plastic. She favored them with one of her rare smiles.

"I was just showing Steve and Matthias something I discovered today. There's something buried here," she tapped the ground with her foot. "It's about twenty meters down and I'm pretty sure that it's part of the transporter's instrumentation."

"So far from the cave?" Dierdre said, absently. Her mind was elsewhere. Hannie nudged her. "Oh, yes. Matthias, this is Hannie Meersma. She'll be taking over as your guide and escort. She's the best bush guide we have."

"I'm, ah, very pleased to meet you." Pflug's eyes were slightly bugged and he seemed to have difficulty keeping his lower jaw all the way up.

Dierdre squinted at Hannie. It was hard to tell under the floodlights, but she seemed to be blushing furiously. Blushing!

"I'm sure we're going to get along," she said, twining a blonde lock around one finger. She smiled with what seemed to be twice as many teeth as any human mouth should hold.

A loud, bellowing honk split the outer darkness.

Pflug started. "What was that?"

"A styracosaurus," Hannie said. "One of the hornheads. You haven't seen any of our dinosaurs yet?"

"As a matter of fact, no." Pflug was getting over his shock, but he still couldn't take his eyes off her. The other three looked back and forth from one to the other like spectators at a sporting event, following a ball in play. "I haven't had time yet."

"Know what's the best way to see them, the first time?" She took a step closer to him, so that he had to look up to maintain eye contact.

"How?"

"By moonlight. Shall we?" She stepped closer yet. Manfully, he didn't step back.

"It's pretty, uh, *untamed* out there, isn't it?"

"You're not scared, are you?" she breathed.

"As a matter of fact, yes." He swallowed hard. "But, what the hell, let's go."

"That's the spirit." She put an arm around his shoulder and began to guide him toward the gloom. After a moment, his own arm slid around her waist.

Forrest gathered his scattered wits. "Hannie, there's

only two of you and it's after dark. We have standing orders—"

She turned and smiled with her mouth, but he saw violent death in her eyes.

"—I mean, be careful, you know? Pick up a beamer at the guardpost."

She waved and the two walked away. Dierdre studied her retreating back and and wondered whether Hannie had chosen the most flattering outfit. She looked good, but with her arm up like that, her deltoid bulged like an eight-pound-shot.

"Just when you think the universe has yielded up all its secrets," Sieglinde said, "something comes along to surprise you."

"I hope they'll be all right," Dierdre said. "Neither of them is exactly dressed for the outback."

Sieglinde smiled. "From the look of her, it's not going to matter much how they're dressed, once they get beyond the perimeter."

"I suppose strange pairings shouldn't surprise us," Dierdre noted. "Look at Derek and Antigone."

"Must be something in the air," Sieglinde mused.

"The dinos are the least of his risks," Forrest said. "That woman has real spinecracker thighs."

"You'd know?" Dierdre said sweetly but with a faint snarl, beginning to move closer.

Forrest kept a straight face. "I practice hand-to-hand with all my team members, you know that. Hannie's got a mean scissorlock."

Dierdre wondered whether she was playing this right; maybe she should come back with a line like, "You think she's the only one?", but that might be a little *too* blatant and, anyway, it was time for him to make a move. She checked the wind to make sure he would get the benefit of Hannie's perfume.

Sieglinde watched the two of them, slightly bemused. If Hannie's courtship was characteristically meteoric, this was not a totally unexpected development. The two who had become her principal assistants were like cats, alternately hissing and purring. It had been a question of which would break first, Dierdre's pathological distrust, or Forrest's stiff-necked reticence. As she had expected, the increasingly stable girl had made the first move. If Forrest blew this one, Sieglinde would lose some of the considerable respect she had for him.

Steve turned to Sieglinde, his eyes not focusing quite correctly. "Ah, Dr. Kornfeld, do you think you could spare us for a while?"

It would have been easy to tell the utter truth; that she had not really needed anyone since childhood. She decided to be kind instead. "No, this will keep until tomorrow. You two run along."

He smiled at Dierdre. "Let's take a walk." Arms placed identically with the previous couple, although with a certain inevitable mirror effect, they walked toward the edge of the illuminated area, choosing a different direction.

Sieglinde looked after them and was astonished that her eyes stung faintly. All her lovers and good friends were dead. Even her best enemies were gone. Unless she got the matter transmitter perfected, she would probably never see some of her children again in the flesh. She shook her head, disturbed at the sudden surge of maudlin emotion. Yes, there was definitely something strange in the air tonight. She would have to have atmospheric tests run.

She looked back into the face of her odd instrument, its transparent surface crawling with her personal, obscure symbology. No question about it, there was something down there. Tomorrow, they would commence digging.

When the sun came up Dierdre walked out onto the veranda, yawning and scratching. The air smelled fresh and she was alert and ready for anything, unlike most mornings. She felt sore but happy. Below, she could see two people coming up the slope, past the sheep and the maize field.

It was Hannie and Matthias, and while she wasn't exactly carrying him, she was helping him on the steeper parts. At last they reached the steps and trudged up to the veranda. At the top Hannie planted a solid kiss on his face, spun him around and sent him off toward his quarters with a pat on the rear.

As she walked past Dierdre she muttered, "Unpadded."

NINE

Dierdre set the specimen flask on the lab table when she heard the knock. The flask was all but invisible—a molecule-thick polymer produced at the southern petroleum fields. Stripes had been painted on its sides and around the lip to give the user visual orientation. More and more such items were being produced on-planet. Using the transporters, transportation for the smaller objects was virtually cost-free.

"Come on in."

It was Matthias, looking distracted and worried. But then, that was the way he looked more often than not. "Dee, we're getting some anomalous data from the station on Tithonus." Tithonus was the outermost planet of the system, an insignificant rock ball of no discernable use or exploitability. Even so, the aliens had left a transporter there, connected to the great polar relay station.

"Anomalous data is the only type we've been getting for years," Dierdre said. "What makes this notable?"

"It's something big, and it's headed toward us."

Something atavistic made her scalp prickle. "A comet, maybe?"

"The trajectory doesn't fit. It seems to be under

guidance, whatever it is. Every few hours there are minute alterations of course. Velocity, course and course corrections indicate a rendezvous with this planet."

"One of ours?" she said weakly. "Maybe one of the other expeditions changed its mind and decided to head for Delta Pav."

He shook his head. "Wrong direction. Even if it was one of the expeditions that broke off all contact, they'd have had to start from the Sol system. Nobody could have passed us, turned over, decelerated and changed course, and come back from that direction. There hasn't been enough time."

"They're coming back, aren't they?" Somehow she had known it would happen, from the time she had found the transporter.

"*Somebody's* coming," he said. "ETA is about a year from the first sighting."

When he left she finished labelling her specimens and putting the sample bottles in the sterilizer. Her mind was buzzing as she washed her hands and since, as usual, she had forgotten to get any towels from supply, she dried them on the seat of her pants. Beneath her hands she felt a layer of soft padding that hadn't been there a few months before. She would have to get out of the lab and get some exercise, maybe get Sieglinde to turn her loose for a few weeks, let her guide an expedition into the bush. The guide force was shorthanded now. Hannie had headed up for orbit last week, since pregnancy was something no sane woman wanted to experience in major planetary gravity.

Turning the lights off, she left the lab and went out onto the veranda. The hot, muggy climate outside was as natural to her now as the shipboard environment of her childhood. The last time she had been up to visit her family had been a claustrophobic experience, something she could not have conceived of a few years before. It was unsettling, when you had always thought of yourself as a spacer.

Below her the base sprawled down the slope for half a kilometer, its vehicles and personnel rushing about in the streets in the last minutes before quitting time. People would be gathering in the *Happy Stegosaurus*, a bar strategically located between the lab complex and the base, next to the agricultural station. Something just under five years had wrought changes at a dizzying pace.

It made her feel hemmed in and left out, being confined to the lab so much of the time while the base became crowded. People who had sworn never to leave space had come down anyway, lured by the excitement of frontier life. She had intended to spend at least ten years as a first-in explorer before settling down and taking an administrative job. On the other hand, there were some definite advantages to her current position. She was about to experience one of them. A man and woman in Survey uniform approached her along the veranda, obviously wanting to talk to her but waiting for her to address them first. Yes, it was nice, being deferred to.

"Miss Jamail," the man said when she nodded, "the presentation on the 82 Eridani report is set for 2030. Will you be presiding?"

"I'll be glad to," she said. It was nice not being the lowest-ranking and least-favored of Survey's minions. She was Dierdre Jamail, famous explorer and first human being to travel by matter transporter. More importantly, she was Sieglinde Kornfeld-Taggart's right hand. Sieglinde was phenomenally busy these days, even for Sieglinde. Dierdre not only assisted in the lab, she ran interference with the rest of humanity. At last, she had found a socially useful employment for her generally antisocial leanings. She was perfectly willing to face up to the most prominent and powerful of government or industrial figures and tell them to leave her boss the hell alone, she was busy.

It was an ideal pairing—Dierdre had the gall and Sieglinde had the prestige.

"This one's the strangest yet," the woman said. "I thought the last few were the limit." Of the last twelve expeditions to report in, eight had found Earth-type planets. Of those, three had human primitives in residence, two were nuclear wipeouts, and another had apparently been annihilated by poison or pestilence. Whether the last was done by its own inhabitants was still unknown, but they had achieved a high level of technological culture. That seemed to be the pattern everywhere so far—continuing primitive culture or technological suicide. All except for Earth, and they knew how narrowly that had been avoided.

"I've just heard something that may be far more important," Dierdre said, "but it'll take more data before we know."

"We've heard," the woman said. Dierdre wasn't surprised. News travelled with incredible speed in the new planetary societies as well as in Island World society, where official secrecy was considered more abhorrent than official corruption. Suddenly, she felt the need for company. "I think I'll go down to the *Steg* and see who's there. Come along, I'll buy you one."

The two looked surprised and flattered. "Of course," the man said. "We're off duty now."

As they walked down the slope Dierdre's belt unit beeped in a familiar pattern. She unclipped it and raised it to her mouth. "Steve?"

"It's me. We're halfway up the volcano. Got some good holos of the little reps and protobirds that live up here. I may be back soon. I don't think this bunch will last the full ten days."

"Good. Run them hard tomorrow and maybe they'll give up. I miss you."

"At least you're back there with the air conditioning. See you soon." It clicked off and she clipped it back to her belt.

"What a liar," she said, smiling. "He'd never come out of the bush at all if he could avoid it."

"Don't you two ever get to trek out together?" the woman asked.

"Only when Sieglinde's off-planet. She always wants one of us around. Usually she prefers me because Steve isn't assertive enough with the Survey bas—" She gave their uniforms a wry look "—well, you know what I mean."

"We understand," the man said, laughing. "We plan to sign on with an independent as soon as this hitch is up."

"You can't get into first-in work without connections, these days," the woman said, "and who wants to be a flunky? I think you were the last one to make it in by screwing up."

"Jesus, Sara!" the man said, faking horror.

Dierdre giggled girlishly. Maybe these two weren't as twerpy as she had assumed. "When's your hitch up?"

"Three years," the woman said. "We came in on a pair-hitch." This was an arrangement allowing couples to stay together on assignments. If they had a falling-out in the meantime, tough.

"About that time, a bunch of us from Derek Kuroda's old team will be forming our own company. Look me up then. I might have something for you."

"It'll be something crazy?" the man said, eagerly.

"Derek and Sieglinde are charter members. I won't tell you any more about it." Official secrets were anathema, but commercial secrets were quite different. No ambitious firm surrendered an edge. The couple were so overjoyed at the prospect that, when they got to the Happy Stegosaurus, they insisted on buying the first drink.

Dierdre ordered white wine in a tall, chilled glass and sipped at it slowly. Unlike some of her friends, she drank abstemiously. Alcoholism and hangovers were things of the past, but her tongue and temper were difficult to control sober. Alcohol weakened her repressive capacities and led her into undiplomatic behavior.

People came in from their shifts, most of them calling greetings to Dierdre. She knew just about everybody. Some were her friends, but the old Task Force Iliad/Team Red crew was diminishing all the time: promoted, transferred to other assignments, invalided because of injuries, married and shipped out with their new mates. Work at the base had become routine and the one thing none of them could abide was boredom.

A quick beeping from her belt unit told her it was time to begin the evening's presentation. She waited for the go-ahead light. They no longer needed the amphitheater. Most of the permanent residences and workplaces were now equipped for full-environment holography. The teams in the bush could pick up the broadcast on their portable units. The flashing red ball appeared over the table before her and she began.

"Dierdre Jamail here, bringing you the straight stuff. For those of you who have been in a coma for the last 48 hours, the 82 Eridani expedition has reported in. At last, someone's found an advanced technological society that hasn't wiped itself out, but wait'll you see why. This one isn't as visually spectacular as some we've received, but we're giving you the full-environment treatment anyway. The 82 Eridani expedition spent several months exploring and putting this together before they sent it out. Pay close attention if you've ever felt any nostalgia for the good old days on Earth when life was simple."

The scene opened with a view of metallic structures and frames. The black sky, crystal-clear light and sharp-edged shadows indicated a vacuum environment. The voiceover began: "This is Gildan, the smaller moon of Abbatas. If you're wondering about the names, they're native. The Abbatans speak a language we can pronounce, so we didn't have to delve into Earth mythology to come up with names, for a change. It should come as no surprise to learn that Gildan translates as 'lesser moon' and Abbatas as 'the world.'

"Both moons were visited in the past by the Abbatans. And when I say the past, I mean it. These ruins are in such good shape because of lunar conditions. They are at least three thousand years old. These space ventures flourished for less than a century, then were abandoned."

The scene shifted to a planetary locale: an immense, sprawling metropolis of low buildings. And yet somehow metropolis did not seem like the right word. Another word occurred to them all, an old word, one from the histories: *slum*.

It was not that the place was filthy; on the contrary, it seemed quite clean. There was public transport in the streets in the form of long, segmented vehicles, and a large number of animal-drawn carriages. The streets were thronged with people, still too distant to see in detail, but overcrowding seemed to be no great problem. The buildings were shabby, functional, utterly without beauty or grace. The city lacked even the squalid attractions they associated with the holos of the legendary slums of the past: the sullen menace of New York, the raffish colorful charm of Shanghai, Paris, New Orleans, the cheerful decadence of 1920s Berlin, the disorderly splendor of ancient Rome and Byzantium.

"The entire planet is like this," continued the voiceover. "It's a true planetary culture, so ancient that only one language is spoken, without a single dialect or regional variant. Architecture everywhere is just as you see it here. As for art, it practically doesn't exist. There is music . . ." Replacing the voice came a rather unpleasant atonic sound of stringed instruments accompanied by a thumping, monotonous percussion. It was faintly ragalike, but without the intricate improvisation of the true raga. "There seem to be only four or five basic themes, upon which the musicians work minor variations. It's played at religious functions, to use the term rather loosely. These people have an all-encompassing religion, but it has no god or gods. In fact, it has no supernatural entities at all, nor a theology, cosmology or iconography. Apparently, it limits itself to ethical teaching."

The scene shifted to street level. For the first time, they had a good look at the inhabitants. For scale, a standard measuring rod had been set up and they could see that the natives were only slightly more than a meter in height. There seemed not to be a centimeter's difference in height among adults, and differences between male and female were so slight that only close examination revealed gender. They were rotund, with round faces and narrow eyes, and their earlobes dangled almost to their shoulders. Hair was black, growing in tight balls rather like a bushman's peppercorns, but the balls were marble-sized and rose to a peak in the center of the scalp. Skin was yellowish, with a bluish undertone. They looked amazingly like conventionalized Buddhas. Costume for both sexes was a loose, short, sleeveless robe and sandals.

"They aren't clones, although they look it. Genetically, they are so similar that some sort of genetic standardization must have occurred somewhere in their past. It's difficult to tell, because they don't bother with history very much. We found a few who could tell us something."

The scene shifted to a city park. Passersby glanced at the hulking shuttle parked on its spidery legs, but they revealed only flickering curiosity. Children stared with more interest, but were soon tugged away by parents. A male of indeterminate age sat cross-legged on the grass, facing an invisible interviewer. The man's words were computer translated, with a different voice used to supply words with no English equivalent. His lip movements did not, of course, match the words they heard. It seemed to be a language with few labial sounds, for his lips scarcely moved at all.

Interviewer: You are a scholar?

Native (with a shrug and duck of the head, seemingly slightly embarrassed): I know a little. It is a hobby, learning of ancient things. It does not set me apart. I am by trade a smith. I make metal shoes for our [draft animals].

Interviewer: And how is old knowledge preserved?

Native: One finds books here and there. They are nearly indestructable. The ancients were ignorant of the Great Cycle. They were unaware that it is unnecessary to record history, since all that has happened will happen again and again through infinity.

Voiceover: A search has been instituted for these books.

Interviewer: We have encountered other humans similar to ourselves, but never a culture so utterly homogeneous as yours. Nor one that had turned its back on high technology.

Native: Once we were much like you, full of vain desires and aspirations. There were many different types of people, as I can see is still true of you. When we discovered the Way, we learned that there is no need for these devices. The only correct use for technology is to produce fertilizer and agricultural machinery, so that there may be more people to follow the Way. Once we reached for the stars, but there is nothing to be learned out there. We look inward now.

Interviewer: What became of the other types of human beings on this planet?

Native: When the Way was discovered, it was decided that all this diversity was unnecessary, that it led to unjustified conflict. Genetic knowledge was used to create a single, stable type, so that all the world would be in harmony. At the same time, we were reduced in size, so that individuals would consume less. That way there could be more people.

Voiceover: This has been confirmed. Ancestral Abbatans were more than twice the size of these, and were of diverse racial types.

Interviewer: What became of artistic creativity? We've come across no cultures devoid of it before.

Native: These things are vanities. They serve no useful purpose and they set people apart from one another. One who seeks to create something new deceives himself and others. From what the ancients say of the aesthetic sensibility, it was not shared by all, and of what merit is anything which cannot be universal? Thus we have dispensed with such triviality.

The scene faded. "It is difficult to believe," the voiceover continued, "that we could cross the void and discover other human beings who have achieved a high level of technology, even space travel, and find them boring. And yet this is the case. A day's study of these people will put you to sleep. They are the most complacent, self-satisfied lotus-eaters imaginable, devoid of creativity, curiosity or ambition. Their sole aspiration is to achieve nothing at all, and they have been successful at this for millennia. All their ideals and goals are negative: no war, no conflict, no surprises. The standard of living planetwide is abysmal, but they consider that fine as long as there is no real starvation or want. Population is static: as many people as the planet can support without famine or resorting to a level of technology any higher than the late nineteenth or early twentieth century on Earth. They have no disease, apparently part of their genetic standardization, and their medical practice is adequate to deal with the occasional injury."

"And yet," said another voice, "it was not always so. In the more remote parts of this planet, we have found ruins of ancient cultures." The scene became one of carved stone walls upon which human warriors battled monsters, armies clashed with sword and spear. In a desert, the stumplike remains of temples were still surrounded by a forest of statues, mutilated but with enough remaining to hint of their once great beauty. In a snowy waste, a broad mosaic floor had been uncovered, its colors still dazzling. The beautiful figures were enigmatic, but the ritual poses suggested a complicated mythology in which battle and blood played a great part.

"These are the remains of pre-technological cultures, bronze and iron ages most likely. By their spacefaring period, it seems the Abbatans were no longer building so massively, nor with such enduring materials. Nearly every structure we've found is richly decorated with immense skill and imagination. They must have been an extremely bloody-minded people, but that has never been a bar to great art. On the contrary, it seems to be one of the sadder aspects of human history that ages of great art are also ages of great aggression and brutality."

Now they were looking down on a string of islands, apparently uninhabited but with many flat, geometrically regular areas. "This was a space launch facility," said a third voice. "Analysis of blast effect still detectable in the substrata reveals that they reached the stage of chemical-propulsion heavy lifters. There is no sign of development past that stage. They seem to have ceased space ventures abruptly."

Now they saw a distinguished-looking man in what appeared to be a library. A label identified him as Prof. Lars-Erik Engstrom. "This is the final report of our findings before we transmit our summary. We have located and translated some of the surviving texts and the tale they tell is depressing. Paradoxically, these people achieved just what many Earth historical theorists used to claim was an ideal progression of events. Their industrial revolution was followed by a period of booming population growth and huge, worldwide wars. But, unlike Earth, they achieved world peace and population control *before* they reached a technological level allowing space travel. Thus, space was never militarized; it was explored for purely scientific purposes.

"The religio-ethical system the Abbatans call the Way arose at the same time that the planet was being demilitarized. It began in the more backward areas of the planet, but was quickly adopted by the intelligentsia of the more advanced regions. Its doctrine of passivity and standardization appealed to the war-weary populace, but it was inimical to space exploration; to all technological progress, for that matter. All wealth not expended on giving a maximum population a minimal standard of living was deemed immoral. Space ventures were abandoned in less than a century. The new science of genetics was used to reduce the population to a single genetic type that would be immune from disease and birth defect, and with a standard level of intelligence. There would be no more subnormal intelligence, but there would be no more geniuses, either. Such extraordinary individuals upset harmony.

"Art was abandoned at the same time. Painting and sculpture, music and drama, all these things were vain frivolities, distracting people from their contemplation of the Way. It was deemed better to do nothing at all than to do anything that might upset the balance of harmony.

"We do not intend to stay here. This planet already has as much population as it can support, and the inhabitants have not the slightest interest in anything we can manufacture. We will study here for a few more months, while we replenish our resources from the other planets and asteroids in the system. Then we shall choose a new star system for our destination. This has been a disappointment, but now that we know of the abundance of Earth-type planets in this part of the galaxy, we can be fairly sure of finding something better. One thing we have discovered here: there is a previously undreamed-of method for humanity to commit cultural suicide.

"We shall notify you when we have settled on a new destination. At the moment, we favor Beta Hydri, to join the expedition already headed there. This is the 82 Eridani expedition, signing off."

The lights came back up and Dierdre resumed her talk. "Just when you thought we'd seen everything, huh? It can't be said that what the Abbatans have chosen is worse than nuclear annihilation, but it sure as hell isn't much better. This is Dierdre Jamail signing off, and hoping the next expedition to check in brings us something a little less depressing." The red ball winked out.

She finished her wine, ordered another along with a large beaker of Steinhäger and lime. Carrying both, acknowledging waves and invitations to tables, she left the bar and walked uphill toward the largest building in the lab complex, a little apart from the others. She found Sieglinde in the big lab, seated at her console and looking haggard, the way she did most of the time these days. If people still smoked like in the old holos, Dierdre thought, she'd have a big tray in front of her, piled high with butts. She looked up wanly when Dierdre plunked the beaker down in front of her.

"Good morning, Dee." she took the beaker, sat back and sipped. "That's good, even if it is a little early to be drinking."

"It's evening, Doc. Late."

"Oh. I lose track of time these days."

"It figures, since you spend days at a time in this lab. What's the problem, Doc? Why be so obsessive about this thing?" She waved an arm at the banks of instruments and power plants.

"Because I can't figure out how they did it! Look at this stuff! Great, massive power plants, all the facilities of my energy transmitter at my disposal and

I still can't reliably transport matter for even a short distance. And yet they did it with minimal instrumentation, things so simple that I can't figure out how they did it!"

"They had a whole culture, Doc, and who knows how many eons of time to work out all the bugs. I've known people to get frustrated because they can't get a job or finish a project or be a media star, but you're the only person I know who gets all wrought up because she can't be God."

"Even I'm not that ambitious. I just want to figure out something somebody else did, and they can't be that much smarter than I am."

"They just had more time. Hell, Doc, it's beginning to look like you may just be able to ask them. Did Matthias tell you about what's headed this way?"

"I've heard. I was going to look at the data later. I'm not ready to jump to any conclusions yet."

"Keep saying that, Doc, I need to hear it."

Sieglinde's eyebrows went up. "You mean you're afraid?"

"My God, yes! We've found humans, but they're experiments of the aliens, and maybe so were we. We've yet to encounter any real aliens, and these are unimaginably powerful. And we've been messing around in their laboratory. I feel like Goldilocks and now the three bears are coming back."

The first crop of bananas had been harvested at the ag station, and for days they had all been eating them like monkeys. Food programs had been scoured for new banana recipes. The novelty was beginning to pall, but they weren't quite tired of them yet.

"What I want to know," Fumiyo said, forking up a last bit of fried banana, "is how they spotted this alien vessel, if that's what it really is." She was managing a large bio lab on the mainland these days, but managed to visit at least once a month. "If it's taking them that long to get here, they must be a good-sized fraction of a light year away. I didn't think we had anything that could detect a ship-sized object at such a distance." She paused to think. "It *is* ship-sized, isn't it?"

"About the size of Avalon," Pflug said.

"That's a relief," Fumiyo said. "If it was big enough for us to *see* the damned thing, I was going to steal a ship and head for Sol."

"How'd they do it, Matt?" Dierdre asked. "I asked the doc but she just grunted and said she didn't have time to explain."

Pflug sipped at an experimental wine made from a native berry, soon to be marketed as *Dino Red*. "It was one of her devices, as you might've guessed. A development of the defense field she invented to protect us from particle collisions at high speeds." The field had made interstellar travel practical. At near-light speed, a solid particle massing a single gram packed the explosive power of two kilotons of TNT. The Kornfeld field would repel any particle approaching the ship. The faster the approach and the nearer the object got, the stronger was the repulsive power of the defense field.

"I still don't get it," Forrest said, picking up a beaker. A computer had dredged up an ancient African formula for making banana beer. He sipped, winced and pushed the beaker away. "Force field physics isn't my favored study." He punched in an order for conventional, grain-based beer.

Pflug grew expansive, glad to have a subject he could lecture on. They still made fun of his clothes. "It's like this: so long as the mass of the approaching particle is negligible relative to the mass of the asteroid ship, the field works perfectly. All but an infinitesimal proportion of interstellar objects are microscopic. But, if we ran into a rock with a mass comparable to that of the ship, the ship would receive a severe jolt since repelling the rock means that the rock will be repelling the ship with equal force. Newton's third law of motion works perfectly in space: action and reaction. At speeds like that, you don't want *any* kind of jolt. That's where the detection system comes in."

"How does it work," Dierdre pressed, motivated by her own irrational fears, "and how does it tie in with spotting this alien ship?"

"It's an adaptation of the same principle that makes the repeller field work. It monitors the wave-pattern of matter through indeterminate n-dimensional space, same as the defense field. N-dimensional detection is instantaneous, limited only by the operating speed of your recording instruments.

"Take one reading, you spot the approaching object. Another reading taken an instant later gives velocity and direction of approach. The ship can then make minute course alterations to miss the rock. At those speeds and distances, it takes only the slightest alteration of course to miss a whole planet, if you just have enough warning."

"And that's what detected the alien?" Dierdre asked.

"Right. As soon as Sieglinde learned of the transporters, she had the particle detectors on all the ships set to scan the approaches to this planet and had them monitored constantly."

"But suppose," Dierdre said, betraying her nervousness, "the aliens traveled by some technology unknown to us? The transporters certainly came as a surprise."

"Then," Pflug said, "we'd have been in a fix, with no way to protect ourselves or even prepare. However, you have to go with what you have, and in this case it was enough to give us a little warning."

"So how far was the alien ship?" Fumiyo queried.

"Half a light year away, which was at the limit of our detector. For all we know, it started this way years ago. As it's been decelerating from quasi-luminal velocity at about one gee, it will arrive about one year from first sighting. Sieglinde thinks it probably started on its way about the time Dee first used the transporter. She probably triggered some sort of superluminal alarm system."

"Still getting us into trouble, eh, Dee?" Forrest said. He smiled to soften the remark, but it hurt. Dierdre wondered if she was growing too sensitive.

"Why was it so close? It hasn't been all that long. Giving it time to start, build up to near-luminal speed, then turn over and decelerate and reach orbit within a year from now, it didn't start from all that far away."

"Maybe they have a base nearby," Pflug said. "Or maybe it's a patrol ship. When they get here, you can ask them."

TEN

"Pack up," Sieglinde ordered. "We're moving operations."

Dierdre's head jerked up. "Are you serious? We're in the middle of a dozen experiments and there are three expeditions out in the bush."

"Not them, just the two of us. Delegate the experiments in progress to your subordinates. Neither of us have looked in on the bush expeditions in weeks. That operation can take care of itself."

"But Steve comes in in less than a week. We were going to take some vacation time—"

"The aliens may be here before then," Sieglinde cut in. "This takes precedence."

Deirdre's stomach went queasy. "Where are we going?"

"The polar transporter complex. I'm fairly certain that was their base of operations when they built this place. That's where they're most likely to check in when they get back."

Dierdre sighed, resigned. "I was afraid that's what it was. I'll call Sims, tell him we're coming in and arrange for quarters and lab facilities."

"Do it. Call the orbitals, have them standing by to send down instruments and equipment as I order them. Actually, we may not need much. It would be like tribal witch doctors trying to figure out a space ship." She stood for a moment, staring at nothing. "But then, we owe it to the species to see that the best witch doctor around is on hand."

The next few hours were hectic ones for Dierdre; not that it was a new experience. Sieglinde frequently launched into new projects with little or no warning and expected all preparations to be attended to without fuss or complaint, and at maximum speed. Dierdre arranged for flight clearance, told the choleric Sims to boot some VIPs from their quarters if he had to—he knew damn well that Sieglinde always had highest priority—and browbeat Survey logistics into keeping all possible equipment free for emergency standby. This last was difficult, because with exploration of the planet now in full swing, nearly everything was allocated on tight schedules. By the end of it all, Dierdre was wishing she were out in the bush getting chewed by bugs and nursemaiding a bunch of criminally incompetent researchers.

Last of all she made a tearful call to Forrest and told him to join her as soon as he got in from the bush. She hadn't cleared it with Sieglinde, but she figured that the boss wouldn't fuss. Four hours after getting notification of the move, the two were settling into Sieglinde's personal shuttlecraft. As the craft lifted, Sieglinde looked over the list of preparations Dierdre handed her.

"Not bad. You know, you're the best assistant I ever had. Would you like to make it permanent?"

Dierdre thought a moment. "I don't know. I've never been proposed to before. Do I get a ring or anything?"

Sieglinde actually laughed, a genuine rarity. "Ten thousand professional scientists and management specialists would cut each other's throats for that offer, and you have to smart off."

"It's my nature. Seriously, Doc, I'll have to think

about it. It's not as if I didn't appreciate the opportunity, not to mention the honor. And I like working for you. It's just that for years I had my heart set on exploring and I only got a little taste of it. There's still a lot of exploring to be done. And there's Steve. Absolutely no way is he going to give up bush-busting, not even to live blissfully with me in whatever lab you've set up as headquarters."

"Men are that way, aren't they? Take your time. Depending on how our first encounter works out, the question may not be worth worrying about."

First encounter, Dierdre thought. It was an old expression, one much used in the early days of space exploration. It might even have dated from before that time. It meant mankind's first meeting with alien intelligence. So far, there had been none. In defiance of all expectation, all the intelligent creatures contacted thus far had been human, with a yet-unexplained common origin. Evidence of the aliens was abundant, but the creatures themselves remained enigmatic. And now it was going to happen. So many firsts since they had established orbit around this planet, and Dierdre had been present at more than her share. It was enough to make a person believe in destiny.

The polar base was a sprawling facility as large as the one on Dinosaur Island. Its landing port seemed unusually active, with craft from various agencies and corporations in evidence. As they settled, Sieglinde's gaze swept the field, then sharpened on a line of three shuttles with profiles that were low, angular and, Dierdre could think of no better way to put it, *menacing*. They were matte black, with red insignia depicting a stylized Greek helmet, its graceful, curving crest offset by sinister, slanting eyeslits.

"What are *they* doing here?" The vessels belonged to the military Salamids. The nucleus of the old Island Worlds fighting force, detachments of them had accompanied most of the interstellar expeditions.

Over the years, with little fighting to do, they had developed into veritable warrior-mystics. Their Spartan lifestyle had become an end in itself.

"Maybe they're just giving the troops some arctic training." Dierdre said, hopefully. A couple of years before, the Sals had requested permission to rotate their companies down to Dinosaur Island for tropical maneuvers. Sieglinde threatened to shoot down their shuttlecraft if they came in range. Dierdre wasn't looking forward to this meeting.

Sims greeted them as they descended the shuttle's ramp. "Good evening, Dr. Kornfeld." He shook Sieglinde's hand, then seized Dierdre in a bearish hug. "You too, Dee. Haven't seen you in too long." Sims had put on weight, and in his neat Survey uniform he looked much more the ranking administrator he was now than the hell-raising young explorer he had been such a short time before. Sieglinde's magic touch and the celebrity of their discovery had jumped many of them into positions they might not have reached in decades.

"What are the Salamids doing here?" Sieglinde demanded as Sims escorted them toward the main facility. In their thermal suits and gloves, they felt the cold only on their faces. Even so, coming directly from the tropics, it was a shock.

"They came in yesterday," Sims said, grimly. "Claimed that there's something in their charter and the Articles that gives them the right to demand quartering and observation facilities when they have reason to believe military action may be called for. I told them to stay the hell away from my base and keep to their ships and I'd have them arrested if they tried to come into the main facility."

He grinned bitterly. "All bluff, of course. I always thought I was as tough as any other working stiff, but the Sals scare the hell out of me. They're like those sickleclaw dinos we used to see on the island—not much for brains, but the claws and teeth work fine."

"I'll pull their teeth," Sieglinde promised.

There was a knot of officials standing in the glassed-in reception area just off the landing pad. It was connected to the main facility by an umbilicus along which wheeled vehicles moved freight and personnel. Heads turned as Sieglinde approached. Dierdre noted that the prospect of battle banished Sieglinde's weariness. She walked with spine erect, all but bouncing on the balls of her feet. If she had been a cat, Dierdre thought, the fur would have been standing up along her spine.

"Ah, Dr. Kornfeld, how good to see you." It was an Althing functionary, a smoothie Dierdre remembered from previous encounters, named Wyeth.

"Why are they here?" Sieglinde demanded, jerking her head toward the orderly group in military uniforms. There were a dozen of them. Ten were heavily-armed enlisted personnel, the other two were officers in coveralls, armed only with pistols. They all wore chameleon camouflage that blended with any background.

One of the officers came forward. "Dr. Kornfeld, it's an honor—"

"Kornfeld-*Taggart*," she corrected. It wouldn't hurt to remind them that her late husband's grandfather had founded Sálamis, and that one of her sons, a Salamid officer, had elected to stay behind with the original Sálamis, to help defend the Island Worlds that had remained in Sol orbit.

"Dr. Kornfeld-Taggart, of course. I am Colonel Singh, CO of the 25th Ala, Salamid Rangers. We are here in accordance with Article Thirty-Two, which states that, should the general staff agree that a possible military situation exists, they may petition the Althing for a position of observation and counsel, with the option to assume command should hostilities become imminent. The staff have so petitioned and the Althing had acceded." He held out a document bearing the Althing seal. "This man," he nodded at Sims, "is being difficult."

"You just think he's difficult," Sieglinde said. "Now I'm here."

"Dr. Kornfeld-Taggart—"

"Sieglinde is OK, as long as you get the point."

The officer made a strangling sound. "Sieglinde, there is no cause for friction. For the time being, we are only here to observe. No action will be taken without consultation between the general staff and the Althing."

"Don't try to bullshit me. I know what you'll do. You'll wait until you think the situation warrants it, then you'll jump in without consulting anybody and justify yourself later, if there is a later, on grounds of 'military necessity.' I've played a key role in two major wars, Colonel, don't think you're dealing with an amateur. My husband was the premier diplomat in the formation of the Confederacy. My sons and daughters all served in important commands in the last war, and I operated at the highest levels of command in both wars."

"Goddammit, Sieglinde! Nobody's talking about fighting! All we have here are myself, my adjutant, and a light squad of Rangers. Even you can't be paranoid enough to think this represents some sort of military coup!"

"It has to start somewhere, doesn't it?"

While this was going on, Dierdre was studying the Rangers. She had little contact with the military, and she found them interesting. The one closest to her was a young woman, no older than herself. She wore the usual camouflage and armor plates. Her face was almost pretty, framed by a helmet that swept down to outline her cheekbones. Blonde hair showed beneath its neckguard. As Dierdre studied her the woman looked back, alert but utterly uninterested, her blue eyes like ice chips. She was draped with armament and carried an awesomely powerful beam rifle.

Instinctively, Dierdre rested a hand on her own pistol, which with explorer's habit she wore whenever she was away from base, along with her comm set and medkit. Even as she did it, she realized how idiotic the gesture was. She had only fired her pistol in practice. What chance would she have against this professional killing machine? Not to mention the other nine. Plus, of course, the officers, who were probably just as deadly.

"Sieglinde," the colonel persisted, "I don't propose to argue with you. We have our orders, not only from staff but from the Althing. Argue with them. We are being approached by an alien power of unknown intentions, and it is our duty to be prepared."

Sieglinde looked at him wonderingly. "Prepared? These creatures build planets! Do you think they can't disassemble any fleet we can throw against them? You must be joking!"

"Guarantee of victory has never been a prerequisite for defense," the colonel insisted. "If attacked, we must do whatever we can, however futile it might be."

"Dr. Kornfeld," said the colonel's adjutant, "if I may interject a comment?"

Sieglinde eyed him coolly. "Go ahead."

"Major Quivera, at your service. What, Doctor, makes you so certain that the approaching vessel holds the same aliens who built this planet? It could be another race entirely, and one more nearly our equal in military capability."

"And they just happened to stumble across the same planet that we did, out of all the billions that must exist in this galaxy? Do you play poker, Major? If you bet like you think, I'd like to play a game with you. I'd clean you out within five hands."

The major flushed, and Dierdre decided it was time to step in and smooth things over. It was not her usual capacity, but she had done it before, with some success. "Excuse me, but we seem to be at something of an impasse here. I don't think it's to be resolved by a lot of teeth-baring and chest-thumping. As I see it, Colonel Singh has the authority of the Althing and the Articles. Dr. Kornfeld-Taggart's authority on the transporter bases is absolute. Why don't we dismiss the troops, retire to a bar someplace and work this out like sensible people?"

Wyeth spoke up again. "Miss Jamail, isn't it?" As if he didn't know perfectly well. "I believe Dr. Kornfeld's authority is more assumed than genuine, but you make an excellent point. Adjournment to a suitable refuge to sort matters out is a hallowed tradition and I propose we do just that."

Singh cocked a graying eyebrow toward Dierdre. "Jamail? You're the one who tried out the transporter without authority?"

"I'm afraid so," she admitted. The old celebrity status. It always worked like a charm.

"Pleased to make your acquaintance. If you'd been under my command, you'd still be in the brig."

She shook his proffered hand. "I guess my service still appreciates initiative."

"We do too. But," he jerked his head toward the file of his soldiers, "considering the capabilities of our troops, we can't afford to allow such latitude."

Dierdre pretended to study the soldiers closely. "I see you have a point. I wouldn't want them making any rash decisions in my vicinity." She turned to Sims. "Bobby, this is your base. What's convivial but not too noisy?"

"The *Icebreaker* is the first stop on the shuttle bus. It's fairly quiet at this hour."

The troops were given liberty and the officials climbed into the seats of a bus. It seemed to work pretty well, just as Sieglinde had taught her: *first show your teeth, then turn on the charm.* Of course, Sieglinde wasn't always so good in the charm department, and Dierdre had to work at it. But, by the time they reached the *Icebreaker* and ordered their drinks, the initial hostility had dissipated without either side yielding any points. Soon Sieglinde and Singh were trading stories of relatives in the last war. Family connections were always important among the Island Worlders. Quivera wanted to know all about the famous Team Red expedition. For the thousandth time, Dierdre obliged. Some of the Rangers drifted in and took a table, including the icy blonde Dierdre had eyed earlier. With their rifles propped against a wall and helmets on the floor beside their chairs, they behaved like any other group of raucous young people, except for a certain air of deadliness. For sure, nobody was going to start a fight in this place tonight.

Later, at their quarters, Dierdre asked Sieglinde: "Why do they do it?"

"Why does who do what?" Sieglinde seemed to be in a good mood. She had established a moral ascendancy over the Salamids, which they had acknowledged, even if they weren't quite sure how she had done it.

"The Salamids. I can see how you can dedicate your life to actually *doing* something, but there's been nothing for them to do for decades. They work and train like maniacs, and there's nobody for them to fight. For all they know, we may never have to fight enemies again. They could be wasting their lives."

"It's a self-contained way of life." She pulled clothes from a bag and tossed them onto her bunk. "They're like monks, only instead of religion and salvation, they're motivated by a sense of duty. In theory, it's their duty to be prepared, and they've discharged that duty if they've remained prepared to fight. Whether they actually fight in a war is irrelevant."

She sat on her bunk and looked at Dierdre. "But, you're right. They see their lives slipping away with no opportunity to exercise their special skills. Secretly, maybe unconsciously, and they'd never admit it, they're itching for a fight. It would be vindication. It would justify a lifetime of sacrifice and self-denial. People give them a hard time. Every one of those young troopers could tell you of parents, friends and family who were shocked at their career choice, who told them that they were wasting their lives."

"And now they're hoping the aliens will be hostile?"

"Yes. And that's why I want to keep this bunch on a tight rein. I'm afraid that open hostilities may not be necessary. They'll jump at implied hostility, and that would be the end for us all."

A few days later they had the first clear holographs of the alien vessel. It floated above them in full-environment holo, a translucent ellipsoid of immense size. It glowed from within, a soft radiance that silhouetted a lacy framework of struts, probably an internal bracing.

Sieglinde was studying a fast-flashing readout as she scanned the ship. The room was full of officials and scientists. Some were really there, others were present in holograph.

"It's huge!" said a physicist named Renko. "Even larger than our largest asteroid ships."

"Look at its mass, though," Sieglinde said. "Like it's made out of soap bubbles. That exterior skin must be about a molecule thick. The inner structure can't be much more substantial."

"How do they cope with radiation?" someone wondered.

"It may be unmanned," said someone else.

"Then why did they leave the lights on?" Dierdre asked. "Electronic equipment works fine in the dark."

"Maybe I'm letting my imagination play tricks," Sieglinde said, "but does anyone else get the same impression I do, that this ship is *old*?" The emphasis was clear in her voice.

"I was about to say something of the sort," said

Landru, a famous archaeo-anthropologist. "Despite the translucency, it has a battered look and"—he made an eloquent gesture—"it simply has the feel of antiquity."

"So how long has it been in space?" Sieglinde wondered. "Has it been travelling all this time, or did they take it out of mothballs?" Nobody seemed inclined to answer. In the absence of any data, a judicious silence was observed all around.

These were tense times. From first word of the aliens' approach, rumor and speculation had run through the Island Worlder's ships, orbitals and planetside bases with incredible speed, variety and recklessness. Some regarded the advent of the aliens with fear, others with awe, others with near-religious hope. Sometimes it seemed to Dierdre that everyone had sent rationality out through the airlock and replaced it with a sort of apprehension little short of hysteria.

Dierdre had to admit, though it pained her to do so, that she was not immune to the current atmosphere of unreason. She knew that she was being egocentric, perhaps to an unhealthy degree. Nevertheless, she had the nagging feeling that because she had been the first to use the transporter the aliens had come looking for *her*. Borrowing her own phrase, Sieglinde had named this the "Goldilocks syndrome" and threatened to publish a paper on it someday, when she had the time. Considering Sieglinde's schedule, there was little chance of her carrying through on the threat, but Dierdre felt that it constituted blackmail, all the same.

"Course alteration," said a technician, studying a continuous readout. "Still consistent with approach to planetary orbit. Deceleration constant. Three days, four hours, fifteen minutes to a stable parking orbit. Give or take a few hours, depending on the altitude they select. Optimum time estimate is for the lowest stable orbit."

"Wonderful," Sieglinde said. "Three more days to sit on our hands and wait for them to make the first move."

"There's no rush," Dierdre said, shakily. "I'd just as soon they take their time. I sort of like the leisurely approach; give us time to get used to each other, maybe after a year or two, we could open a dialogue."

"Easy, Dee," Steve said from behind her, *sotto voce*, "you're getting bad for morale."

She fumed. He would never take her seriously. She knew that there was no real reason why he should, but it still hurt that he was so insensitive. There were some feelings for which a person should not be required to supply a rational explanation.

It had started a few nights before. He had been restive, jittery, the way he always was when he had to spend an extended time away from the bush. It was especially hard on him here in the arctic, where you couldn't even walk away from the base without a lot of cold weather gear, and then there was nothing to see except ice and snow. She was, however, tired of sympathizing with him, and wanted a little sympathy for herself, which was not forthcoming.

"I can't help it, I'm scared! We've seen what they can do, they're like gods! And I messed with their property."

"We've been messing with their property since Derek tripped over their power packs. What makes you so special?"

"The transporter took me apart and reassembled me. They may record transmissions and have a complete genetic readout on me."

"So what? Don't you think it's a little self-important, thinking that a race of gods have come from who knows where just to hunt you down?" He smiled his maddening smile. It was amused, superior, and it infuriated her. Before she could erupt, he wrapped his arms around her. "Putting on a little weight, aren't you?" He pinched softly here and there and soon she was giggling and after that it was better, for a while. But, things hadn't really changed.

And now the aliens were nearing.

After the alien ship analysis session, Sieglinde began giving orders for cessation of operations. "I'm shutting down the transporter labs until we know where we stand with the aliens. We may have to leave this system fast. Everyone we can spare is going on leave and that means up to the orbitals."

"We should have started this operation as soon as the alien ship was detected, then," Dierdre said. "It would take weeks for everyone on-planet to get back into space." She thought for a few seconds. "Back, hell, we even have some that were *born* down here." There had been cases where some back-to-nature types had insisted on trying natural childbirth under full-grav conditions, usually much to the mother's regret.

"I've floated the idea to the Althing for weeks," Sieglinde said. "But, since it's a political or at best free-choice matter, rather than a scientific question, my influence is marginal at best."

"What were their objections?"

"Several. Some are convinced that the aliens must be wise and benevolent. That's a reasonable surmise, but an unwise assumption. Nothing to bet your life on, anyway. Others don't want an unseemly show of timidity, especially one that might quickly degenerate into panic. There's certainly good reason for that point of view. And some are just unwilling to look scared. Our population is overburdened with that type."

"Steve's that way," Dierdre admitted.

Sieglinde leaned back in her chair and steepled her fingers, frowning. "I was hesitant about pushing a cautious attitude myself. Not because of the aliens and what they might do, but because of the Salamids. If they could say the great Sieglinde Kornfeld is worried that the aliens might prove hostile, they'd have that much more excuse to demand a greater role and more discretionary power." She looked less self-assured than usual. "I don't know, maybe I was wrong to soft-pedal the danger. I hope I'm not letting my fear of military action cloud my judgement."

"Does the Althing really have the power to order an evacuation?" Civics had never been one of her strong subjects.

"No. For some reason, nobody took this into account when the Articles were drawn up. The Island Worlds are technically ships, and the commanding officer on duty can take unilateral action to assure the ship's safety without consulting the Board of Navigation or the governing council, but ordering an evacuation of a planet or a system would call for a referendum. Which, knowing us, would take forever to arrange. What we have is a cooperative system agreed to by near-anarchists, not a true government."

"I've always had trouble getting along myself," Dierdre admitted. "I guess I'm not as different from everyone else as I used to think."

"I wish some of Thor's diplomatic skills had rubbed off on me," Sieglinde said, with a genuine sigh.

This was interesting. Sieglinde seldom spoke of her husband. "As I understand it, diplomacy is sort of a lost art. He was good at it, huh?"

She smiled. "He was the best. Anyone he couldn't charm he could browbeat or simply outlast. Once his reputation was established, just seeing him across the table was enough to half-defeat the other side's negotiators. I think he was the only diplomat in history to conclude a war by letting the other side pretend they'd won."

Intrigued, Dierdre said, "There've always been rumors about the First Space War. What's the story on that?"

Sieglinde smiled. "Not a chance. We all swore to secrecy, the dozen of us who worked out the agreement. Our various memoirs get uncorked twenty years after the last of us dies, and I'm the last one alive."

"You mean the conspiracy theorists have been right all along?"

Sieglinde ran a hand through her short hair and her smile turned wry. "Sometimes I think all of human history comes about through conspiracy. Other times I think the conspirators are just fooling themselves. I've been involved in a few, and often as not the result would have come about whether we'd schemed and made deals or not. Or else we got what we wanted and the end result was something totally unexpected. And now this."

"What do you mean?" Dierdre asked, mystified by the last remark.

"We're coming up on an event for which all planning and plotting is futile. This will be one of those unique incidents of history; the meeting of two utterly separate races, cultures, histories. There's no precedent and no way we can prepare for it. Except to keep an open mind." She turned very grave. "And the option of flight."

"That option sounds better to me all the time. Doc, what do you say we pack up and move operations to something mobile and really fast?"

"No. Our duty lies down here. The consensus is that the aliens will first contact us in space, probably in orbit, and most likely at our largest orbital colony, to wit: Avalon. I don't think so. I may be going out on a wild flight of fancy, trying to second-guess a species unknown to us, but I think it's going to be here, at their main transport system on this planet. From now on, one of us is going to be on duty in the main transport chamber at all times."

Dierdre felt a little sick. "Just the two of us?"

"Others can help if they want. I'm not going to coerce any of them into staying, but besides whoever else is in the chamber, one of us will be there, in charge."

"Why me? I mean, I'm flattered, but you have plenty of more experienced, better qualified . . . "

"No, I don't," Sieglinde cut in. "What's called for here isn't any scientific or technical expertise. Any we have is paltry compared to what the aliens have. I need someone with me who is attuned to my thinking and my temperamental quirks. I'm almost a hundred years old, Dierdre. In all that time I've gotten along better with you than with any other human being."

Dierdre was stunned. "Are you serious?"

"Absolutely. I include Thor. We loved one another, but we never really got along very well."

"I know the feeling," Dierdre said, thinking of Steve. Then another thought occurred to her. "You know, Doc, I've heard lots of people gripe about how impossible you are, not naming any names, of course, but I've never found you hard to get along with. Come to think of it, I've never worked for anybody who chewed me out less."

"We're two of a kind, although there is a disproportion of degree. Oddly, in most cases neither of us gets along with anyone who resembles us at all. You grew up thinking yourself a misfit, but I was a genuine freak. I was not merely possessed of a true scientific talent and genius; I was immensely valuable. I had no parents, no peers, and, at first, no self-definition except as the most valuable little girl in the solar system."

"I guess I've had it easy compared to you." Dierdre admitted.

Sieglinde looked at her strangely, as if doing a double-take. "Do I sound self-pitying? I didn't intend to. Actually, I never felt deprived when I was younger. I couldn't imagine the lives of other children, so I felt no envy. I did feel manipulated and endangered. So, when I was still a child, I escaped, disappeared and went into an underground of my own creation."

"That's why there's no record of you at all, prior to Island Worlds independence?"

"Right. I needed a place where I could live as I wanted, where I could do the work that had to be done. Ugo Ciano made it all possible. Martin Shaw was the great rebel, Thor was the statesman, Chih'-Chin Fu was the propagandist, and Sálamis supplied most of the military expertise, but I created the Confederacy because I needed a place to live. Later, when even space was no longer safe in the Sol System, I made it possible for the whole republic to escape. Does that sound egotistical?"

"It sure does. I've never heard anything like it, but then I wouldn't expect humility from you." Then, "I guess it's just as well. What's coming is likely to be too demanding for weak personalities."

ELEVEN

Another night in the main transporter chamber. It was the aliens' largest artifact on the planet, but it was drab, just an expanded version of the simple chamber she had found on the island. Of course, the whole planet was some sort of artifact; its surface was, at any rate.

These long watches were hard to take. After the exciting life of an explorer, and then of being Sieglinde's assistant in her frenetic, never-ending work, this was maddeningly dull. At first, friends had come to spend time with her, but the longer the immense alien ship hung in orbit the less time they spent planetside. They found excuses to stay in orbit themselves, just in case. She didn't blame them.

The first few nights, it had reminded her a little of the long night watches when they were camped on the island, but here there were no night sounds, and there was none of the camaraderie of the team to sustain her. Sometimes she would run old entertainments on a one-wall holoscreen. Sieglinde had forbidden any whole-environment holos, lest she miss something happening in the chamber. She studied a great deal. There was always need for study, and she concentrated on history, both Earth and Island Worlds, amazed at the depth of her ignorance. Like most of her contemporaries, she had concentrated on specific, utilitarian skills, rather than things like history and philosophy, art and the humanities. If nothing else, she figured she might get a well-rounded education out of this experience.

Even Steve hadn't been around for days. They'd had a flaming blowup when she agreed to stay at the transporter site with Sieglinde. The monotony of the arctic station had been driving him into terminal brain-burn for weeks, and he had turned her decision into a loyalty test, which she had failed. She thought that, had he at least tried to be conciliatory and used a little persuasion, she might have changed her mind. Once he took the take-it-or-leave-it attitude, though, her pride wouldn't let her back down. That was what she told herself, at any rate. She decided that maybe she wasn't suited to stable interpersonal relationships.

Predictably, Sieglinde had been short on sympathy. She had said that nowhere in the Articles was there any provision for smooth interpersonal relations, and pointed out helpfully that the only times in history when men and women had stayed together predictably had been when women were virtual slaves and nobody cared how miserable they were. Still it seemed unfair that two people with as much in common as she and Steve had couldn't get along, when two as appallingly different as Hannie and Matthias enjoyed apparent bliss. Sieglinde had had a few words to say about anyone who expected life to be fair, too.

She decided not to think about it. There was nothing she could do about it just now. Her life, like everybody else's, had been put on hold until the aliens made their intentions clear. If the aliens were actually in that ship; there was still debate on that point. If they were the same aliens. Sieglinde thought they had to be, but Dierdre wasn't so sure. There was always the chance. And this planet had been here, in its present condition, for uncounted years. Others might have found it in that time, and left their own detection systems, and now be coming back ("Who's been sleeping in my bed?").

The chamber where they had set up the lab was unique in this facility in that it had only a single transporter. There were dozens of chambers in the great master facility, some of them with scores of transporters set into the walls. Some of the gateways led to stations all over the planet; others to sites on the moons and on other planets and sizable bodies in the system. There were a few through which the robot probes had ventured, never to return, from which no signal had ever been received. The transporter in the lab chamber was one such, and had been marked with the ancient skull-and-crossbones device as a result.

She switched off her educational program and got out of her chair. It was time for her hourly sweep of the facility. One after another, she looked into the transporter rooms, each one deserted and silent. She stifled a yawn. It was too early to yawn. She had five hours left on this watch.

She returned to her chair and noted the uneventful sweep in the record. She thought of calling one of her friends on the planet, or in an orbital, to talk to. She decided that she really didn't have anything to talk about just now, and she was damned if she'd call up somebody just to entertain her.

She chose another holo, one about the early days of the terraforming of Mars, a period she was weak in. It was just getting to the part about the terrible first year of the settlement at Tarkovskygrad, complete with music by Holst, when she felt the familiar electric-shock sensation, the same thing she had felt hundreds of times since that first time in the island transporter room. Only Sieglinde had forbidden any transporter use until the current crisis was resolved.

She didn't want to turn around. The transporter

was behind her, and she was afraid of what she might see. Horrible pictures went through her mind-images from old holos, older movies. Beaks and tentacles, razor-edged teeth, hard, shiny carapaces and blobby, amorphous bodies with multiple eyes. Whatever it was, if it was there and she wasn't imagining things, it made no sound and didn't seem to emit any horrible smell. She tried to swallow but her mouth had gone dry and she couldn't reach for the water beaker inches from her hand. Her heart thudded and her breathing grew ragged.

After a few seconds she found she could still move her feet a little. She didn't want to see but she had to know. Moving her feet in tiny increments, she began to swivel around, turning off the holo screen.

At first she felt a vast relief, because it didn't look all that bad. Then there was a great suspicion. Was someone trying to play an awful trick on her, someone like Steve, maybe? Because not only did it not look horrible, it looked rather—*human*, that was the only way she could put it. Not quite like a real human, but you could do a lot with holos, and nobody could tell the illusion from reality without actually touching the projection.

Not that she was about to touch it. Despite all the self-reassuring things rushing desperately through her brain, she was terrified as she had never been in her life. She knew it was real.

It was tall, over two meters. There was something not quite right about the shape of the face, the flexibility of the neck. The hands were a little wrong, too, something about the proportions of fingers and thumb to the palm. It appeared to be male. She was sure about that. It wore clothes, but they resembled blue paint. Yes, male. Definitely. And human, or at least an excellent approximation.

She reminded herself that, in some of those old movies and stories, the aliens could adopt human form, the better to accomplish their nefarious ends.

She wondered whether she was going insane, or just hysterical. She had never been truly hysterical before. Its skin was the color of bronze, its hair also bronze but lighter, growing rather long on the scalp, dipping to a graceful peak on the brow, and forming a short, soft fluff along the broad cheekbones. Its eyes were golden, extremely large but not round; more of a rectangular shape, only not angular.

It—she corrected herself—*he* was not quite the sort of human she was accustomed to, but he looked far more human than the primitive hominids they had discovered. He was, she finally decided, quite beautiful. That put her even further on her guard. Legend was full of beautiful, deadly creatures: sirens, vampires and the like.

He walked toward her. Even his walk was graceful, a smooth stride full of springy muscles and supple joints. It made her feel clumsy and awkward just watching him. She wanted to run, to hit an emergency transmit switch, to yell. Instead she sat as if paralyzed, her breath coming in choking gasps. He stopped no more than a pace in front of her.

"You are the Dierdre?"

God, what a voice. The greatest Shakespearian actor who ever lived sounded like a howler monkey compared to him. His accent was odd, but sounded wonderful. The use of the article before her name betrayed a certain lack of assurance with the language, as did the phrasing of the question, but he had the rising inflection down pat, so there was no doubt that he meant it as a question.

It also meant that her worst fears had been realized. They had recorded her and had tracked her down for violating their property. She saw no point in evasion. They undoubtedly had a complete genetic readout of her, probably all her memories as well, her whole wretched school record, everything.

"Yes," she croaked. Great. First word spoken by a

human to an alien and it was a croak. But was he really an alien? He didn't look it.

"Or is it the Jamail? We have not yet mastered your titling protocol." That voice again.

"Either is fine." That came out all right. "I like Dierdre better. Just Dierdre, no *the*."

"Dierdre, then. I am being sorry. This will take time."

"You're doing fine. I guess I'm the first of us you've talked to?" You're babbling like an idiot, she thought, stop it.

He considered that for a while. "Except for"—passive—"yes, you are first direct."

"Another first for me," she muttered.

"I am sorry?"

"Oh. Excuse me. I'm not quite myself. You must want to talk to someone important. I can contact the Delta Pavonis council. That's what we call this star, you know: Delta Pavonis."

"I know."

"The council's in charge while the Althing isn't in session. We call our legislative body the Althing. Or you might want to talk to my boss, Doctor Sieglinde Kornfeld-Taggart. She's been our greatest scientist for a couple of generations."

"No, not yet. I wish to speak with you."

"I was afraid you'd say that. Because I was the first to go through one of the matter transporters?"

"Yes, that is one reason."

"Actually, I didn't know what it was at the time. It looked interesting, that's all." God, she thought, I have to get out of here. "Really, I wasn't supposed to try out any alien apparatus. It's against the rules." It was getting worse.

"I know."

"You seem to know a lot. Have you been monitoring our communications?"

"Yes. There is still much we are not understanding. The—cultures—are too different."

"It's going to be a problem. We'll work it out, don't worry." She wasn't feeling so scared now. If she had to be alone with an alien, she couldn't have asked for a better-looking one. Or a nicer one, so far, at least. She wanted to keep it that way.

"Why did you do it?"

"What? Use the transporter?"

"Yes."

"That's what they all wanted to know. I knew I wasn't supposed to, but there it was. For that one moment, see, I was in sole possession of something unique in human experience. I just had to see what it would do, before anyone else." She wondered whether it was wise, talking like this. They might get the idea that humans were all lawbreakers like her. Perhaps she should refuse to say any more, tell him he would have to do any further talking to officials.

Oddly, she didn't want to do that. She was not over her fear yet, but this was another experience she was reluctant to share. Here was the first alien to contact mankind, and she had him all to herself.

"Could I ask you a few things?"

Again that slight pause. "Yes."

"Let's start with something simple. What's your name?"

"It is quite long. M'ats is an acceptable short version." There was a glottal stop after the first consonant.

She reminded herself to be careful of her phrasing. It would not do to use anything that might be interpreted more than one way.

"Forgive me if this sounds strange—is this your true appearance, and not a look you've adopted to be diplomatic?"

"This is my true appearance—the appearance of my species." There was no way to tell from the sound of his voice if he was amused, shocked or bored. His facial expressions were equally enigmatic.

"Oh, good! But, tell me, we never expected to find anything away from our own solar system that would look remotely like us. We were prepared to meet intelligent species that were vaguely humanoid—upright, bipedal with manipulative appendages and a brain and sensory organs concentrated in a head at the top, but you can have all that and not look much like us. The humans we've discovered on other planets came as a surprise, but they seem to be related to us, somehow. How is it that you resemble us so closely?"

Another pause. "There are some things—that will want time to explain. Not so much at once."

"I can go along with that. But, pardon me, I'm not being a very good host. Would you like to see our facility here?" She felt uncomfortable with the way he looked at her. Not a stare, really. His eyes were so wide it was hard to tell whether he was staring or not. But he seemed to have an eagerness, as if he were seeing something he couldn't have gotten enough of. Well, she was the first Earth human of his acquaintance, after all.

"I would be liking that."

"We're going to have to get your tenses straightened out, but you're doing fine so far." She got out of her chair and, to her utter surprise, he pulled back a little, as if he were alarmed. That would be a laugh.

"I'm sorry. Did I do something wrong?"

"It is nothing. You move very fast. I was—startled."

Things connected in her mind: the little pauses, the slow speech, which she had attributed to unfamiliarity with the language and deliberation in choosing words, the stately, gliding walk. The alien sensed time differently. To him, her speech must seem rapid, her movements abrupt. She told herself to gear down a little.

"Excuse me. I'll be careful. Are you comfortable? I mean, we keep the temperature rather warm here, compared to the outside, both for our own comfort and to preserve our equipment from the humidity."

He didn't look dressed for the climate. He didn't look dressed, period.

He made a graceful, flicking gesture that took in his paintlike garment. She was going to have to count the joints in his fingers. There seemed to be too many of them. "This is—protective. Heat or cold, no matter." She liked watching his lips when he talked. They weren't broad, but they were beautifully shaped. Something was a little different about the teeth, though.

"Well, this is your own facility, of course. Ours starts—you *are* the people who built these transporter chambers, aren't you?"

"Oh, yes." This time he almost smiled, a very human expression. She was surprised at how little expression his face seemed to register, and wondered whether it was racial or cultural. She knew that there had been some peoples who made it a point to be stonefaced in front of strangers.

She didn't think that was the case with him. She tried to put a word to his expression and the one she kept coming up with was *serene*. Not the fatuous, Buddhalike serenity of the Abbatans. That had been mere boneheaded complacency. No, he had the look of someone who had seen just about everything and wasn't thrilled to see more.

She knew she was reading far too much into the apparent blankness of his face, but she couldn't help herself.

"Come this way." He walked along beside her as they left the chamber. They were in the ice corridor before she remembered that she should have notified Sieglinde that she was leaving. The event seemed to transcend her orders.

She shivered slightly in the chill, but her companion didn't seem to be bothered. At one point he drew a little ahead and she admired his back, which was as sleek and limber as an otter's. Like his neck, it seemed to have too many vertebrae. His hips were absurdly narrow, his buttocks as tightly muscled as a dancer's.

She tried to shake off a storm of incredibly unprofessional thoughts. It occurred to her that the dissipation of her fear-adrenaline must have brought on a hormone rush. What she was thinking was probably anatomically impossible. But then, his clothing didn't hide much in front, either, and from that angle it looked very possible indeed.

"This is the facility we built here to study the main transporter chambers," she said as they entered the man-made area. "We had to melt thousands of cubic meters of ice to do it. That was accomplished with orbiting parabolic mirrors." Empty corridors, offices and labs stretched ahead of them.

"Are you here alone?"

"Not quite," she said, improvising quickly. "We're operating on minimal staff right now. Everybody else is away for the holidays."

"I see." Was there a trace of irony there?

"Dierdre, are you going to introduce your friend?" She jerked around. It was Sieglinde.

"Oh, hi, Doc." She was getting too many shocks today. "Doc, this is M'ats. He's an alien."

"So I presumed. Welcome." She showed her customary *sangfroid*.

"You are being Dr. Sieglinde Kornfeld-Taggart?" M'ats asked.

"He's having a little trouble with tenses."

"Yes, Dierdre. Calm yourself." Then, to M'ats: "I am Dr. Kornfeld. Are you the sole inhabitant of your ship?"

"No. There are many others."

"Let me assure you before anything else that we have no aggressive intentions, and I can imagine no basis for conflict between our peoples."

He left a longer pause. "I believe you. Others may not."

"An honest answer. Do I have your assurance that you have no hostile intentions toward us?"

Dierdre was a little put out at having to share him so soon, but she had to admit that Sieglinde asked sensible, pertinent questions, instead of babbling.

"You have," he said, then, enigmatically. "We have no need."

"Do you mean that we couldn't hurt you if we tried, and if you wished to hurt us, there is nothing we could do about it?"

Pause. "Not-exactly."

"We'll leave it at that for the moment. I should tell you that there are some among us who would not be averse to a fight, and that none of us are in control of all the others."

"We deduced that from your—transmissions. It is difficult to understand. You are—interesting."

"You are more than merely interesting to us. There are incredible amounts that we want to know. But there is no rush, is there?"

"No, time is unimportant. It means much less to us than to you."

"Doc, I was showing him the facility. Maybe we should continue."

"By all means. I'd offer refreshments, but that might be unwise at the moment. Dierdre, shouldn't you be at your post in the transporter chamber?"

"Uh-uh. He's what we were waiting for and I'm not letting him out of my sight."

"You can be insufferable. Come along, then."

M'ats watched this byplay bemusedly. Dierdre figured it was one of those oddities of the human temperament that the aliens found intriguing. Something occurred to her.

"M'ats, up to now, we've been thinking of you, I mean all of you, as 'the aliens.' But you're not, really, although that has yet to be explained. What can we call you?"

"Our comprehensive word for those like me is being—no, *is*, *Arumwoi*."

"That's nice," Dierdre said, "kind of Greek-sounding. Means 'the people,' right?"

"Not quite. Not that primitive. Your word 'human-kind' would be the better transliteration."

" 'Translation' is the word you mean." Dierdre said.

"You say 'those like me' " Sieglinde said with her usual grasp of pertinent detail. "Does that mean that there are among you those who are *not* like you?"

He seemed suddenly discomfited. "Yes, but—this is not where/when the explanation should be. It is very complex. There are many peoples, but the *Arumwoi* are *your* people among us. It is not easy to explain, and I should not do it now."

Sieglinde turned to face him squarely and he jerked at the abruptness of the movement. For the first time, Dierdre saw the exercise of intuition, the leap of insight that distinguished a mind like Sieglinde's from that of an ordinary genius. "You're not an official envoy, are you, M'ats? You're doing this on your own, and when your superiors find out, you are in deep trouble, am I right?"

He stared at her, and now there was no question about his expression. Dierdre understood that, while he may have come from an incredibly ancient and advanced culture, he was out of his depth intellectually.

"Yes. It is true. And I underestimated you."

"You won't be the first."

"Hey, don't worry," Dierdre reassured him, "she's not typical."

"Dee, shut up!" Sieglinde said. Well, hell, there was no making some people happy. She watched M'ats closely. He had recovered his composure.

"This event is unique in many ways. Not just your first meeting with—aliens. Certainly not ours. Our—relationship is completely different. This is important to remember. I had expected to find you—what is the proper word—?"

"Naive?" Sieglinde said. "Unable to encompass a culture as ancient as yours?"

"That must be it. I was wrong. This one—" he turned to look at Dierdre—"she is much what I expected."

Well, thanks a lot, Dierdre thought.

"But you are not. You are like—," he made a sound for which there was no human equivalent. It came through as an aural blur.

"You'll have to explain that later," Sieglinde told him. "Our problem right now is to figure out a way to justify you to whatever ruling system you have, and to make ourselves some sort of semi-official diplomats. Under the Articles, the Althing is empowered to make such appointments."

"This is amazing," M'ats said. "Do not think me—wrong—we," he seemed to back off, take a breath, "we do not expect innocence. But such—sophistication and"—he needed longer to find a word this time—"flexibility are not what we expect of a culture as, excuse me, as primitive as yours."

"Is that why you've taken your time in contacting us?" Sieglinde asked. "Because you want to analyze our oddities first?"

"Not—exactly. We are not having been, no, I correct that, we are not *being* slow, by our standards. You people rush, do everything very fast."

"It's what happened with many of your experiments, isn't it? They developed too fast."

Dierdre looked from one to the other, realizing that Sieglinde was using M'ats' slower reaction time against him, trying to press him into parting with information he did not want to give. She resented it, while understanding that her personal feelings were of no importance in such an event.

M'ats shook his head, a slanted movement made possible by his flexible neck. It was unclear whether this meant negation, or protest. "No. You should not have space flight yet, not for millennia. Last time we sent probes, you were not yet building cities." He seemed to rein himself in. "I must go now. I will be back."

He turned and began to head back for the transporter.

"But we didn't finish your tour, yet." Dierdre protested.

"Will conclude later. Perhaps, soon, I may show you our ship."

"When will you be back?" Sieglinde asked.

"Soon. No more than one rotation. I will speak to you two, no others yet."

"We'll keep it quiet," she assured him. By this time they were back in the transporter room.

He turned and held out his hands awkwardly. Sieglinde understood and clasped his hands in her own. Then he took Dierdre's. He held her hands somewhat longer, which suited her very well. His hands felt good. Then he turned, manipulated the controls with incredible dexterity, and was gone.

Dierdre took a shaky breath. "See, *they're* not afraid to use the transporters. What are you doing?"

Sieglinde had rushed over to an emergency medkit and began scraping at her fingertips with a small probe. "When he took my hands, I scratched his palm slightly. With luck I may have got some epidermal cells."

"Now why didn't I think of that?" Dierdre said.

"It doesn't look like you've been thinking at all."

"I was taken by surprise. To be honest, I was absolutely horrified, until he turned out to be so friendly."

"It was more than fear at work." She put away a small sample packet. "We'll run an analysis on this later. Right now let's look at the holos."

Dierdre handled the desk controls and they watched a one-wall holo of M'ats appearance and the subsequent events in the transporter chamber and ice tunnel.

"God, did I look like that?" Dierdre said, embarrassed. A series of comical expressions chased one another across her holographic face.

"Don't worry, he's not yet experienced enough to read our expressions, any more than we can read his. Now, this is interesting." She watched as Dierdre's expression went from fear to fascination to more than fascination. When she saw Dierdre give M'ats the once-over in the ice tunnel she glanced sideways, eyebrow raised. "A little loss of scientific detachment, there?"

Dierdre stared at her hands in her lap. "Ah, I was just getting over—," it started out as a whisper, but quickly gained strength. "Ah, hell, boss, I don't know what happened. One moment I was so scared I could barely talk, the next all I could see was how beautiful he was in the middle of the most unbridled feelings of lechery I've ever experienced." Her hands gripped together nervously. "This isn't easy. I've always been pretty conventional that way. More than conventional."

" 'Repressed' is the word I would use. Don't worry, it's a common defense for people who know they're different. I was that way myself, a virgin in my mid-twenties."

Well, wasn't this the day for revelations, Dierdre thought. "If you hadn't shown up when you did, I might have taken him to my quarters and locked the door."

"That might not have been such a bad idea. An interesting experiment, and we would have ended up with a lot more than just a few measly epidermal cells."

"I hadn't thought of it that way. But, he's an *alien*, for God's sake! Even if he is pretty. Am I getting bent or something?"

Sieglinde leaned forward. "Dee, whatever he is, he's no true alien. He's a human male of enormous sexual allure. You think I didn't feel it? I may be old, but there's nothing wrong with my biological equipment."

"Good. I was beginning to think—are you sure he *could*?"

"That's never certain, even for our sort of human. However, he seems to have the wherewithal. Now, let's rerun those first minutes again. This time, let's concentrate on him instead of you."

"I suppose we won't be able to announce this for a while?" Dierdre said as the holo ran again.

"Shh. Don't be such a glory hound. Not if we're going to protect him, not to mention ourselves. What do you think of the way he's looking at you?"

"You said yourself we can't judge their expressions yet. I was too scared at the time to take much notice. I was expecting long, sharp teeth or something. He does look sort of—what do you think?"

"If he was one of ours, I'd say he's taken a fancy to you."

"Do you think so?" Come to think of it, he did have a sort of appreciative look. More than Steve had, the last weeks.

"He did ask for you by name."

"But I was the first one to use the transporter. And I was all over the media for a while, and they've been monitoring them."

"Why should that mean anything?"

"I don't know. Doc, are we really having this conversation or have we both gone vacuum happy?"

"I wish I knew. Come on, let's go to my quarters and have a drink. I'll toss these samples into an analyzer and see what turns up."

Sieglinde's quarters were larger than Dierdre's, but most of the extra room was taken up with instruments. "There's beer in the cooler. Open us a couple."

Dierdre untopped two of the new full-grav containers—long cylinders that were much more convenient than the old bulbs. Sieglinde scraped her samples onto a tray and inserted it. A few seconds later a readout flashed on the screen.

"What's it say?" Dierdre asked.

"I don't know. I'm not a biologist. Let's run it through a layman's program to interpret it."

Ordinarily, Dierdre would have been unnerved to find that there was a science Sieglinde hadn't mastered, but she was still preoccupied with her reaction to the alien. Sieglinde took notice.

"Sit down, Dee. I've been thinking about this. Now that I've had time to consider it, your reaction, and mine, make perfect sense."

Time? Dierdre thought. *Forty-five minutes, maybe? Sieglinde never needed much time.*

"It's like this: Mentally, we may stand between ape and angel, but biologically we're still just another species that wants to give its own genetic material the best chance to survive. The wider your gene pool, the better chance your species has. Any time we come upon a new people, there's always this urge to get together and mix genes. Historically, it's been men who did most of the exploring, so they had most of the fun. They kept it a secret, of course."

"The hell with this!" Dierdre protested. "I don't want to be just a bubbling vat of body chemicals, yearning to swap DNA with another one!"

"Like it or not, it's how we are."

Dierdre thought about it for a while. "Now that *would* be a first."

TWELVE

"Do you ever get the idea, Doc," Dierdre asked, "that this little piece of the galaxy we've explored has turned out a lot like those old movie and television entertainments we used to study in media history?"

They were waiting for M'ats to make another appearance. Sieglinde was going over the bio data to pass the time. "How's that?"

"Well, in a lot of those old shows the aliens looked human, maybe just made up a little, and often as not they spoke English. Everybody responsible said how stupid that was and pretty soon you didn't see that any more, when cheap holo effects could make really believable aliens. Now we're out here and what have we found? Humans."

"M'ats hinted that there are many other species. I want to hear more about that. And now we've had a look at this planet we can be pretty sure that human life didn't just spring up spontaneously wherever conditions were favorable. M'ats has the answers and I want them."

"I'm still not sure about all this. A little unauthorized exploring is one thing, maybe a bit of surreptitious experimenting on the side, no big deal. But what we seem to be doing now is opening unofficial negotiations between humanity and an alien race. It's an order of magnitude bigger. People might get the wrong idea."

"Remember what I told you about the role of conspiracy? Besides, neither we nor M'ats are empowered to speak or negotiate for our respective species. As long as that's understood, I don't see that any harm is being done. When the *Arumwoi* finally decide to make official contact, there'll be a lot of caution, lots of time tied up in ceremonial, things like that. This way, we'll be learning something in the meantime."

Dierdre stood behind Sieglinde, bent to look in the screen. "Does the bio readout make any sense?"

"It's puzzling, and it'll stay that way until I can consult some specialists on this. As near as I can tell, he reads out as nearly human, but not quite. Too close to be coincidence, but not close enough to indicate common origin."

"That makes no sense at all. How can they be that close without common origin?"

"It looks like we're going to have to rewrite the books on evolution again. We've been handed evolutionary anomalies by the bucketful since humanity reached the nearby systems. We may be back to square one where evolution is concerned."

"I can't buy that. The rest of evolution seems to work out. It's only human evolution that seems to have gone crazy."

"Well, that was the only kind people really raised hell about. The religious types could mostly get along with the idea of animal evolution, expecially when geological evidence was irrefutable. It was when Darwin postulated a common origin for man and animals that the uproar started. If, as seems to be the evidence now, humanity is *not* part of Earth's evolution, we may be arguing with the same people all over again."

Dierdre sat and scanned her fingernails, which she

had just trimmed and then, on an impulse, lacquered. "Still, what we're looking at here is a long way from some sort of divine origin, creation by a supreme being in his own image. I never could figure out what that last part meant, anyway."

"Don't be so certain. We've already noted that our aliens have what amount to godlike powers. If not up to Old Testament creator-of-the-cosmos standards, at least they're of Greek pantheon level. By the way, I like your necklace."

"Thank you. What's keeping him?" She started to brush nervously at her hair but stopped herself, not wanting to disturb her antique shell combs.

"He was pretty vague about when he'd get back. I'm not sure how to read this." She frowned, studying the screen before her. "There must be some way to interpret his olfactory perceptions."

"Why is that important?"

"He might not like that perfume you're wearing. Even among us, not everyone likes the same scents."

"I hadn't thought of that. Should I go wash it off?"

"Dee, have you utterly abandoned your sense of humor? I was teasing you."

"It wouldn't be the only sense I've lost. Look at me." Sieglinde had already looked. Besides perfume, jewelery and hair elaboration, she had dressed in a party suit and applied cosmetic, none too expertly. "I feel like a fool. To them, we're probably ugly. Ugly and primitive. I might as well have put a bone through my nose."

"Just consider it an anthropological experiment, if it helps to salve your pride. You know, if the rest are like him, we may be in for some real trouble. How are our men going to take it if all their women get itchy for aliens?"

"My God! You know, I've been going over those old books and cinemas and holos; from *War Of the Worlds* on, Earthmen-alien wars were a theme. Usually, the issues were conquest, territorial ambition, silly things like that. I don't think sexual jealousy was ever a factor." She began to nibble a fingernail, winced at the taste of fresh lacquer. "That may not be the worst of it. What if their women are as gorgeous as he is?"

"Civil war between the sexes. Of all the things we never expected to run into out here. Oh, well, let's not get ahead of ourselves. One catastrophe at a time."

"You're the big genius around here," Dierdre said, wanting badly to change the subject. "You've had a whole day to study our new evidence. Come up with any conclusions yet?"

"Even I need more evidence than this." She leaned back in her chair, propping her feet on a console. It was an incredibly relaxed pose for Sieglinde, so Dierdre knew that she had something important on her mind. "If it's speculations you want, though, I have a few. I think the common origin is still there. For us, for the other humans we've found, and for the *Arumwoi*. Right now we have a few chicken-and-egg questions to settle, but the answers are there. Countless times we've come up against phenomena that seemed to have no rational explanation, and each time it's turned out to be that some vital evidence was missing. Once the evidence was supplied, everything else fell into rational place.

"I don't believe in magic, nor in divine intervention in natural affairs. What's missing here is information. When I get it, everything will make sense, rationally and scientifically. The *Arumwoi* are tremendously advanced, but they need ships to travel through space. They don't create matter out of nothing, and at least one of them is operating without the others' knowledge, if we're to believe him. They're powerful, but they aren't gods."

She stabbed a finger at the screen with its abbreviated biological readout. "I have a feeling that a lot of the answer is in there, and it's not my field of expertise. I'm not going to be able to call anybody else in until we reach an understanding with M'ats, though." She snorted frustration.

"Some people wouldn't be so scrupulous," Dierdre said. "The prospect of immortal fame is tempting, as I well know."

Sieglinde shrugged, an Earthie gesture retained from the Mars of her youth. "I'm already famous. Probably the most famous human being of my generation. Besides, that was never important to me. I spent most of my first three decades trying to stay obscure. And when I give my word, I mean it. I'll keep faith with M'ats as long as he does the same with me."

Despite their preparation and long wait, they still jumped slightly when the alien in question made his appearance.

"Good day, M'ats," Sieglinde said. "It is M'ats, isn't it? For all I know you all look exactly alike."

"It is M'ats," he confirmed. "And we do not all look alike. In fact, we seem to differ rather more than you of Earth origin."

Dierdre noticed something different from the day before. The small pauses before his responses were diminished if not absent entirely.

"You've taken something to speed up your response time!" she said. Then it occurred to her that it might be a rather impolite observation.

He smiled. Either he had been practicing, or the expression was the same for both species. "There are treatments. To me you seem slowed down, which is a relief. The difference in timing could prove mutually irritating, over a prolonged time."

"We wouldn't want that," Sieglinde said. "Your grasp of our grammar has improved since yesterday as well."

"We have techniques of information absorption as well. The last—that is, yesterday, I had not prepared properly. It was most unusual for me, for any of us, to take such, I should say precipitate action."

"Are you a society of conformists, then? Rule-followers?" Dierdre asked.

"Not as you might think. We are quite individual in our interests, in much private and interpersonal behavior. In some ways, you would consider nearly all of us rather—eccentric. But certain behaviors regarding the social pattern—how shall I put it? Let us say that our language no longer has an equivalent for 'foolhardy.' I may have to reintroduce it to describe what I have done."

"You have only a single language?" Sieglinde asked.

"For our entire race and culture, yes. Many for smaller groups. Some practices and fields of study are so arcane that their practitioners require a separate language as well."

"We've become that way ourselves," Sieglinde said. "Just what is it you *have* done?"

"I have stepped outside the bounds of the social consensus in contacting you on my own. The action is not really what you would call criminal; we no longer have that concept. But it is 'other-than-expected,' which is a great perjorative among us."

Dierdre faced him, wondering what lay behind his beautiful, impassive facade. "Do you think the reward of what you've done will prove worth the price?"

"Oh, yes. It already has."

"It has?" Dierdre was mystified. He had done nothing so far except show up and cause them a lot of puzzlement.

"What did you wish to accomplish by coming here?" Sieglinde asked.

He looked at Dierdre. "To meet you. And I have."

It was, to say the least, stunning news. She decided he must still be having difficulties with the language.

"You mean, to contact us, don't you? You wanted to be the first to make contact with Earth humans?"

"No, it was to meet you personally."

This was a little more than she had expected. "Boss, I think I'd better sit down."

"Go ahead, dear. M'ats, of all the motivations I might have ascribed to you, this is about the least likely. Not that Dierdre isn't attractive, in her fashion, but, isn't this rather a . . . a . . . grand gesture?" To Dierdre, the shock was almost worth seeing Sieglinde at a loss for words.

"Not really. You will need to learn more about us, and you shall. I am sure that I am not the only one to have this urge, I am just less disciplined than most. I was the first to see her. I was monitoring the detection system when the signal arrived. I was in suspension, along with most of the crew, and it woke me. It has been so long since our detectors found anything, and this! After the failure of so many others."

That last remark was going to take some explaining, too, Dierdre thought. She was still dazed by his proclamation of—what? She couldn't be sure what it meant. Although she was pretty sure that it couldn't be as good as it sounded.

"M'ats," she asked, "just what did you see when the system woke you?"

"I saw you at the transporter controls, having just made the transition and not yet aware of what had happened. Later, when I replayed the whole sequence, I saw you from the moment you entered the chamber. Our cultures are not so different that I could not see how frightened you were when you first touched the controls. Yet you did it anyway! Later, I watched as the others did the same. By that time, the more remote sensors had been activated and we made a record of what happened outside the cave as well."

"And what conclusions did you draw?" Sieglinde asked.

"First let me describe. I woke the controllers and specialists and we made immediate course change. It took little time for your language to be translated;

our instruments and specialists have thousands of years of such experience at such tasks. We heard the arguments and the justifications, and the fact that you were determined to proceed with your exploration despite the risk and in defiance of authority."

"Did you understand," Sieglinde asked, "that this was a very young, undisciplined and irresponsible group?"

He smiled again. "We quickly discovered that, compared to us, you are *all* very young, undisciplined and irresponsible."

Oddly, it was Dierdre who first voiced the big question. "And is that bad?"

"Not to me. We must persuade the others as well."

He left quickly, leaving Sieglinde bemused and Dierdre all but stunned. "Boss, tell me this didn't happen. Is that alien really hinting that he's *in love* with me?"

"Difficult to say. I haven't studied many aliens. He might be tricking us, I suppose, able to read our minds and tell us what he knows we want to hear."

"If that's the case, wouldn't you be the one to flatter, rather than me? I'm a nobody while you're the great wonder of the age. If they've studied our transmissions and delved into our memory banks, they must know that."

"Love is strange. Besides, if they had recording devices outside, you're the one he's seen romping around naked in that pool."

"You're right. Maybe I wasted all this artificial allure." She looked down at her body and sighed. "At least I was in good shape then, plenty of exercise and sunlight. Doc, let's be serious; I am not the sort to launch a thousand ships, or even tempt one putatively human alien into a terrible transgression. What's happening?" She was on the verge of tears, shaking from suppressed fear, confusion and a complex of emotions she could only feel and not name.

Sieglinde stepped up behind her and placed her

hands on Dierdre's shoulders. The strong, competent fingers were soothing, bringing a measure of sanity to an increasingly insane situation. "I wish I could tell you, Dee. I need someone to tell me. But I'm glad I'm not going through this alone, even if it's hard on you."

Dierdre got hold of herself and felt, for some reason, much better. She looked over her shoulder at Sieglinde, covering one of the thin, wiry hands with her own. "Why's that, Doc? I thought you were the most self-reliant human being in existence."

"That may be true, but there are limits, even for me. I hardly ever hear from my sons and daughters from one year to the next. I'm glad I have you with me now."

Deirdre felt the tears returning. "I wish I could tell you how good that makes me feel. I've felt so alone, lately."

"Dierdre, I'm going to pretend to be a physician and prescribe you a sedative. I want you to return to your quarters and get a minimum of eight hours sleep. I can manage here for the next shift."

Dierdre got out of the chair, feeling a little woozy. "I guess I could use some sleep. It's been an eventful twenty-four hours, hasn't it?"

"I think you've been up for about forty, and I shouldn't have permitted it, but I was flustered and anxious, too. Right now, fatigue won't do either of us any good." She went to the med chest and withdrew a dose tube, pressing it against the skin inside Dierdre's elbow. "Tired as you are, you're probably too wrought up to sleep. This'll make sure. Now go on. At least eight hours, remember?"

"Sure," she said, sleepily. "You'll wake me if he comes back, won't you?"

"Of course, now go lie down."

Sieglinde watched as Dierdre staggered off toward her quarters. A few minutes later, she looked in and saw her assistant sprawled across her bunk, fully dressed and snoring. Sieglinde tugged her boots off, drew a blanket over her and turned out the light before she closed the door behind herself.

Dierdre didn't get eight full hours of sleep. After seven hours, Sieglinde woke her. The aliens had made official contact.

THIRTEEN

It felt strange to be in space again. Dierdre had only been up a few times since first taking the shuttle down to the planet. Each trip had been increasingly uncomfortable. She had become acclimatized to planetside life and space was fast becoming an unnatural environment to her. The people of the orbitals and the free-ranging ships had looks and habits that now seemed strange. Zero-gee made her queasy and she had to take anti-nausea medication.

The alien vessel had altered its orbit, gradually approaching Avalon. It would rendezvous within a few hours.

Dierdre gazed through a port at the great asteroid-ship that had been her home during her later school years. It was an irregular mass of hollowed-out rock and artificial structures, landing docks and drive units. It was the largest of the old asteroid colonies, and the largest vessel ever sent by humans out of the Sol system. The alien vessel was not yet visible.

They docked at the North Polar Facility, the shuttle's landing pods cleated to the surface although the centrifugal effect generated by Avalon's spin was absent here. The planetoid-ship had one Earth normal spin-induced gravity in its outer layers, near the equator lessening to near zero-gee close to the center and the poles. Inhabitants could choose whatever felt most comfortable.

A corrugated umbilicus extruded from a lock and fastened itself over the shuttle's exit hatch, fattening as air pressurized its interior. A gong sounded as the hatch opened and the passengers unstrapped themselves.

"Come on," Sieglinde said. "We might as well get this over with."

"What do you mean?" Dierdre asked. "The *Arum*—" she caught herself. "I mean the aliens won't be arriving for a while yet."

"Watch your tongue. I doubt that anybody's spying, but plenty of snoopy people have sensitive ears."

"Sorry."

"It's not the aliens I dread just now." They left the shuttle and entered the old customs area, unused for its former purpose since the diaspora of the Island Worlds. It was not, however, deserted. A subdued uproar began with Sieglinde's appearance, and the crowd surged forward. It was largely made up of people wearing optical headgear and accompanied by hovering camerabots. In a word: newsies.

"Dr. Kornfeld-Taggart!" a man shouted, "what will the aliens do next?"

"How the hell should I know?"

"Dr. Kornfeld," a woman said, "are we in danger?"

"You know as much as I do."

A camerabot swooped within a meter of Sieglinde's face, an extreme rudeness by Island World standards. Dierdre drew her pistol and leveled it at the buzzing device. "Get that thing out of her face or I'll shoot it down!" The camerabot swooped away, the crowd parted to both sides, clearing her line of fire, and the noise quieted. There were times when her wild-woman image was a real help.

Wyeth, the Althing man, came through the newly-cleared path, a conciliatory hand thrust forward. "That isn't necessary, Miss Jamail."

"Maybe not yet." She held the pistol at high port, finger off the firing stud.

He smiled ingratiatingly. "Please, put it away."

With a show of reluctance, she jammed the weapon back into its holster. She glowered at the newsies. "If you want to ask Dr. Kornfeld any questions, you do it quietly, one at a time. I don't know what you expect anyway. The aliens have yet to open official contact." There, she hadn't actually lied.

"Where will you be staying?" Wyeth asked her as Sieglinde talked to the newsies.

"At Sieglinde's suite in the Kuroda stronghold. The old Ciano lab is too far from the Althing chamber if things start breaking fast." Ciano lab was a separate rock attached to Avalon. Sieglinde kept her usual orbital residence there. "You can keep in contact with us through our belt comms. We'll have them with us at all times. Don't bother using the Avalonian comm system, it might be too slow."

Wyeth addressed Sieglinde, who had dismissed the newsies with promises of a full interview as soon as First Contact was concluded. "Dr. Kornfeld, if you think it's necessary, we can arrange for quarters next to the Althing chambers."

"No. If they rush us *that* badly, it will probably mean hostile action. In that case, the Salamids will take over and the rest of us had better just keep out of the way."

"Let's hope it doesn't come to that."

They walked into the tube station and stepped into a passenger car. "What's the Salamid position since things started happening?" Sieglinde asked.

"It has been decided that a liaison setup could be too slow and awkward under the circumstances. The Chief of Staff will be present in the Althing chamber during all ceremonies and negotiations. He will take no part unless authorized by the Speaker," Wyeth told her.

"Who is Chief of Staff these days?" Sieglinde said.

"A General Moore."

Sieglinde nodded. "I knew his father, back during the First War. Met him my first day in Avalon. He was with Thor and Hjalmar Taggart and that da Sousa woman. Thor looked like hell, he'd just come in off a raid." She smiled at the memory. "The father was a General Moore, too. An easy man to deal with, as I recall. Let's hope the son's the same way."

"Could you make anything of the alien's transmission that the others couldn't?"

She shook her head. "It seemed straightforward enough." It had been broadcast in the clear, merely a series of numerals giving time, velocities and rendezvous coordinates.

"Except as regards intentions," he said.

"No, they're giving very little away. Perhaps they merely have a keen sense of the dramatic."

"That's an inordinately anthropomorphic speculation, coming from a scientist."

"I'm not an ordinary scientist." She fiddled with something at her belt and the figures scrolled upward past her face. "They're also coming terribly close, for such a large vessel."

"It didn't escape our notice," he said.

"I think we can assume that they have the expertise to pull it off, considering the other capabilities they've displayed."

The car stopped at the Kuroda stronghold, where Wyeth took his leave of them. A serious-looking young man greeted them at the landing.

"Aunt Sieglinde," he said, bowing stiffly.

"Dierdre, this is Massimo Kuroda, Derek's nephew."

"Miss Jamail," he bowed again, this time not quite as low. He had light brown hair and a wispy mustache. She could see no resemblance to Derek. "Aunt

Sieglinde," he continued, "your suite is ready. It has been swept and declared secure, for whatever good that does in this situation."

Sieglinde raised an eyebrow. "Is the clan on wartime status?"

"Since the situation is unknown and tense, we have gone to standby alert." They followed him through the massive main door of the stronghold. "Since you will be very busy and your schedule is likely to be crowded, there will be no formal family functions. Just come and go as suits you, and ignore the rest of us. You, too, Miss Jamail. Ordinarily, we are very keen on family ritual. Please don't feel neglected. The clan chiefs have ordered that you are not to be bothered or detained in any way."

"That is most thoughtful. Shoes off, Dierdre." She took off her own and lined them up next to a dozen pairs of footwear ranging from boots to sandals. "Tell Anastasia that when this is over, we'll have a big family get-together and I'll bring everybody up to date."

Knowing Sieglinde, Dierdre thought, she'd probably have the news conference at the same time. That would conserve on time and let her get back to work all the sooner. She examined her surroundings with fascination.

The Kuroda stronghold had been carved from the rock of Avalon in the early days of asteroid settlement, when times had been decidedly unsettled, with feuding, claim-jumping and outright banditry not uncommon. The place was a fortress, its nearest neighboring dwellings separated by many meters of rock, its accesses tightly controlled. The extended Kuroda-Ciano-Taggart-da Sousa clan was dominated by the Kurodas, and the Kurodas had never considered peacetime to be more than a temporary aberration. The stronghold had never been penetrated in either of the two wars nor in innumerable subsequent intrigues.

The floors were covered with tatami, woven reed mats unknown among the Island Worlds except for Avalon, where the reeds were grown and a family of craftsmen practiced the art. Scrolls of Chinese and Japanese calligraphy hung here and there, and a rack of ancient swords stood against one wall.

Sieglinde led her through a labyrinth of corridors and down a flight of stairs to a suite of rooms furnished in the more familiar Avalonian style—flimsy, light-gravity furniture, mineral-fiber carpeting and colorful, holographic decoration. Dierdre dropped their bags and sat on a low couch. They had not bothered to pack more than minimal articles. They could buy anything they might need in Avalon.

"Low-grav's going to take some getting used to, but it's sure easier on your back and feet."

"Mm? Oh, yes. It is." Sieglinde seemed decidedly abstracted.

"Doc? What's wrong?"

"I feel my instincts are slipping. I didn't think that they'd make their first move at Avalon. I thought they'd use the main transporter facility."

"They did. One did, anyway, so consider yourself half-right. And we can't be really sure that M'ats wasn't sent ahead by their authorities. Maybe they wanted to check us out in person before making a public move."

"Maybe. We'll probably know pretty soon." She changed mood. "Do you know where you are?"

"Where?" She had been enjoying these odd mood shifts of Sieglinde's since the sudden, unexpected intimacy of the evening before. She suspected that it was a part of Sieglinde's personality usually hidden from others.

"It's the Kuroda fort. Legendary, of course, but pretty much as I pictured it."

"You're also directly below Antigone Ciano's suite. We'll go up there later, if we have time. She's probably in residence considering the circumstances. If you can survive the decor up there, nothing the aliens have will shock you."

"The Cianos do have a certain reputation. Will Derek be there?"

"You can never tell with those two." Sieglinde yawned. "I'm going to try for some sleep. How about you?"

"I'm all right. I may look around, if that's all right with you." She was determined to explore *something*, even if it was just the Kuroda fort.

"Go ahead. You'll have the run of most of it, and anywhere they don't want you to go, you won't be able to. Be ready to move fast, but I doubt we'll have to. If the rest of them are like M'ats, they're the leisurely sort."

After Sieglinde retired, Dierdre freshened up, reapplied her makeup, reminding herself that M'ats might be among the delegates, and set out to get her bearings. She could never be comfortable without knowing the layout of her surroundings.

There were people everywhere; the family gathering for a potential crisis. Everyone nodded politely but ignored her otherwise. That suited her, because she wasn't feeling especially sociable.

She came to a long, tatami-floored gallery, devoid of furniture except for a slightly raised dais at one end. Against one wall were ancient armors, three Japanese and one European. Against the facing wall were eight obsolete spacesuits: one Lunar, one Martian, the rest of an early asteroid prospector design. Plaques beneath the suits identified the former wearers. She recognized some of them. The frontier nature of space settlement had restored the importance of cohesive, interdependent families, largely lost in the fluid societies of Earth.

She told herself that she would contact her own family, as soon as she had time.

"Miss Jamail?" The voice broke into her reverie. She looked up to see an extremely tall, stately woman with gray eyes and long, chestnut hair. She looked about Sieglinde's age, which could mean she was anything from thirty-five to a hundred or more. Something about her bearing gave her the look of senior years.

"Yes, I'm Dierdre Jamail." The woman looked interesting, and Dierdre didn't mind her intrusion.

"Forgive me, I know we're not supposed to bother you or Linde, but I wanted to welcome you. I've greatly admired your work planetside."

"Please don't ask me to forgive you." Dierdre took the proffered hand. "I have nothing to do at the moment, and nobody to talk to."

"Then let me offer my services. I'm Anastasia."

Dierdre was taken a little aback. "Then you're the, ah—"

"Yes, I'm the titular chieftainess. We elders take the position in rotation. There has to be a chieftain in residence in Castle Kuroda at all times. After a year or two you get castle fever and pass it on to some unfortunate relative who's reached sufficient years."

For once, Dierdre had no urge whatever to make flippant remarks. "I'm honored to be here. I know that very few people outside your allied clans have ever seen the inside of this place."

Anastasia laughed. "We're not all that exclusive. And the bloodlines don't count for everything. We've expelled unworthy clansmen, and when we see talent we want we marry or adopt it into the family."

"That's one way to maintain quality. I have relatives I don't enjoy sharing the same solar system with."

"Exactly. When did you last eat?"

Dierdre thought. "Let's see, Sieglinde woke me about six hours ago, and we spent most of the time getting ready, flying to the coast and catching the shuttle up here, and—I guess it's been a while." Suddenly she realized she was ravenous.

"Come with me." Dierdre followed Anastasia, admiring the black silk pantsuit the chieftainess wore. The wide trousers gave it the look of a gown, severe yet at the same time luxurious. She sighed, knowing that it took the woman's tall, elegant build to make the outfit look so good. They entered a spacious room furnished with low divans, its walls hung with what appeared to be genuine Gobelin tapestries. Even to Dierdre's inexperienced eye, it represented wealth unimaginable.

"Make yourself comfortable while I order us something from the kitchen." Anastasia filled two glasses with white wine at a sideboard, speaking a code number into an archaic voice-grille. She turned and handed Dierdre a glass. "A lot of our equipment here is old, but it all works. Cheers."

Dierdre, normally suspicious of unfamiliar people, felt relaxed. No one of this woman's stature had anything to gain from flattering her, so she was sure that the goodwill was sincere. Seconds later, a servobot of truly antiquated design rolled in on fat little wheels.

It was little more than a covered serving table with a rudimentary electronic brain, just sufficient to maneuver from the kitchen to readily accessible rooms. Its top deck bore covered dishes of decorated silver.

"As I said, old but efficient." Anastasia lifted a cover, releasing steam and fragrance. Much of the fare was seafood, raised in Avalon's huge salt-water tanks. There were few synthesized items, another evidence of the family's wealth.

Dierdre loaded a plate and bit into an enormous butterflied shrimp. The flavor almost brought tears to her eyes. It had been a long time since she had eaten like this.

"It's rather commonplace, I'm afraid," Anastasia said, "after you've been used to living on dinosaur meat."

Dierdre began to laugh, then to choke, while Anastasia thumped her back. "We only did that once!" she said when she could talk, "but nobody'll believe us. They think we're carnivorous cavemen down there."

"I suspected that. Yet you seem to have come through the deprivation and drudgery well."

"I wish I could have had more of it." It occurred to her that this might sound disloyal. "I love the work with Sieglinde; among other things it's the greatest education anyone could ask for. But I miss being out there in front, seeing things nobody has seen before. Things only happen for the first time once."

"I know what a thrill it can be. Still, you can't stay a hell-raising young adventurer forever. I know far too many who have blighted their lives by trying to remain as children for too long. You showed mature judgement in accepting Linde's offer to become her assistant. Your record shows that you would not bend to authority from mere submissiveness."

Dierdre found it difficult to react to sincere praise. She had experienced adulation, in her time, and had little use for it. This was different. "At least she keeps me too busy to be bored."

"And, a public persona has its uses, when dealing with the public. I saw your little display at the port today. It's good to see a little bravura in these pallid times."

Dierdre grinned, feeling about ten years old. "I wish they'd left it there, I'd have shot it down. I hate those things. That would've given them something for the late-shift news and made them leave Sieglinde alone."

"Well, there's no reason you have to grow up *too* quickly." She became more serious. "We have been very impressed with Linde's reports about you."

"Reports? She was sending in evaluations on me?" This was new.

"Oh, it's all quite informal. Nobody spies or keeps dossiers or anything like that. But Linde's a collateral member of the family, as a Taggart widow. And we do like to hear about promising new talent. I did mention that we adopt."

Dierdre was speechless. She didn't know whether to be flattered, angry or just shocked. "I already have a family," she said, finally.

"Most of us have several, it's no impediment."

"Did Sieglinde mention that I'm attached?"

"She did mention something about you and Mr. Forrest. She also said that it was not likely to last long, something about an excessive similarity between the two of you."

Dierdre felt her ears burning. It was an improvement. A few years before, it would have been a full-blown rage. "She seems to know quite a bit."

"She doesn't miss much. I realize that this is sudden, and that you have a great many other things on your mind just now. Think about it when you have time. There's no rush. And don't be angry with Sieglinde."

"She's told me a little about her ideas on conspiracy."

Anastasia smiled again. "It's not much of a conspiracy. Sometimes, Linde gives us a recommendation. She doesn't have to, and we don't have to act on them. It's a family thing."

"Thank you for the offer. It's something unique in my experience and I'll need time to consider it. In the meantime, however I decide, I'll always appreciate the honor." Tact. She was actually acquiring tact. She thanked Anastasia for her hospitality, then pleaded fatigue. Anastasia gave leave as graciously as she had extended welcome.

On the way back, Dierdre pondered this new turn of events. Was Sieglinde trying to manipulate her personal life, or was she just looking out for Dierdre's interests? She was always generous in promoting the careers of her students and subordinates, but no one had ever mentioned her sponsoring someone for inclusion in the clan. It was hard to figure, because Sieglinde just wasn't a normal human being. Dierdre had always considered herself different, an outsider, but she was positively conformist compared to Sieglinde.

What it was, she decided, was that her life had become an exercise in surrealism, ever since that Survey woman, whose name she could no longer remember, had, against her own better judgement, allowed Dierdre a planetary assignment. It seemed like decades ago. Between then and now had come dinosaurs, sabertooth cats, matter transporters, Sieglinde, and an alien whose intentions toward her were unclear. It wasn't the sort of thing they prepared you for back at the Academy, especially when you were pursuing a degree in topographical analysis.

When their belt units woke them, Dierdre felt oddly refreshed and ready for anything. Something had broken while she slept. It had fallen away and now she was free of it. She wasn't sure yet what it was, but she felt good.

Sieglinde noticed. "You're looking joyous for someone with such an uncertain future."

Dierdre brushed out her hair. It was almost elbow-length now, as black and glossy as obsidian. "Nobody's future is certain. But in a little while, we'll be doing something while almost everyone else has to sit and watch. We'll be taking the active role."

Sieglinde beamed. "That's my girl. You make me feel young again."

"You make me feel grown. Come on, Doc, we'll be late for the big show."

They dashed for the tube landing and caught a car just in time to hear a voice over the intercom: "The alien delegation will be received at the South Polar main lock. Althing members and authorized personnel are to proceed there at once. All others are to stay away. All proceedings will be shown by live holocast."

The message was repeated as they got off at the next landing and switched to a car going in the right direction.

"Why the South Polar dock?" Dierdre wondered. "I don't think it's been used since the big jump."

"It still gets used, from time to time. It's mainly for bulk freight. The locks are much larger. Maybe they want to make a grand entrance."

The landing at the port was thronged, as crowded cars disgorged everyone at once. There was much cursing and muttering as pages tried to sort people out and direct them to appropriate positions. Sieglinde saw a man in Salamid dress uniform: a matte-black coverall emblazoned with the red Greek helmet design. The crowd parted for her almost unconsciously as she crossed the landing to stand before him.

"General Moore? You must be. I knew your father. You favor him."

The Salamid saluted her informally. "He always spoke most highly of you, Dr. Kornfeld."

"I trust you will act with utmost restraint in the next few hours, General."

"We are not warmongers, despite what civilians think."

"But I suppose you have ships out there somewhere, on alert status?"

"We're not fools, either."

"Good, and I . . . " she broke off as Wyeth came up to them, sweating and understandably agitated.

"General, Dr. Kornfeld, you had better come inside now."

Neither seemed inclined to do so. Moore glanced up momentarily, seemingly looking over Wyeth's shoulder but actually checking an eye-implant scanner. "It's not urgent yet. Still twenty minutes to docking time. Let's let things get sorted out in there, then we can make a suitably dignified entrance."

"That sounds fine to me," Sieglinde said, then, to Wyeth: "Do they really intend a docking maneuver with that enormous ship?" She seemed amused rather than alarmed.

"So it seems, if we're interpreting their latest communication correctly. It only came in minutes ago. And we had the Althing chamber all set for a formal reception. We expected some sort of shuttle to deliver them to the North Polar dock." He shrugged. "Well, if they won't send a delegate ahead to arrange protocol, they'll just have to put up with what we can throw together. We've never had much experience at that sort of thing anyway. But the media people are going frantic in there, trying to set up their equipment in time."

A page stopped them by the entrance to the docking area. He stood guard over a rack draped with pistols and knives, even a sword on an ornate baldric. Some Island Worlders went armed as a religious tenet or just from a sense of personal style. "Check your weapons, please. None allowed inside."

Moore removed his pistol belt and handed it over. "I suppose it wouldn't do to terrify these planet-builders with these deadly things." Dierdre followed suit.

The interior of the dock was in an uproar. There weren't all that many people, considering the size of the place, but its acoustics were terrible. The holographic technicians were putting the finishing touches on their equipment, and everywhere Dierdre could see phantom objects appear and flicker out as units were tested: tiny ships, tigers, a Lunar mountain, even one of her favorite dinosaurs, a brilliant-faced triceratops. Then they all winked out and a voice sounded over the intercom: "Media net now complete."

Wyeth unclipped his belt unit and spoke into it. "Please evacuate all media people except those who are authorized delegates or the cage crew."

Dierdre glanced up toward the cage: a glassed-in box overlooking the dock, ordinarily used for directing dock operations but now swarming with technicians and commentators.

"Be careful of your expression," Sieglinde warned. "They'll be doing closeups of you."

The docking area was a vast, flat expanse, large enough to handle a dozen standard freight pods at once. There was a double hatch large enough to admit a small spaceship, although the whole dock would have to be evacuated for such an event. More often, pods were admitted through the outer hatch; the lock was pressurized and they were towed in through the inner hatch. Above the hatch a thick, curved window twenty meters high and a hundred meters wide gave a magnificent view: a section of the planet and a broad starscape. Had they been turned toward the sun, the window would have opaqued automatically.

"There it is!" someone almost shouted. The ellipsoid ship came into view, gradually blotting out the starscape. It was no more than a hundred meters away. There was a mass inhaling of breath, tightly-held. Ordinarily, ships of such size were never allowed to approach so closely. Collisions were always catastrophic in the unforgiving environment of space.

Small holographic displays winked on around the assembly. Some showed the alien vessel alone, others showed the ship and Avalon together in smaller scale. Sieglinde and Dierdre stood in the midst of the scientific delegation and everyone wanted to talk at once.

"No speculations yet," Sieglinde said, quietly. "Just stay quiet and observe. We'll all have plenty to talk about later." Obediently, the hubbub died down.

"It still looks old," Dierdre said. "Older than any man-made object I've ever seen. I don't know how, but I don't think I'm imagining it."

"Nor do I," Sieglinde said. The huge ship began to project a wide, telescoping umbilicus. Its rectangular mouth was surrounded with winking, colored lights. "In fact, this reminds me of something I saw when I was a child."

"What might that be?" Moore asked. He stood at ease, hands lightly clasped behind his back.

"On the holos from Earth, I once saw the King of England meet some foreign head of state. The visitor arrived in a space-plane of the latest design, but the king, William the Fifth, I think it was, arrived in a horse-drawn carriage. And I remember seeing holos of the Pope being carried on a palanquin by twenty or thirty men."

"A deliberate archaism for diplomatic purposes?" said Moore, who seemed to pick up on such things far more quickly than Wyeth, whose supposed job it was. "That would make sense. It's always been popular with the military; trooping of the guard, old-fashioned dress uniforms and such."

"They might also be trying to spare us culture shock," Dierdre said. "Maybe they don't want to shock the natives with something our poor, primitive little brains can't comprehend."

"That could well be," Sieglinde said, "and they could be right. More than one Earth culture simply disintegrated upon contact with one more advanced, more powerful. When you think your nation is at the center of the universe and your god-king its most powerful being, it's a shock to find that you're a tiny, backward country in an obscure corner of the world."

"Umbilicus contact established," said a voice from the cage.

The Althing Speaker, a man named Kimathi, spoke. "Docking Authority, can you tell us how they did that?" He had a directional mike on him and did not need to use a manual unit.

"Either they built the thing for the occasion, or it's adjustable. The mouth is of the remora type, lined with a flexible material that conforms to the irregularities of our outer lock surface, where it seems to form some sort of molecular bond. It's quite sophisticated."

"Sophisticated," Wyeth agreed in a low voice, "but not quite what we might have expected from people who have mastered matter transmission."

There were groans and mechanical noises from the lock. Apparently the aliens' umbilicus-tunnel was pressurizing. Dierdre felt excited, tingling all over in a way she hadn't in too many years. The fear, the sick dread she had been feeling was gone. Whatever was coming, she was ready.

A voice echoed through the dock. It did not come over the intercom, but seemed to have no point of origin. It was a rolling, mellifluous, gorgeous voice. Dierdre found herself smiling broadly, and she hoped that nobody was watching her on holo, and wondering why she smiled. It was not the same voice, but she knew the type.

"Island Worlds Starship *Avalon*, this is *Arumwoi* Starship *Shining In The Void.* Have we your permission to come aboard?"

Wyeth's mouth dropped open. "God must have sounded like that when he spoke to Moses."

Moore smiled wryly. "Nice of them to ask. They could probably open this thing like a beer bulb."

A small man stepped up next to Kimathi. This was the moment of glory. He was *Avalon*'s Spacing Master, the man in charge of all the vessel's actual movements through space, and its titular captain. Ordinarily, he was an obscure functionary. He spoke crisply. "This is Roland Lau, commanding. Permission granted."

"I wish we'd have given this ceremony stuff more thought," Wyeth muttered. "We could have had a live orchestra, all sorts of honors."

Sieglinde patted his arm. "They're calling this one. You've done your best."

Dierdre was certain that nobody was paying any attention to all this byplay. All the holo instruments and the eyes of everyone actually in the dock were fastened on the inner lock hatch.

Slowly, majestically, it opened. Light poured like liquid gold through the gateway. Sparkling motes danced in the light. Everyone sighed in admiration.

It might be stage-managing, but it was expert stage-managing. Island Worlders appreciated such things.

The hatch swung wide. The light was almost a controlled fog now, amorphous but not straying from the area just before the lock. Dierdre almost expected to see a red carpet come rolling down the ramp, but there was no such spectacle.

The general humming stopped. The main show was about to begin but the aliens, true to form, were making everybody wait. Dierdre felt a nudge in her ribs.

" 'Starship' " Sieglinde said. "They must have given our files a real going over. That's a word from those old holos of yours."

"So what?" Dierdre said. "It's a good word. I like it."

"Hear, hear," Moore said. "I wish we had more words like that one. We're too prosaic these days, if you ask me."

It occurred to Dierdre that Salamid officers could be as crazy as anybody else.

A shape appeared amidst the golden glow. It descended slowly, a platform supporting a number of massive seats, each a throne.

"Anti-gravity?" a scientist said, whispering. Nobody commented. The aliens on the platform held everyone's attention, and there was little to spare for their conveyance.

All over the system, spectators were seeing the aliens in holographic closeup. There was a collective sigh from the onlookers in the dock. Dierdre knew how they felt. Like her, they had been prepared for bizarre, repulsive or at least strange aliens. These delegates were, if anything, even more beautiful than M'ats. There were both males and females, and a few whose gender was indeterminate.

Their garments were flowing robes of glimmering material and they wore a variety of jewelery, all of it beautiful and elegant. Except for Dierdre and Sieglinde, the viewers bore a look of stupefaction.

"Anything else," Wyeth said in a strangled voice. "I would have expected anything else. Not just human, but Greek gods."

"Let's not take anything at face value," Moore cautioned. "We can produce pretty convincing effects with holographs ourselves."

Sieglinde spoke into a handset. "Analysis?"

"They're real," said a voice from the cage. "There are some peculiarities to their skeletal structure and internal organs, but they're closer to us than any of our nearest primate relatives back on Earth. None of these has any mechanical or biomechanical implants." Another voice came in. "Whatever is holding that platform up is a field totally unknown to us. Antigravity may not be a myth after all."

Dierdre leaned close and whispered to Sieglinde. "My God, Doc, look at those women! They make every holo queen who ever lived seem ugly." The aliens showed great diversity in physiognomy and pigmentation, but none was less than dazzling. In size they ranged from a woman more than two meters tall with carbon-black skin and silver hair to a man little more than a meter in height whose skin was ruddy, his hair a blue cloud.

The platform made its stately way toward the awaiting delegation. Ten meters from Kimathi, it settled silently to the deck.

"I wonder," Sieglinde said, *sotto voce*, "if that's their genuine formal dress or if they just know what looks impressive to us?"

"Doc, if you could custom-build a planet, would you *try* to impress us?"

"Shh! Something's happening."

The *Arumwoi* were standing. They did this with great aplomb, swiftly but without regimentation. In the light gravity their flowing garments swirled lazily about their limbs, sparkling faintly. One of the men, a two-meter specimen with golden skin and violet eyes, descended a short flight of steps to stand two steps from Kimathi. His gaze swept the assembly, regal as a lion's. When he spoke, it was with another of the amazing voices.

"We are the *Arumwoi.*" He did not speak loudly, but his voice was amplified in some fashion. The accent was strange, but as attractive as everything else about the aliens. "We welcome you to this system. We also extend our congratulations. You are the first of our experiments to reach us."

Kimathi was nonplussed for a moment, then began his prepared speech. "On behalf of the now-migratory Confederacy of Island Worlds, I welcome you aboard *Avalon*, our largest republic." He added: "I'm afraid you'll have to explain that last part."

"There will be time. We *Arumwoi* are well acquainted with time. Accept my assurance that there is not, and shall not be, any cause for alarm or hostility between our peoples."

Whatever knowledge-absorption system they had, Dierdre thought, it was efficient. He spoke with perfect assurance. She glanced over Sieglinde's shoulder at a readout coming from the cage. She had switched to visual in order to keep her ears open for the parlaying. Among other things, the readout affirmed: "No translation device operating. He is speaking as we hear him."

"I am Dedane Kimathi, Speaker of the Althing, which is our deliberative body. We arrived here as part of a great migration from our home system. Our intentions are peaceful. By the Articles to which we all agreed upon leaving our system, we may not remain in a system inhabited by intelligent beings who do not wish our presence. Although we do not know whether this is your home system, we have seen ample evidence of your prior claim. If you wish us to leave, we ask only ample time to make our preparations."

The speaking *Arumwoi* made a graceful gesture with one beringed hand. "I have said welcome, and I do not withdraw it. Stay for a day or an eon. Our races have a great deal to communicate to each other, and it will require time. Much of what you shall learn, you will find disturbing. Prior to establishing contact, we studied the transmissions you broadcast. We wished to have knowledge of you prior to contact. It was not—spying." For the first time he seemed unsure of a word.

"It is public information," Kimathi replied.

"We know now something of your nature, also of your history, from educational broadcast and files. We have not had time to meditate upon these."

Kimathi took a moment to clear his throat. "Mmm. Our, ah, history has been turbulent. I trust you understand we have matured as a species."

"But such history. To have crowded so much into so little time."

"It seemed like a long time to us, your, ah, shall I say, excellency?"

"Our naming and titling system is complex. Short names would be best. I am Dastan, a much-shortened form of my name. I have been chosen to speak because I have mastered your prevailing language best. These are delegates from our—forgive me, a precise translation is not possible—our *disciplines*. This does not represent what you would think of as government, although we are empowered to speak for our race. These things are done differently among us."

"These things are barely done at all among us," Kimathi said. "Our home system had a long diplomatic tradition, but we Island Worlders have had no practice at it for many, many years. Forgive us if we seem clumsy and unprepared. Our race has never made contact with another intelligent species."

"You will have to learn a redefinition of that word 'species.' That may come later."

"We, ah, look forward to it. However, it *is* customary to give honored visitors a guided tour of a vessel. May we show you Avalon?"

Dastan smiled, a fully human expression. "I propose a mutual visit. Perhaps some of your scientific personnel would like to be first to visit our ship?"

"I think that would be most agreeable," Kimathi said. He turned and studied the scientific contingent, most of whom were clearly salivating with eagerness.

"We would especially like to have the Doctor Sieglinde Kornfeld-Taggart who figures so prominently in your recent history. She is here?"

Moore whispered urgently to Wyeth: "We can't be sure of their intentions. I counsel we don't give them custody of our best scientific mind!"

"Don't be absurd, General," she chided. "I'm probably a witch-doctor by their standards. Besides, my best work is behind me. I have to see the inside of that ship." She stepped forward, signalling for Dierdre to follow.

Dastan saw them as they drew near. "Yes, and with her is the Dierdre Jamail."

He has trouble with the articles, too, Dierdre thought.

Kimathi turned his dark face toward her. "Our Miss Jamail has attracted your attention, too?"

"She was the first of you we saw," Dastan said.

"How many of us can you accomodate?" Sieglinde asked.

The very tall, black-skinned woman stood. This close, they could see that her eyes, like her hair, were silver. "I am Al'assa, and I shall be your—guide. I think that ten would be a good number for the first group." It was the first *Arumwoi* woman's voice they had heard. It was, predictably, beautiful. Sieglinde turned and named eight more to accompany them. They came forward without argument.

A group of *Arumwoi* followed Dastan off the platform and the Island Worlds scientists climbed up. To Dierdre's surprise, the small, ruddy man stepped forward and took her hands in his. "Welcome, welcome. I am Binat. We have waited so long for you." He seemed reluctant to release her hands and she was terrified of insulting him by pulling away. Keeping one hand in his, with the other he touched her face, her hair. "I am sorry. My command of your language is not yet good. There is so much we must speak."

The tall woman turned, her arm around Sieglinde's shoulders. "There is time, Binat," she said, smiling, "there is time."

To Dierdre's surprise, the other scientists, regardless of age or gender, were getting the same treatment. The aliens couldn't seem to help touching them. To Dierdre, who had never enjoyed this sort of physical familiarity from strangers, it was distressing. It made her feel self-conscious. She envied the ones who kept Italian or Russian customs, and didn't seem to mind at all.

Rostov, the gravitation specialist, bearhugged a man of his own height and kissed him on both cheeks. "This platform! How does it work?"

The *Arumwoi* erupted in the most musical laughter Dierdre had ever heard or imagined. "Patience!" Al'assa said. She had shifted her arm to Sieglinde's waist, but still held her close. "Some things we will explain, others not. But we will always tell you why we do not explain."

The platform was in motion and Dierdre hadn't noticed. It had lifted to about two meters and rotated toward the hatch. It was absolutely soundless, without vibration. She knew that all the holos in the system were trained upon them, but she had attention only for the tunnel ahead, filled with liquid golden light.

The umbilicus had an organic look, made up of translucent circular sections with no apparent rigid bracing. The gold light was all around them but the mist had no detectable substance. They drifted into a large room with a domed roof and the platform slid into a slot in the continuous floor. When it halted, there was no way to see where the platform ended and the deck began.

"Welcome to *Shining In The Void,*" Al'assa said, "the last of our great ships of exploration."

"Does that mean you no longer explore," Sieglinde asked, "or that you no longer explore by ship?"

"Both, I am afraid," Al'assa said, in a voice of great sadness. "But, of that you shall learn."

There were more of the *Arumwoi* gathered in the docking area. All of these wore the paintlike garments Dierdre had seen before, and few of them wore jewelery. Like the emissaries, they came in a great variety of sizes, shapes and colors, all of them beautiful.

Al'assa made introductions among the emissary party, then gestured to the gathered crowd. An *Arumwoi* came forward.

Al'assa turned to Dierdre. She was still holding Sieglinde close. "This is Junior Technician M'ats, whom you two already know."

M'ats had a look Dierdre could only describe as sheepish, although he carried it off far better than any ordinary human. "They found out," he admitted.

The other scientists looked at them. "I'll explain later," Sieglinde told them.

"Since our M'ats and your Dierdre share something in common—a great desire to be first, he may be her escort." Al'assa said.

Reluctantly, Binat released Dierdre's hand and turned her over to M'ats.

"It's good to see a familiar face," she said.

"I am glad they have made me your escort. It must be that I am back in the good graces." Without awkwardness he took her hand and slid the other around her waist. This time she didn't mind a bit.

With swift assurance, Al'assa paired off the visitors with guides, retaining Sieglinde for herself. She sent them to different parts of the ship and dismissed the assembled crowd. The other *Arumwoi* went reluctantly at the conclusion of her songlike speech.

"They cannot get enough of you," Al'assa said. She, Sieglinde, M'ats, and Dierdre were now the only inhabitants of the dock. "I had to assure them that they would have ample opportunity to mix with our visitors."

"Why?" Dierdre asked. "Are you all so scientifically-minded? We find you unbelievably beautiful, but I'm sure you can't think the same of us."

Al'assa stroked her fingertips down Dierdre's cheek. "We know of your concepts of beauty—of symmetry of face and body, grace of movement and melodiousness of voice. We prized these things ourselves once, and built them into our genes. Now we scarcely notice them. But to us, you shine like stars in the void."

"But—"

"I will let M'ats explain some of this to you. He is more your—age, although that is not quite accurate. It is an affinity."

Sieglinde looked up at Al'assa. "You are our creators, aren't you?"

Al'assa blinked, her first sign of surprise. "M'ats told us you were swift, that we would need a speeding-up treatment just to converse with you comfortably, but this—"

"She isn't just fast," Dierdre said, "she's intuitive. You can't match that with any treatment."

"Intuitive," Al'assa said. "Yes, that is something you have. We, too, once, long ago. Come with me."

They left the dock, entered a corridor walled with what looked like flowers, then a ballroom-sized chamber with walls and floor and ceiling textured subtly in ripples and waves so that the eye was drawn along to differing arrangements in much the way that the ear was beguiled by music. Dierdre was astonished at the degree of sophistication required to come up with something like this and she asked about it.

"An art form we practiced once," Al'assa said. "Now we sometimes use it for decoration. You see it static now. When it moves it is far more amusing."

"Where is the control room?" Sieglinde asked.

"There is none," Al'assa said. "The ship is voice-controlled by specialists in its language."

"You don't use your matter transporters for long-distance travel?" Sieglinde pressed.

"I've said that we will not reveal everything. Many things you must discover for yourselves. We would not cripple you by giving you everything we know."

"I was afraid of that," Sieglinde said. They came to a room shaped like a bubble on the side of the ship. It was transparent and faced the planet beneath.

"We're not rotating," Dierdre observed. "But we're standing on this floor at what I judge to be about point-seven-five gee. How's that?"

"I fear we cannot—" Al'assa started.

"Reveal everything at once, or ever," Dierdre finished. "I think I know the spiel by now."

Al'assa chuckled richly. "So impatient. Suffice it to say that you still have much to learn about the nature of gravity and how it may be manipulated."

"Poor Rostov," Sieglinde said. "He'll be going crazy about now. Back to my question. Don't worry that you'll upset us with this one, because it's been upsetting us for centuries. Long ago, most of us outgrew the religio-mythological explanations of our origin. The scientists have been arguing about it ever since, mainly because of an extremely spotty fossil record. That we were part of Earth's natural environment we no longer question. How we fit into it is a matter of some dispute. When we landed on that planet"—she jabbed a finger downward—"the debate blew up again. It's been raging ever since, gaining fuel each time the other expeditions came across hominids or humans on other planets. Different races, but all seemingly of the same species, or at least a subspecies of the same. Why?"

Al'assa hesitated for a while, then, "I will give you some of the explanation. You may decide how much to inform the others. Yes, we—made you. I will not say 'created'; we are not gods to make something from nothing." She leaned a hand on the sill below the great bubble window and seemed to organize her thoughts.

"We are the *Arumwoi*. It is a very ancient word, not even of the language we speak now. It means 'the First.' We are not from this arm of the galaxy. We originated in another arm, closer to the center. It was an area of stars far more ancient than these near your home star. Our homeworld had been reabsorbed into its parent star long before there was life on your planet. We have been star-rovers for a long, long time, and much of our earliest history has been lost. We do know that we were the first humans.

"In our explorations of this galaxy—and there is much of it, the great bulk, that we never reached—we found life in many places, and all organic life is very similar, easy for us to manipulate. Our history was very slow compared to yours. We must have had many millennia of the Stone Ages, many more of metal ages and mechanical centuries before we developed space flight. We never had your urgency.

"And sheer time wore us down. We grew weary, we lost our creativity, our ambition. But we felt that we should not be the end of human evolution. We did not deceive ourselves that we could create a higher form, but we thought that, by developing variants of ourselves, starting far back in our phylogeny, we might bring about humans more versatile, more capable and imaginative. With you, we succeeded better than we could have hoped. I suppose it was inevitable that you would be other than predicted. We wanted something different, after all."

"It didn't work as well with all your experiments,"

Dierdre commented, remembering the bombed-out cities of the sterilized planets.

"You developed so fast!" Al'assa said. "We made this great laboratory to experiment with the organic life of the planets we had found suitable for human life. We kept specimens of the various stages of evolution, natural and forced, as controls in case something should fail and we would have to go back to an earlier phase to begin again."

"As you said," Sieglinde commented, "you're used to dealing with time."

"In the end, it was all we could deal with. When we had definite hominids, ones that we could be sure would develop into something resembling us, we seeded the worlds with them. In small numbers, of course, in keeping with the natural workings of evolution."

"And you used your own genes for these experiments?" Sieglinde said.

"Yes, you are our close relatives, despite a period of retroevolution. But we never thought you would develop so fast! When we last looked, you were fully human, but had only recently developed language. You were not living in villages. We had thought that by now, at most you would have rudimentary agriculture. We never expected spacegoing technology while you were still children, socially speaking."

"So," Sieglinde said, "you didn't foresee that we would have the means of planetary suicide while we were still mentally at the level of feuding tribes. It must be a disappointment."

"Oh, no. We wanted something different. We were not trying to recreate ourselves. Your history is violent and tragic, but I think it is wonderful that you have arrived among the stars while you still have this ferocious vitality."

"Already," M'ats added, "you have delved into areas where we never went. We have never developed artificial intelligence as you have, for instance."

"This is going to come as a shock to our more insistent guilt-mongers," Sieglinde said.

"Thus, you can imagine the shock that went through our race when you arrived here. We were prepared to wait another hundred millennia for definite results from our experiments. We were quiescent in—another place when the alarm woke Junior Technician M'ats and he saw this radiant child in our transporter."

To Dierdre, who remembered well how she had looked that day, the description was more than flattering. But by now she knew that *Arumwoi* aesthetics were different from her own.

"We activated this ancient vessel and made our way here. We had means of reaching *Shining In The Void* with little delay, and once activated it was but a short flight here at near-light speed."

"We wouldn't consider that a short flight," Sieglinde said, "but a few years means little to you. I gather there was some reason why you didn't want to arrive by your current means of travel?"

"It would be rather more—spectacular than would be truly suitable for a first contact with you."

"Don't dazzle the natives, eh?" Sieglinde said. "Well, you've done some dazzling already. Could I see the drive units on this vessel?"

"Certainly. They will mean little to you, but I will explain what I may."

"I guess that's as much as I can ask for. Please, lead on." She turned to Dierdre. "Dee, you and M'ats get better acquainted for a while."

When they were gone, she was alone in the bubble room with M'ats. He was still holding her close, but she broke away, gently but firmly, and turned to face him.

"I still don't get it," she said. "I've never been strong on glamor, even among my own people. With you *Arumwoi*, I feel like an ugly, primitive, filthy, lice-infested ape! You look the way the ancient Greeks pictured their gods, the way Renaissance artists pictured angels. You even sound that way. But you can't keep your hands off me. None of you can keep from touching us. Why?" She was almost in tears, although she couldn't have said why.

"Dierdre, we are old. *Old*! We are so tired and discouraged, and for hundreds of thousands of years you have been our only hope! You are human beings as we once were, only better! You will accomplish a thousand times what we did in a tenth of the time."

He came close to her again and took her by the arms, and she did not draw back. "Can you have any idea how it feels to one of us to stand close to someone like you? You are the embodiment of youth and strength, enthusiasm and joy. Even your terrors and your sorrows seem joyful to us! You are the youth of worlds and being so near you is to bathe in that force. It is too late for us to rejuvenate, but we can enjoy this sensation for a little while. It is as—Al'assa said, to us you are as stars in the void; the great, beautiful stars that for a million years have been the objects of our adoration."

She put her hands against his chest, but not to push him away. It was more to brace herself. "This is all a little much."

He laughed and the sound sent a shiver through her. How, she thought, are we ever going to be content with each other after seeing and hearing these people? She answered herself: *We never liked each other all that much anyway*.

"A little much! I wish there were some way I could describe how I felt when I saw you in the transporter! Not just your beauty, but the courage it took to do what you did! You and your companions afterward; the unbelievable courage and determination to risk your terribly short lives just to do something no one had ever done before, to learn things unknown, and to do it in defiance of authority."

"But," she protested, "most people thought it was idiotic!"

"Yes, isn't it wonderful? We love even your contradictions and confusions! I had to find you, to make contact. Like you, to be *first*! I flouted thousands of years of accepted custom to do it. I waited until we were within safe transporter range, then when I knew you were alone in the main chamber, I came to meet you."

"Well," she almost whispered, "maybe it isn't too late for you to rejuvenate." She looked at the entrance to the room. "Does that door close? You came across space to find me. By now you know I don't do things halfway." She couldn't tell how he did it, but the door closed like a descending eyelid.

Later, she stood with Sieglinde at one of the broad windows in Avalon's old museum. From here they could see the way the umbilicus connecting the two ships rotated with Avalon's spin, turning at some mysterious, unexplained joint at the *Arumwoi* ship end. With artificial gravity, the *Arumwoi* ship needed no spin. All around them hulked the old asteroid-ship, once the most advanced work of mankind. Now it seemed a clumsy hunk of artificial buildings and drive units. It was entirely appropriate, Dierdre thought, to a race of star-travelling cavemen.

"Where will they go?" she asked.

"Al'assa says they may migrate to another galaxy. Long ago they sent out expeditions to other galaxies and never heard from them again. They feel they can leave the galaxy now that we've turned out successfully. Not any time soon, though. They want to teach us a few things, although they're being cagey about it. Hell, they just want to hang around us. They can't get enough of us."

Dierdre laughed. "You don't know half of it!"

"Don't be vulgar. You know, they just got too old, they lost their enthusiasm and curiosity. In that short tour she gave me she didn't think she was revealing much, but I saw a half-dozen areas in matter transmission alone where they never developed promising technologies. They just let time and momentum take care of most of their studies."

"So, they're just a bunch of old travellers, looking for the fountain of youth?"

"They're beginning to think they've found it. They certainly make *me* feel young!" She almost sounded girlish.

"Getting the old enthusiasm back, Doc?"

"I told her, when they get to that galaxy they're planning to try for, they'll find we got there ahead of them."

"That's the way I like to hear you talk." She looked at the alien vessel, so incredibly old, so beautiful inside, but so unchanging. "You know, Doc, they're our parents in a way, and I love them, but being beautiful and benevolent isn't enough, to my taste. We may not live as long, but we're going to do *lots* better than they did."